Journey
through
Magic
River

ALSO BY ANN MARIE PICHE

Spiritual Journey of an Ordinary Girl

Book design by Jessika Hazelton
Printed in the United States of America
The Troy Book Makers • Troy, New York • thetroybookmakers.com

To order additional copies of this title,
contact your favorite local bookstore
or visit www.shoptbmbooks.com

ISBN: 978-1-61468-835-8

Journey through Magic River

ANN MARIE PICHE

Contents

Massachusetts 1690

THE TWELVE-YEAR-OLD NATIVE AMERICAN girl sat on a buckskin blanket alongside a big oak tree a few feet from her family's long-house where her mother was weaving a basket. The young girl's legs were crossed, and her back was straight as a board. Her eyes closed as she conjured up visions. She could see a young, dark-haired woman with a brown spot shaped like a heart on her wrist and saw that she used her magical powers for good. Only anger could change the course of her powers. Then a mature woman with a young face appeared. Her long red braid traveled down one shoulder. The woman showed a gentle spirit, yet profound sadness followed her.

The young girl began to feel the rumble from the ground. A thunderous sound of horses approaching with loud yells of men and screams from women and children. She opened her eyes and saw the cloud of dust just beyond the longhouse. She jumped up, running towards the entrance just as a swipe of a shiny sword flung through the air slashed her mother's throat.

The young soldier held the blade dripping with blood in horror at the carnage he just inflicted. He locked eyes with the girl as she saw shame on his face. He slowly retreated, saying the words, "I'm sorry. I'm so sorry." to the girl holding her mother's bleeding, life-less body. The soldier's gaze stayed frozen on the girl.

She shouted in her language words he could not possibly understand. "You will be cursed!" she cried out. Then the wind blew with the sound of rushing water, and a mist filled the air. Her tribe called her Catori, which means Spirit, and she possessed the powers of a seer.

Chapter 1

I AM YOU

Massachusetts November 2021

EMILY STANFORD ENTERED THE MAPLE RIDGE town offices and was directed to a room with the name Mark Johnson, Editor and Chief on the smoked glass door. As Emily sat inside the office, she began to feel nervous. Voices came from the adjacent room talking about building plans and pending taxes on upcoming projects.

Mr. Johnson's office consisted of two rooms. The one she was sitting in had two desks, each situated on the opposite side of the room, facing each other. Against one wall was a set of filing cabinets with shelves above the cabinets, showing framed pictures of the town and books that looked randomly placed. To her left was the other room where all the chatter was taking place. The room she waited in felt too warm, and then Emily spotted the source of the radiating heat coming from a cast iron radiator under a window with its view blocked by pine trees. She tapped her restless foot trying to settle the negative thoughts that did their best to consume her mind. The clock ticked loudly on the wall, and the more she waited for someone to come in, the more doubts she was having. "What in the world I'm I doing here?" she mumbled under her breath.

She was hoping for a chance to be a column writer for the *Maple Ridge Gazette* historical page. She loved history even though she had no education in the field. Emily had a high school diploma and had gone to college for her nursing degree. Although she hadn't studied history in college that wasn't going to stop her; history was in her DNA. Her deep family heritage was everywhere in Maple Ridge, mainly alongside the Magic River that ran through the town. Emily was always surprised that the town wasn't called Stanford. The town was dotted with places like the Stanford Library and Stanford Lane leading across the Shady Brook Bridge and over the Magic River to the Stanford Park Square.

She leaned towards the desk in front of her noticing the latest copy of the *Maple Ridge Gazette*.

"This is ridiculous," she said, intimidated by the professional looking paper as she continued to allow those defeating thoughts to run rampant. Her thoughts were quickly interrupted by a man who pushed the door open from the other office with several people spilling into the room in which she was waiting. Their conversations continued among themselves as they quickly walked past her, leaving Emily alone again. She craned her neck to see if anyone else was coming out of the other office, when suddenly a man appeared sporting a beer belly with an un-lit cigar hanging from his mouth. He reached to shake Emily's hand as she shook his unpleasantly damp grip.

"My name is Mark Johnson, editor and chief of the town paper and in charge of the historical column along with many other things around here."

"How do you do, Mr. Johnson? I'm Emily Stanford."

He waved a hand, gesturing towards a chair for Emily to sit. "Please, call me Mark." Mark had a rough voice and displayed a down-to-business attitude, which told Emily that he didn't have time for nonsense.

Emily did her best to hide her nervousness as Mark looked over her resumé. She decided to use her well-known maiden name in hopes of getting the job. She tried reading his face for approval, but she could find no such expression.

"Hmm, so you have only a high school diploma and a nursing degree, I see."

Emily felt dread at that moment but immediately decided to

give her best pitch. "Yes, I know my education is lacking in English and history, but I have a lifetime of experience with the older generation," she said gesturing towards her resume. "As you can see by my resume, I've worked in the Maple Ridge Nursing Home for several years before retiring about two months ago."

Mark looked up from her resumé, squinting his eyes with interest. "Are you related to the prominent Stanford family that dates back to the eighteenth century around here?"

Now there was a glimmer of hope with his question. She was glad she had used her maiden name.

"Yes, I am. My seven-times great-grandfather immigrated from England, becoming one of the wealthiest men in Massachusetts by starting up his own sugar cane industry. He bought all this land." She looked around the room as if the walls were transparent. "Back then only a few homes along the river existed, and he turned it into a town."

Silence fell over the room. She could hear Mark Johnson breathing and wished she could hear him thinking.

"So, your ancestors founded Maple Ridge?" Mark asked and then added, "Very interesting."

Emily nodded and then shared more knowledge of the area's history. "My five-times great-grandparents married in 1776. A woman named Isabel was an indentured servant for a British captain when she met one of my ancestors."

Mark twirled the unlit cigar in his mouth. "You seem to know quite a bit about your ancestors. Ancestry.com I presume?" he asked while picking tiny pieces of the cigar from his lips.

She didn't particularly like the remark about how she supposedly found her information. Emily remained professional; she wanted the job or a least have the chance to give it a try.

"I've always had an interest in researching the Stanfords given they founded Maple Ridge," she said.

Emily felt more confident, and she certainly knew a lot about the Stanford family tree. She had read strange stories surrounding the Stanford history dating back to the seventeenth century, tales considered legends today but most likely scandals back then. She even wondered if they were true but found them interesting nevertheless. When she was much younger and before the Internet had taken over the world, she had looked up her family history in the Stanford Library archives. It was there she had come across those myths and legends. For the most part, though, the information was military related. Even later on when she could go to the Ancestry.com website there had been missing information, such as no mention of her two-times great-grandparents. The Civil War information of her ancestors only named an officer, Marcus Stanford, who had a wife and two children. All three were unnamed with no dates of their births or deaths. She came to the conclusion that most of the information pointed towards military history.

Mr. Johnson looked pleased with Emily's unique family history and stood to give Emily another sweaty handshake. "Perfect," he said. "You have the job and be here first thing in the morning for your first assignment."

Emily stood with excitement. "Oh, thank you, Mr. Johnson, for this opportunity, and I assure you that I will do my best with my first assignment."

Mr. Johnson sat down and took the cigar out of his mouth. "Mark. You can call me Mark."

The next morning Emily looked at her first assignment. Mark wanted her to do a story on the old Maple Ridge Elementary School building she had attended as a child that was located across the street from where the Magic River ran. It was a huge red brick building dating back one hundred fifty years. Since it had been an abandoned building for several years, she had to call the owner and wait for the key to let her in. She sat in her car to stay warm from the bitter cold of late November. "Oh, God, I hope this works out," she said in anticipation over the assignment.

She looked in the rearview mirror for any signs of the owner coming up the road but saw nothing yet. Emily needed this job to keep herself busy after retiring a couple of months ago. It was essential for her to stay active and challenge her mind enough to forget her husband's tragic death in an auto accident a year ago. If only I could have prevented him from going on that call that day, she thought, always agonizing over the same scenario.

She saw a beat-up old truck rattling down the road, and it pulled in front of her car. A man jumped out. Emily kept the windows rolled up uncertain about the man approaching. He tapped on the window, peering through the glass at Emily. He had a handsome face and looked roughly the same age as herself. He had thick silver hair, deep blue eyes, a five-o'clock shadow and well-worn clothes soiled with dirt and sawdust. His appealing looks were not diminished a bit by his untidy appearance.

"You the historian who wants the keys?" he shouted through the closed window.

Emily got out of the car and straightened her coat. She stood as tall as she could even though she was extremely shorter than the man in front of her. She reached out to shake his right hand, only to notice it was missing.

He offered his left hand with an air of confidence. "Name's Rick and you're...?"

Emily swung the strap of her pocketbook over her shoulder. "Emily Stanford, and you're the owner of..." She pointed to the old school building.

"Yeah, been working on the old dump for a little over a year, feels like an eternity, though." One side of his mouth turned up in a half grin as he passed the key to her. "Lucky for me I'm left handed."

She thought he must have noticed the concerned look on her face when she tried to not look at his missing hand.

"Iraq...beginning of the war," he said in answer to the same question Emily assumed he had probably heard a thousand times.

"So sorry," she said. "It must be hard to work on construction."

He looked up at the building, and Emily saw a look of regret on his face. "I have a lot of help, thank God." Rick leaned on Emily's car. He was well built and seemed overly confident when she noticed his gaze wandered from her face down to her waist and back up again. She was sure he was sizing her up, and she couldn't decide whether it made her uncomfortable or flattered.

"Well...ah, I'll just hang out here till you're done," he said.

Emily nodded and walked towards the front door, turning to see if the handsome man's gaze was still on her. He smiled with a nod as he leaned against her car with his arms crossed. Emily felt the heat coming to her cheeks and gave the man a nod back.

Emily entered the old school building. Immediately, she felt a slight breeze and heard a rushing sound of a waterfall. She started to feel disoriented as she took another hesitant step forward. A strange mist with the image of a woman's face appeared before her and then quickly disappeared. She closed her eyes in hopes that when she opened them the strangeness would be gone, but instead she heard children's voices. She opened her eyes and saw freshly painted brick walls with several posters and a United States map. The large vent in the floor beneath her released warm air, which felt rather good as it drifted underneath the dress she was wearing. She could feel the difference in the fabric. Not the shirt and pants she had on a few seconds ago but a dress from another era. The kind her mother would have worn when taking a shopping trip. What in God's name is going on? she wondered.

"Oh, how marvelous, you're here." A woman approached Emily from what appeared to be an office. "You must be the substitute teacher for our first-grade class."

Emily continued to feel disoriented and confused. "I—ah, I'm Emily Stanford," she said.

The woman appeared to be stunned for a moment. "How interesting. We have a student by that name. As a matter of fact, you are subbing in that class today." She stuck her hand out to shake Emily's. "I'm Marge Billings, the principal."

Emily shook her hand feeling a sense of deja vu. I've met this woman before, she thought. Emily was certain that Marge Billings would detect the confusion on her face. Emily could hardly speak, still in disbelief as Mrs. Billings escorted her to the classroom.

Emily knew the building was supposed to be under construction and hadn't been a school for over fifteen years. Emily felt as if she had entered *The Twilight Zone* somehow. She wasn't sure of anything. All she knew for sure was that something bizarre just happened.

The classroom was enormous, with six tall windows that almost touched the ceiling. The old school was built in Victorian style and was quite beautiful. Her faded memories from years ago came to life as she looked around the room. The student desks lined up perfectly across the room in five separate rows. Mrs. Billings wasted no time with introductions. She clapped her hands to get the children's attention.

"Good afternoon, children. This is your teacher for the rest of today. Her name is Miss Stanford."

Emily smiled as all the children spoke in unison. "Hello, Miss. Stanford." Mrs. Billings handed her a big folder with the lessons for the day.

Once again, Emily had difficulty speaking, and her thoughts kept running in so many different directions. Where am I? What is this all about? Why am I wearing strange clothing? What is happening to me? Mrs. Billings left the room, and Emily put the folder on the desk, opening it to a writing assignment. The first graders had to write a three-word sentence using words they had been learning. Emily decided to go along with all the strange things occurring around her. She took a deep breath to calm herself and turned to face the room full of children.

"Okay, children, get out some paper and write five different examples of three words that make a sentence using your new spelling words." Emily wrote one example on the blackboard: "Can I go?" Which was exactly what she wanted to do at that very moment.

Emily sat down, putting her elbows on the teacher's desk and covering her face with her hands. She peeked over her fingertips, glancing around the room and feeling like she was having an out-of-body experience. Everything looked so familiar. If I didn't know better—this first-grade classroom looks just like mine did so long ago, she thought. Emily got up and walked around the room, finding various things that looked nostalgic. A poster with children and animals, each with their names over their heads. Dick, Jane, Sally, and Spot the dog, Puff the cat and a teddy bear called Tim. A safety-first poster with two children crossing the street with the caption "Look Both Ways." Artwork the children had made covered almost an entire wall. Each child had drawn and colored a picture of a tree. Some trees were green, and others had fall colors. Several had a house next to their tree with stick figures of people or dogs, but one picture stood out to Emily. It was a tree with small squares instead of leaves. In each square was an attempt to draw a person as if it were a photo of someone.

"How interesting. It must be a family tree," she said under her breath. She had a strange flashback of seeing her own hand drawing the same tree. She looked at the name of the child who drew the picture: EMILY STANFORD. She stopped cold, feeling a chill run up her spine. She turned around to look at each child in the room. At the front of the class in row one, a little girl with red hair sat with her back to Emily. She walked to the front of the class to get a better look when suddenly the whole situation crashed down on her. Little Emily looked just like she did at that age. "It can't be!" she shouted, and all the children looked up at her. Emily feebly waved her hand, shaking her head no, "It's okay. Go on with your work."

A little boy raised his hand. "Miss Stanford?" But Emily didn't respond right away. The boy held his arm up resting it on one hand as he waved with the other. "Miss Stanford!" he said raising his voice.

Emily gathered her thoughts by taking her focus off the little girl and putting it on the young boy. "Yes, what is it?"

"Can I use that one?" the boy asked.

His question caught Emily off guard. "Er…what?"

He giggled at Emily. "What you just said. 'It can't be'—three words," he said, holding up three fingers.

Emily could see the kid was a wise guy and probably gave his regular teacher a hard time. "No, make up your own three words," Emily said to the overconfident boy.

She turned her attention back to little Emily and the child she once was. Emily felt a sense of appreciation over how beautiful this little girl was. Yet, she still couldn't believe what she was seeing. It can't be me—can it? Emily then looked at the back wall of the classroom and saw a picture of President Kennedy. She could feel her legs becoming limp. The sight of the picture suddenly anchored her to a time and place that had long passed. My God, it is true—I traveled back to 1963.

Emily's thoughts were interrupted by the same boy raising his hand.

"Miss Stanford, our teacher lets us write the answer on the blackboard," he said.

Emily walked slowly back to the desk and sat down with her legs still feeling wobbly. She began to accept the strange events around her. She looked at the young boy and nodded. "Okay, er—I'm sorry. I didn't get your first name."

"Ricky," he answered.

"Well, Ricky, would you like to be the first to come up then?"

He jumped out of his seat. "Sure do," Ricky said happily. He walked past Emily with a smirk on his face, gave her the thumbs up, and then wrote "Out to play," and proudly turned around to go back to his seat. Emily was slightly amused with the young boy but also thought he must have been a handful at home as well.

One by one, each child came up writing their three words – "Come and see," "Look at me" -- and so on. Little Emily seemed reluctant to come to the blackboard. Emily squatted down to her level. She remembered how she wore her hair like that, off to the side with her favorite barrette. Little Emily's dress was pale blue with embroidered flowers at the waist. It was so surreal for Emily, looking into the past in this strange and unreal way.

"It's okay. I'm sure you'll do fine," Emily said, encouraging the younger version of herself. She also remembered how shy she was and surprised at how apparent it was. Little Emily slowly walked to the blackboard. It was like the whole scene moved in slow motion. Little Emily picked up the piece of chalk and wrote: "I am you."

The younger Emily and the older Emily stared into each other's eyes. Time stood still in The Twilight Zone, some sort of realm that was impossible. The stare was broken by a disturbance in the hallway, and little Emily returned to her seat. Emily looked over by the door and noticed something she hadn't seen before. Written on the blackboard by the entrance was the date November 22, 1963. She blinked her eyes several times making sure she wasn't imagining the date, but there it was, a date she knew all too well, a date no one has ever or will ever forget. The door swung open, and Mrs. Billings waved for Emily to come out into the hallway.

"Okay, children. Um…you can draw a picture of anything you want and color it. I'll be right back," Emily said.

She knew already what Mrs. Billings was about to say. Emily could see the devastation on her face and knew how catastrophic this event was to people at this time. Mrs. Billings appeared to be holding her emotions back as she placed her hand on her chest as she was beginning to hyperventilate.

"The…the…President…he's been shot!" Mrs. Billings put her shaky hand on her forehead in disbelief.

Emily touched her arm gently for comfort. "I'm so sorry," Emily said, not sure if her reaction to the news was dramatic enough. For Emily, the assassination of President Kennedy happened almost sixty years ago. "Is there anything I can do?" Emily offered as she tried to comfort the shaken woman. "Do you need some water or—how about I get you a chair to sit?"

"That's so kind of you," Mrs. Billings said as she took a couple of deep breaths.

Emily could hear the laughter of students and a teacher reading to small children across the hall. Emily wondered if Mrs. Billings had also noticed the sounds of an ordinary day.

After talking to Mrs. Billings, Emily walked back into the classroom to tell the children they were dismissed for the day. As each child left, little Emily struggled to zip her coat. Emily sat on one of the student's small chairs next to the little girl. All the students had left, leaving younger Emily and the older Emily alone.

"Here, let me help you." Emily felt a strange energy go through her arm as her hand touched little Emily's chin while zipping her coat. The unusual energy came with an enormous love for this child. She looked into little Emily's eyes with the same penetrating stare when little Emily wrote "I am you" on the chalkboard.

"I want you to remember something very important, okay?" Emily said as the child nodded.

"Always remember how much God loves you. Can you do that for me?" Emily received another silent nod from little Emily. Emily hugged the child she once was.

Suddenly she heard a noise at the classroom entrance. It was Ricky who returned to get something he had left behind. She nodded to him and said, "God loves you too, Ricky." She thought he had been standing there long enough to hear what she had said to little Emily.

"That's grrrrrreat," he chirped like Tony the Tiger and left with the coat he had forgotten.

She turned once more to look at little Emily and thought of something. "Why did you write 'I am you' earlier?"

Little Emily smiled and gave an answer that was obvious only in a child's mind. "Because we both have the same name."

Ten minutes later Emily walked towards the entrance to leave when Mrs. Billings called out to her.

"Thank you, Miss Stanford."

Emily waved and watched a mist crossing in front of Mrs. Billings, and in her place appeared a young, dark-haired woman. Seconds later, the mysterious young woman completely disappeared. Emily turned to leave and heard the rushing waterfall again.

As she stepped outside, Rick was standing by his truck, waiting for his key. Emily looked back at the old school, totally bewildered over what just happened.

"So, did you find what you were looking for?" Rick asked.

"I hope you weren't waiting too long," Emily asked, not answering his question, and handed the key back.

"Nay, I didn't mind waiting. Besides, you didn't take that long."

Emily had to ask, "How long was I in there?"

Rick looked at her as if she had lost her mind, and as far as Emily knew, she had.

"About ten minutes. Why?" he asked while getting into his truck.

"No reason, and...thank you." Emily opened the door to her car when Rick stuck his head out the truck window.

"Hey, thought I'd tell yah. I used to go to this school when I was a kid. They called me Ricky."

Chapter 2

UNFROZEN TEARS

IT WAS ONE YEAR AGO on a snowy Christmas Eve morning when Lucas and Emily snuggled on the couch by the fireplace while sipping their coffee next to their nine-foot Christmas tree, discussing plans for a Christmas Eve feast for just the two of them. Neither one had parents that were living; they had no brothers or sisters. They had no children, an unfortunate pain they both shared. Emily was unable to conceive, leaving her with maternal loneliness. Over the years, they leaned on each other when the emptiness would creep in, seeing other people's lives fulfilled when having children. The love between them for the past thirty-nine years had been all they needed to get through the sad void of the absence of a child's laughter. Emily was happy for the most part and still madly in love with Lucas, the love of her life.

The aroma of Christmas cookies and the pine fragrance from the spruce tree created perfect comfort for the couple. Christmas music softly played in the background, reminding Emily about roasting chestnuts and receiving nose nips from Jack Frost. Emily felt perfect happiness that very moment in the arms of Lucas. He kissed her gently on the lips, caressed her long, red hair. She returned the kiss and ran her fingers through his thick, dark hair. She touched his mouth as an invitation for more. His dark eyes were enchanting like a magical spell that had captured her heart. Warmth and need for each other were about to be satisfied when the phone interrupted the heat between them.

Emily stretched her legs, complaining, and then moaned, "Oh, don't answer it. This is too perfect to be interrupted."

Lucas patted her leg. "It's fine. It's probably nothing."

He got off the couch and grabbed his phone, talking to someone who needed his help. Emily gazed at her husband, admiring his handsome face and kind ways, still present from the days when she first met him so long ago. Besides a few gray hairs, he was still young as far as she was concerned. His height and well-built frame made him appear younger than his actual age. Lucas had been ambitious in his construction business his whole life, and his ambition made him successful enough to retire by the end of the year. Emily knew he wouldn't entirely give it up; the work was in his blood.

Lucas ended the call. He sat next to Emily, put his arms around her, and kissed her passionately. She gazed up into his face, which had the same look he always had when he was about to tell her something she didn't want to hear.

"What is it this time?" she asked.

"It will only take about an hour," he said.

She couldn't help but complain. "Come on! It's Christmas Eve. Really? It can't wait?"

He looked at her with his beautiful brown eyes and touched her cheek. His expression said it all, and she knew he had to do what came naturally to him: help people.

"Oh, okay," she said, being unable to resist his look or touch.

He handed her the cup of coffee she had half-finished. "Here drink this then have another. I'll be back before you can say 'Merry Christmas'."

Emily patted Lucas on the arm. "Okay, but this better be for a good reason, and whatever it is better be worth it."

Lucas put his boots and work coat on. He got to the door while shoving his hands in his gloves. "Hey! I love you! Merry Christmas," he said.

She laughed and said, "Does that mean you're back already?"

He blew a kiss in her direction, closing the door behind him.

Four hours later, Lucas had still not returned. Emily was worried. She tried calling his cell phone, but he didn't pick up.

Then, just as her clock chimed the noon hour, the police came to the door with the devastating news. She had collapsed, unable to speak, unable to cry. Emily sat on the floor by the door with the police officer holding her hand.

For Emily, Christmas Eve would always mark that tragic event, and that day was today. One year had passed since her husband's tragic death, a sudden passing that gripped her wounded soul with unimaginable pain. Emily stood in front of the gravestone near the northwest corner of the Trinity Cemetery in a newer section not far from the old area, with graves dating back to the Revolutionary War. On any other day, Emily would have found them fascinating, imagining the ancient world in which they lived, but not today. The sadness was too painful; the heartache too great.

It had been a cold, snowy day when Lucas ran his truck off the road into the Magic River. The police told her it was an accident caused by the icy roads, but nothing the police could say would make Emily feel any better. She felt only anger at herself for not stopping him from going that morning. He had blown her a kiss, closing the door behind him, and she would never see him again.

The gravestone was a good size; Emily had spared no expense. She wanted Lucas to have a beautiful memorial and resting place. The stone read:

LUCAS EASTON
BORN: NOVEMBER 15, 1958
DIED: DECEMBER 24, 2020

Emily knelt, placing Christmas flowers in the urn alongside the stone, and then leaned on the cold granite for support. "I miss you so very much, my sweet Lucas." Emily's heartache was as fresh as the day her beloved was killed. She thought she had cried every tear imaginable, but always more tears came without effort. She constantly berated herself about the turn of the events surrounding Lucas's death. The same thoughts kept haunting her: Why didn't I stop you from going? But those regrets and the hurt would never go away.

The cold wind started to pick up in the cemetery, and she was getting cold. The Magic River running alongside Trinity Church and the graveyard gave off a strange mist. She heard the sound of rushing water, a sound similar to what she had heard when she entered Maple Ridge Elementary School four weeks ago. How odd, she thought. Despite the frigid temperature, the river remained unfrozen. It's just my imagination running away again, she told herself. She could hear the Trinity Church bells chiming "Amazing Grace," and she imagined that people were going into church for Christmas Eve service. She glanced once more at the stone. "I wish you were back home safe and sound," she said, heartbroken. A fountain of tears welled up in her eyes, unfrozen tears that could fill the Magic River just behind the grave. She kissed her two fingers and placed them on the stone. "No matter how many times I've said 'Merry Christmas'," Emily sniffled, her voice breaking up. "You still have never returned to me."

The holidays came and went with no celebration. Emily had hoped the new year would be a year of healing for her. She knew the pain would linger for a long time, and all she could do was keep herself busy. Emily kept her mind off her sadness and thrust herself into the article about the old school for the historical column. Between the holidays and staff taking time off, Emily had plenty of time to complete her first article to be published at the end of January. Mark Johnson had given her a deadline of January10, leaving enough time for editing. Emily had it finished sooner, since she had no other plans. No matter how many times she re-read her article, she still couldn't wrap her mind around her strange experience going into the old school and concluded she would forget what took place and put it all behind her.

A few weeks later Emily walked into the office and noticed a stack of the new edition of the *Maple Ridge Gazette* piled on the desk Mark Johnson had assigned to her when working in the office. She took one copy off the top and turned to her first historical column when Mark Johnson marched out of the adjacent office, taking the cigar out of his mouth.

"Congratulations, Emily. I'm very impressed with your Maple Ridge Elementary article," Mark said in his usual loud, no-nonsense tone of voice. "And I like the mention about JFK's assassination—nice touch."

Emily sat in the chair behind her desk, pleased he was happy with her work. "Thank you, Mark. To be honest, I don't know how I did it. The words seemed to pour out of me." Emily knew the raw emotions from that day and had first-hand knowledge of Mrs. Billings' anguish when she had heard the news of the president's assassination.

"I have another assignment that might be right up your alley," Mark said, handing her an address that looked familiar to her.

"Isn't this the old British captain's house?" she asked.

Mark leaned to open her desk drawer, pulling a paper out and placing it on Emily's desk. "I put this in your drawer earlier for you to look at."

Emily scanned the paper showing a list of British soldiers. She glanced at Mark uncertain of her assignment.

"The list identifies British soldiers who may have stayed in Maple Ridge around the Revolutionary War," Mark said. "Your job: find out which captain lived at this address."

Mark plopped himself in the chair behind the desk opposite Emily, wiping sweat off his forehead with a handkerchief he had pulled out of his back pocket. Emily was beginning to wonder if the man had a problem with his sweat glands or if it was simply too warm in the room.

"Thought maybe you'd have some information since your five-times great-grandmother was an indentured servant to one of these guys," Mark said.

Emily took the list, folded it, and put it in her purse. "I'll do my best, and…," she glanced over her shoulder at the window behind her and then back at Mark Johnson. "You might want to crack open that window, Mr. Johnson," she said, walking towards the door. Before she opened the door to leave, Mark Johnson shouted: "Mark! Just call me Mark!"

Emily gave him a lopsided grin and went out the door hoping that this assignment wouldn't cause the same strange events as the last one did.

On a cold February day, Emily drove down a dirt driveway circling the old English saltbox house. Research told her that British soldiers stayed in various places in town during the Revolutionary War, and the address Mark gave her was one of those places. Emily saw a man standing by a wooden gate in front of the house. As she approached, she recognized the beat-up old truck.

"You're kidding me," Emily said under her breath. She parked in front of him and looked over the dashboard at the man. He had his feet anchored firmly to the ground, and his face held a smile, as if he was happy to see her. She got out of the car and took two steps towards him as he spoke first.

"Hey, so we meet again, I see," Rick said.

Her lip quivered nervously as she attempted to smile, drawn in by his handsome face. This time he was dressed more neatly with a clean plaid shirt tucked in and blue jeans sporting a copper belt buckle of a small maple tree logo. His jacket had the same logo.

"You from Canada?" she asked pointing to his jacket.

Oh, nah. I have friends that work for the Maple Sugar Barn outside of town. Guess I just like their logo."

He reached into his left pocket with his one good hand and pulled out a key, this time for the old saltbox house.

She squinted her eyes at the key. "Don't tell me you own this one, too."

"Nope. Not this one." Rick hesitated, looking as if he were deciding something in his mind. "Sorry, I had left out the part where I work for the town as the building inspector," he lifted his chin towards the house. "All the historical sites have keys in the town office."

Emily glanced over at the old truck he drove. "They should at least let you drive a new truck."

Rick gave Emily a sly grin, tilting his head to one side.

"I heard you're a Stanford. Your family goes back a long ways," he said, taking her hand and placing the cold key in her palm. "I can see why Mark gave you this job."

Emily had an unwanted jolt of desire as Rick slowly let go of her hand. She cleared her throat, ignoring her body's response to a man she hardly knew. She quickly cleared her mind to restore some sense of normalcy. "I hope that's not the only reason I got the job, but yes, I do have deep roots in this town," Emily said raising the key. "Thanks for the key I shouldn't be too long."

Rick nodded and gave her a slight wave of his good hand. "I'll, ah...wait right here."

Emily opened the gate and took out a notepad, writing down things about the house's appearance that she could use in her next article. The house had wooden shakes on the exterior and what appeared to be a new roof. A shed-like roof sloped down the front that covered a porch. It had diamond panel casement windows with a simple wooden front door. It was a good-sized place with two floors, big enough to accommodate a large family. In the front yard was a large stump from an old oak tree where an empty flowerpot sat on top.

Emily walked around the side of the house which faced the Magic River that flowed through the yard. She remembered legends told of the river having magical powers on just one day of the year. However, no one knew which day that was. A cornerstone on the side of the house indicated the house was built in 1740.

"Isn't that the old-fashioned way of taking notes?" Rick asked, popping up around the corner of the old house. "What, no fancy phone or iPad?"

Emily looked at Rick and tried not to be embarrassed over her choice of note taking.

"Guess I like doing things the old-fashioned way." Emily put her notepad in her coat pocket and closed her eyes, taking a cleansing breath of cold, fresh air. "I love the sound of the running water trickling through a back yard. It's peaceful," Emily said.

When she opened her eyes, she looked at the mist lingering over the surface of the water. "Did you notice how the Magic River never freezes in the winter?" she asked. "I always wondered why."

Rick walked to the edge of the water and peered in. Emily followed. The two considered the reason.

"Maybe because it has healing hot springs throughout it, or, so I heard," he said.

She could sense he was studying her as she watched the steam coming off the river. "Really?" she said. "I never heard anything before about healing hot springs."

Rick shrugged his shoulders. "I'm not entirely sure if it's true or whether it's just a lot of speculation over the years from way too many people who have too much time on their hands."

The dead leaves left over from the fall blew around their ankles as they walked to the front of the house. Emily shivered while tucking her hands deep into her pockets for more warmth and tried to chase away her anxious thoughts of falling through time again.

"Do you need me to stay or go in with you?" Rick asked. "You kind of have that same ghostly expression on your face you had the day you left the old school."

She was comforted by his suggestion and did have anxiety about what she might see, hoping that nothing would happen. "I'm fine. I can do this," she said while trying to hide her uncertainty.

The cold breeze stirred through the trees, causing Rick's thick silver hair to blow slightly over one eye. "You sure?" he said brushing his hair off his forehead.

Emily smiled and thought about that enthusiastic little boy proud of himself and his first-grade three-word performance. She felt almost certain they were one and the same. "I'm sure," she said.

The two studied each other with barely an inch between them, locking eyes. Neither one moved from their frozen positions. Strands of Emily's red hair with soft blonde highlights blew in the cold breeze even though she had it pulled into a long braid going down past her one shoulder. She became aware of Rick's gaze dropping to her lips and back up to her eyes. Her upper lip began to quiver again, and she ran her finger under her nose, pretending to scratch an itch, hoping he hadn't noticed. "Um—I, ah—hopefully this won't take long," she finally said breaking the stare between them. Emily walked towards the house and wondered if Rick was, in fact, the little boy Ricky. She realized she never got his last name. She turned to look at him. "What's your last name?"

"Miller," he said walking up to her and leaning in as if telling a secret. "A long line of Millers around here, too."

She turned the key to open the door. She stepped inside, feeling that slight breeze and seeing a misty fog accompanied by the sound of rushing waterfalls she had previously experienced when entering the old school. The mist again showed a woman's face for a split second, and then disappeared, followed by another young woman who parted the mist. She approached Emily, sounding pleasant and glad to see her. When the fog cleared, Emily was once again back in time, feeling immediately the weight of heavy clothing. The girl said something, but Emily was confused, trying to process her surroundings. "We have been waiting for ye, Mistress," the young woman said. The girl held out her hand, "I am Isabel."

CHAPTER 3

THE CAPTAIN'S HOUSE

EMILY SAT IN A WINGBACK ROCKER. The warmth of the fireplace was a blessing after feeling the extreme chill that ran through her a few minutes earlier. The room was a good size with the fireplace accommodating another big room beyond where she was sitting. The charred stone fireplace had a large smoked-stained wooden mantle, a big skillet hanging from a spit, and another smaller spit that most likely had to be turned periodically while cooking. Pots, pans, and utensils dangled from wrought iron brackets off to one side. Her whole surroundings appeared to be from the eighteenth century. The skirt Emily wore felt heavy and thick with layers underneath. She ran her hand across the mound of material and felt something in the pocket. Reaching in, she found her notebook, pen, and Rick's key. Best keep this to myself, she thought.

Isabel scurried into the room, pouring water from a pail into the big skillet. "Oh, Mistress, you must be dreadfully tired from your long trip. I shall warm a wee-bit-a water for washing," she said.

Emily stayed seated not knowing what to say as she tried to organize her scattered, confused thoughts. She wondered if this Isabel was her five-times great-grandmother. Then other questions popped into her head. Why am I here? Why is this happening again?

Isabel looked over her shoulder as she set the skillet to the fire. "Though the morning sun barely broke sky, it's no matter to the Captain, he be wanting to speak wi' ye. Dinnae fret yourself none. He's a kind man," she reassured Emily.

Isabel was a tiny woman. Emily thought she couldn't have been more than twenty. She had pale skin with delicate features and spoke with a charming Scottish accent. Isabel was dressed similarly to Emily, and she moved gracefully through the room as if the heavy clothing had no affect on her movement.

Emily stood and strolled around the room, mesmerized by all the artifacts and then realized they were not artifacts to Isabel or anyone else here. She leaned forward to get a closer look at a painting with a small child sitting on the lap of a British soldier.

"Aye, that be the Captain with his wee boy, Oliver," Isabel said, pointing to another picture. "This one be his bonny wife. Ye see, the Captain being madly in love wi' his sweet Mariah. He put on the British uniform for the lass. Of course, he himself has British roots." Isabel shook her head with regret. "I met her once before she died."

Emily narrowed her eyes and gazed at the attractive woman in the painting. "That's so sad."

"Aye, she drowned in the river two years ago along wi' her friend Celina Stanford. Awful tragic." Isabel touched the picture of the little boy as if missing him. "The wee boy was taken back to England to stay wi' his aunt." Isabel seemed to take a weary deep breath and then shrugged her shoulders. "As for the Captain, ye ken he's pure tough enough to bury his grief working all the time."

Emily ears perked up at the name Stanford. She knew from her research that Celina was her six- times great-grandmother who was married to Jacob Stanford, a patriot during the Revolutionary War. What Emily didn't know was how Celina had died. Emily looked for a date on the painting but found only a scribbled signature of the artist. "What year did she die?" Emily asked hoping to become oriented to the time she was in.

"1774, poor thing," Isabel said.

Emily spun around staring at Isabel. She felt the same weakness in her legs she had from the last time she went back to a time she didn't belong. "If she died, two years ago that means we're in 1776?" Emily asked.

Emily could see Isabel's worried reaction as her eyebrows came together. "Aye, that be the year, of course. Why?"

She had no idea how to respond to Isabel's question and luckily the awkward moment was interrupted by creaking sounds coming from a narrow flight of stairs.

"Speaking o' the Devil," Isabel whispered.

From Emily's vantage point she could see only the bottom five steps. The stairs led presumably to where the bedrooms were. As the man descended the stairs, she saw boots that went to the knees with white pants followed by a red coat, a black collar that went all the way down the whole length of the coat. The buttons looked gold, and he had on a white cotton shirt with ruffled sleeves draping over the back of his hands. The man was very handsome, despite the white wig he wore. He also looked familiar to Emily.

"Captain Douglas Miller," he said bowing making Emily feel like the Queen of England.

Emily reached out her hand to shake his. Instead he barely held her fingers as if forced to respond to her gesture. "Mistress," he said smiling. "Isabel tells me you have arrived and sooner than expected, I might add."

Emily felt at a loss for words, not wanting to speak the wrong way and certainly not wanting to draw attention to herself. She decided to keep it simple for now.

"I've had a long journey for sure sir, er, Captain Miller," she said.

"Aw, well, I'm sure Isabel will accommodate your needs until you get settled. For now, I shall write up your duties, and Isabel can explain the details of each day," he said.

Captain Miller seemed to observe Emily with interest, which made her slightly uncomfortable even though she was observing him as well. It was strange to see a man in a wig, she thought and questioned whether this was all a dream.

The Captain offered a slight bow. "Mistress..." At his hesitation, Emily picked up on his curious expression, realizing she hadn't given her name.

"Oh, yes. My name is Emily Stanford."

Captain Miller's posture stiffened, and he took a step back. "Are you related to Jacob Stanford and his son Jeremiah?" His voice had a hint of suspicion.

Emily wasn't sure what answer would be suitable and once again offered a simple one: "No, must be another Stanford."

The Captain abruptly turned, disregarding Emily's answer and walked back up the creaky stairs clearly annoyed about something. Both she and Isabel held their breaths, waiting for him to reach the top step. Then Isabel let out a sigh of relief.

"Did I say something wrong?" Emily asked.

Isabel checked to see if Captain Miller was gone. "He dinnae like Mister Stanford or his boy," she whispered. "He thinks they're American sympathizers and dinnae trust them worth ye life. I think they blame each other over the drowning."

"Why would they blame each other?"

"Guess one expected the other to be there to save the women."

It was late morning when Emily looked at the list Captain Miller had given to Isabel. The duties were mundane and apparently what was expected of an indentured servant. Isabel had been at the Captain's beck and call for five years, which meant she was a mere child when she started. Isabel had to pay off the money it took for her transportation to the colonies. With her debt paid, her time was up. Emily had stepped into the shoes of the person who would take Isabel's place.

Something else more troubling occurred to Emily. Jeremiah and Isabel were her five-times great-grandparents, which meant they were supposed to be married. According to Isabel, she was leaving town for good, and Emily was beginning to wonder what that meant. To get her mind off all the strangeness surrounding her, she glanced at the list of chores and immediately was taken aback by the first thing on the list: making soap. Emily had no idea how to do that, so she asked Isabel.

"Kit is fetching the lye water, and ye can help wi' boiling the grease," Isabel explained.

"Who's Kit?"

Just then a dark-skinned girl walked in with the lye water and poured the contents of the heavy bucket into the large cast iron pot with no effort. Emily thought she was beautiful and suspected she was one of Captain Miller's slaves.

"Are you Kit?" Emily asked.

The girl looked to Isabel before answering. Isabel gave Kit one of her friendly smiles and nodded towards Emily.

"Yes-um, Mistress. I'd be Kit."

Emily offered Kit a friendly handshake, and again Kit seemed to look for Isabel's approval. Isabel nodded once more. Kit hesitated and then held out her hand. Emily could feel the reluctance of her loose grip. When letting go, she saw Kit stare down at her hand in disbelief. Emily wondered if the slaves were not allowed to have formal introductions that included a handshake. For Emily, her twenty-first century manners automatically took over.

"Kit, my name is Emily, and it's nice to meet you," Emily said. "We're very glad for your help today."

The three women worked on the soap making. Later, Isabel grabbed the flat iron and heated it over the fire so she could press the Captain's shirts. Isabel was busy even on her last day. She was leaving town by morning, and Emily kept trying to think of a way to get her to stay. She saw Isabel go to the front window several times, and she even went outside once to see someone. When Isabel returned her face seemed flushed as if she had been crying.

"It was Jeremiah," she mumbled and immediately went back to her work.

Emily wanted to ask if everything was okay but decided to give the girl some space. About an hour later Emily suddenly heard a tiny gasp. When she turned to look, she saw Isabel by the window again.

"What is it, Isabel?" Emily asked as she walked to the window.

"It's Jeremiah. I ken he be here to speak wi' me again." Isabel swirled around with a smile this time. "I must go to him."

As Isabel went out the door, Emily peeked through the window, finding a well-dressed man wearing black breeches with white stockings underneath. He wore a black topcoat over a white waistcoat and a hat Benjamin Franklin might have worn. Twice that day, Isabel had run out to see Jeremiah by the front gate. As Emily looked on, she noticed their faces brightening up as soon as they saw each other. A sense of urgency came over Emily, and she decided the next time she was alone with Isabel she would ask about Jeremiah.

Kit had left the room to clean the privy, or what Emily knew as the bathroom, located outside several yards from the house. When Isabel returned, she and Emily sat in the two rockers by the fireplace, sipping hot tea and taking a much-needed break. Emily closed her eyes and listened to the sounds from the fire crackling and the faint creak of the floorboards from the rocking chairs. Emily was amazed at how quiet the room was when another pleasant sound drifted past her ears. Isabel hummed a tune Emily had never heard before. The sound offered a feeling of contentment and peace. She glanced towards Isabel and saw that her eyes were closed. It's now or never, Emily thought and decided to take this opportunity to ask Isabel about Jeremiah.

"Are you friends with Jeremiah Stanford?" Emily asked.

Isabel opened her eyes and gave Emily a curious look as she put her cup of tea down and pushed a long strand of blonde hair back under her cap. "Why d'ye ask such a question?"

Emily was aware of the sensibilities from this time period, and she certainly didn't want to insult her five-times great-grandmother.

"I noticed him walking past the house, stopping at the gate, and you going out to see him. Both of you looked happy."

"Aye. Ye'd be right. I ken Jeremiah loves me and I him. He is wanting to be wi' me for a long time." Isabel shook her head with a hint of disappointment. "His father widnae have it. An indentured servant would be a stain on his family's name," she added.

Finally, after thinking so hard to come up with an idea to help Isabel, one just popped into Emily's mind. "What if I can talk to his father and make him see reason? I'm a Stanford after all," Emily offered.

Isabel seemed confused. "I thought ye said ye weren't related to them?" Before Emily could answer, Isabel got up from the chair and looked out the window towards the front gate. "Jeremiah first told me he loved me right there at yon gate three years ago," Isabel said.

Emily could see it written all over Isabel's face that she saw the image of that moment.

"Haste ye back, I told him."

Emily had no idea what she just said, and Isabel must have read the confusion on her face. "Aye, it means, 'return soon'."

Emily walked to the window wondering if she could even leave the house. Will I go back to my own time before I can help Isabel? Or will I end up some place else unknown and lost forever. I need to take my chances, she decided. Emily knew from the Stanford Library archives where Jacob Stanford lived at the time. It was still early afternoon, and she knew she had time to go and get back before anyone knew she was missing. In her own time, it was a short two-minute car ride but now, no more than a fifteen-minute walk.

"I can do this," Emily said mostly reassuring herself. "I know things—things that could change his father's mind." Emily took hold of Isabel's arms and look confidently into her eyes. "Trust me, Isabel. Don't leave yet. Stay a few more days."

Isabel looked puzzled over her statement, and Emily could see by Isabel's soft expression that she trusted her strange idea.

"I will wait till ye talk wi' him," she nodded towards the door saying, "Haste ye back."

Emily smiled and hugged Isabel. "Don't worry, I will."

Emily stood at the threshold of the entrance way looking beyond the gate leading to the dirt road. She heard no water fall sounds, saw no mist with the mysterious woman's face, although she felt a slight brisk breeze of what she assumed had been a February afternoon. Melted ice dripped from an oak tree in the front yard as the afternoon sun hit the branches. She was glad there was no snow on the ground, which would make it easier to walk. Emily closed her eyes and could hear the clatter of horse hooves with wagons being dragged along the loose stone and dry mud. Happy sounds of greetings from two neighbors passing by each other echoed through the cold, fresh air. She took two steps forward, then opened her eyes, and could see she was still in the past. She reached into her pocket. I still have my notebook, my pen, and Rick's key, she thought. She felt comforted knowing she was still tethered to her own time.

When she reached the main street, she was struck to see Maple Ridge completely underdeveloped. There was no supermarket. Just a small livery stable with a tiny general store next to it. No homes with groomed lawns and bushes. Only painted houses splattered with dried up mud and dust from the road. The Shady Brook bridge was still there, although narrower and looking unsafe. Emily walked across the wooden bridge leading to a small path and through an overgrown wooded area that eventually become the Stanford Park Square. Only one path had been kept clean, and she followed it. She stopped behind a large oak, took out her small notebook, and jotted down some details she saw firsthand, a perspective she could not find on any Internet site:

Horses pulling wagons through massive holes in the dirt road, yet somehow-they do it anyway. A stone house painted white with bright red trim and large, red front doors. Dried up mud spattered everywhere even on that beautiful white stone house set to close to the road. Old cast iron hitching posts positioned every few feet along the roadway. The Shady Brook bridge looked as if it could barely take the weight of a horse and wagon.

Emily suddenly heard the sound of someone walking towards her and quickly put the notebook and pen back in her pocket. She turned to where the sound was coming from, and a man popped out from behind a bush with huge cast-iron cutting shears.

"I'm sorely sorry if I scared you, Mistress," the man said.

Emily was stunned by the man's looks. The man could have been Lucas's brother. She could barely catch her breath, and she stumbled out from behind the oak tree. The man dropped his shears and sprang around to catch her before she fell.

"Are you well, Mistress?" he asked.

Upon his touch, Emily felt a strange energy go through her. She gazed into the man's eyes, not wanting to let go. "I'm so sorry, I—I think I'm okay," Emily said, trying to pull herself together.

The man looked at her strangely. "Okay? What is this 'okay' mean?" he asked.

She waved her hand as if she were swatting a fly. "Oh, just an old expression from where I come from is all."

The man faced her formally. "William Easton at your service," he bowed politely to Emily.

She knew he must have been Lucas's ancestor by the remarkable resemblance along with the same last name. She had a hard time not staring and began fumbling her words.

"I...er...I'm Emily Ss-Stanford."

William seemed unfazed by Emily's abrupt appearance and instead began a pleasant conversation.

"I love gardening, and it's a good time of year for pruning shrubs," he said swiveling around and holding his hand out in presentation of the wooded area. "I volunteer my time with the intent of turning this wooded area into a park someday, or—as I try my best to do so."

William looked to be between the ages of twenty and twenty-five. Emily remembered Lucas and even herself at that age and longed once again for her deceased husband. William pushed his dark brown hair back, and despite the cold air, beads of sweat showed on his forehead. She continued to stare at him, trying to steady herself.

"Stanford," he said with a thoughtful look. "Would you be related to the Stanfords up the road?"

Emily was able to regain her composure. "Yes, as a matter of fact, I was just going there, so how far is it from here?" she asked, even though she had the general idea where it was.

"Over the bridge," William lifted his chin in the direction of the bridge. "Third house to the left alongside the river."

An awkward silence came between them with William breaking it first. "Well, best be getting back to my work," he politely bowed. "With pleasure, Mistress Stanford." He picked up the cast-iron shears.

Emily watched William walk towards the wooded area and disappear into the brush. He had left her astonished by the strange energy from his touch, causing her to wonder: What kind of magic did William Easton possess?

Chapter 4

THE RIGHT SIDE OF HISTORY

THE WAGONS GOING BY KICKED UP A CLOUD OF DUST, making it almost impossible to breathe. It felt dry for this time of year, which caused the mud to harden on the road. Emily was accustomed to clean air and paved streets. She wished she had taken one of the canteens on the shelf in Isabel's dish cupboard and filled it with cold water. She walked back over the creaky bridge, stopping in the middle to look out over the Magic River. The river's edge showed foot traffic from slaves and servants drawing water for every household need. The same mist that had hovered over the water was there. A river that strangely never froze. She remembered what Rick said about the hot springs going through it. Apparently, from what she could see, that phenomenon had been occurring for over two centuries. Emily walked along the side of the road and tried not to get run over by a horse. Her long skirt felt heavy, making each step difficult. Emily walked for at least fifteen minutes, passing the first house and then the second. She arrived at the third house, which was set back slightly from the road.

The gate was pretty, constructed of wood painted white with a maple leaf carving in the center. She saw slaves digging with pickaxes, working a small field for planting. The Magic River ran through the backyard of Jacob Stanford's home, as it did at Captain Miller's place. A maple tree shaded the front of a large fieldstone Dutch home with its steep roofline and shuttered windows. Two small window dormers perched over the front porch roof, and firewood was stacked off to one side of the porch for convenience. Smoke billowed out of a large chimney at the far end of the house, making it look inviting on such a cold day. The chill, however, didn't stop her hands from sweating and her heart from pounding as she knocked on the front door. A woman about Emily's age opened the door looking disheveled as she wiped her hands on a well-stained apron.

"Can I be of assistance, Mistress?" she asked pleasantly.

Emily cleared her throat, making every attempt to calm her nerves. "Yes, I—I'm looking to speak to Jacob Stanford."

"May I ask who is calling?"

Emily put on her best smile. "Emily Stanford."

"Oh, of course, come in. Have a seat won't you?" The woman pointed to a small chair near the doorway leading to a big room off to the left. She left Emily alone.

The big room had enormous beams and wide plank floors that looked scuffed up from all the traffic that most likely flowed through what appeared to be the main room. I can't believe I'm actually going to see my six-times great-grandfather, she thought. Her nervousness was starting to return when she saw standing in the doorway a small black child with the most beautiful smile.

"I'm-ah, come to fetch you, Mistress. Come follow me," she said in a sweet voice.

She led Emily through a long hallway with a door at the end. Upon entering the room, Emily saw a man sitting in a big chair behind a beautifully carved wooden desk. All the carvings indicated the same theme: maple trees.

"Jacob Stanford at your service," he announced, standing with a bow. "Please," he said extending his hand, offering Emily the chair in front of his desk.

"It's a pleasure to meet you, Mr. Stanford," Emily said nervously.

Jacob smiled, nodding. "You as well, Mistress Stanford. Are we related somehow, given we share the same last name?"

His question gave Emily the opening she needed. She was determined to leverage her knowledge about Stanford family history in hopes of helping Isabel and Jeremiah.

"Your Uncle Vergil took in a very young indentured servant with a child and no husband. Vergil was such an extraordinarily good man. He protected them both by giving the servant and her child his last name." Emily put her hand above her chest. "I am that servant," she said, almost believing her own lie.

Jacob looked surprised but not shocked. He seemed to know this information. His expression told Emily that he was surprised only by his uncle's servant showing up on his doorstep. Emily had records of Vergil adding a woman and child to his household, but no first names were ever recorded. Although Emily never found details about the servant or her child, she did have one document stating that they had disappeared, never to be seen again.

"How remarkable. There was talk of you and your child and that you had drowned in the river," he said.

Now Emily was the one surprised. She hadn't heard that story anywhere yet realized the possibility that it could be true. She felt almost guilty taking on the identity of someone with such a tragic ending.

"My daughter passed on from illness," Emily said. "I became indentured many years ago to another family and now work for Captain Miller. So we did not drown in the river," Emily clarified.

Emily had a difficult time weaving lies in and out of the real truth, which caused her to be nervous again. She overcame her nervousness with one thought that ran through her mind: I have to keep this going for Isabel and Jeremiah's sake. "So, as to why I'm here, sir. First, I believe in true love, which, if true, lasts forever. Wouldn't you agree, sir?" Emily asked.

Jacob looked puzzled. He had striking features with a long, sharp nose and a gray mustache, which traveled down both sides of his mouth. He wasn't overly handsome but had big, attractive brown eyes that seemed to have the capacity to intimidate or lure someone into submission. Neither of which affected Emily at the moment.

He raised his thick eyebrows in agreement with Emily's observation over true love. "I echo your sentiments, Mistress Stanford."

"Now that we agree so far," Emily said. "Here's the truth of it. Your son Jeremiah and Captain Miller's now-former servant Isabel are in love—hopelessly in love." She emphasized her last point. Jacob opened his mouth to respond, but Emily interrupted. "Please, Mr. Stanford, hear me out."

He nodded. "Go on with it then."

Emily sat up straight in the chair slowing her breathing while fighting off the nagging jitters in her stomach. "If you're able to see past whatever misconceptions you might have about Isabel, you would see her good reputation." Emily tried with all-out effort to be as convincing as possible. "You would also see her kindness and beauty, not to mention the love she has for your son. Therefore, I ask on their behalf that you consider them as a couple and give your permission for them to marry."

Abruptly, Jacob stood up from his chair. The veins on his temples throbbed, giving Emily the sense that he was insulted. "I beg your pardon, Madam, who gives you the right to speak to me in such a disrespectful way, presuming I should do what you say, when I haven't the slightest proof of who you are!"

Emily had worried Jacob might have this reaction but only considered it a worst-case scenario. Luckily, she was ready for her next plan, which included using a more powerful tactic, although it was one she hoped she wouldn't have to use. She rose with the same force as Jacob, standing her ground, ready to give the next piece of information that would give her that leverage she needed.

"Does the word 'smuggle' mean anything to you, Jacob Stanford?"

He looked like a balloon that was popped suddenly.

"What are you speaking of? And I suggest you use your words carefully, Madam."

Emily strolled around the room, trying to act coy. She felt the danger but had to be brave even though her insides screamed fear and the urge to run dominated every part of her body. "Don't worry, I have no intention of spilling your secrets," she said pushing past her fears. "After all, you are on the right side of history. I know about the soldiers you're hiding in the basement along with gunpowder and muskets."

Jacob pounded on the big wooden desk and startled Emily. "This is blackmail worthy of treason!" he yelled.

"Yes, in any other army," Emily quickly explained. "But not this army, not in the American army of patriots." As Emily came closer to Jacob, the side of his mouth twitched, diminishing his blustering response towards her. She then softened her tone with an air of understanding in her voice.

"You're fighting for the freedoms of all Americans, so they have life, liberty and the pursuit of happiness. So, Mr. Stanford, as I said, you and I are on the same side."

Emily knew the peril she put herself in but trusted her ancestor. She had full knowledge of Jacob's character and how brave he truly was during the Revolutionary War. Jacob was one of many throughout the region that had smuggled men and weapons for the past year, helping the resistance to sail up the Magic River from the Boston Harbor into interior sections of Massachusetts and elsewhere. The Stanford house was one of those stopovers for the men to rest and to gain reinforcements. If caught by the British, Jacob and his son would be sure to hang from the maple tree standing in front of their house.

"How is it that you come by this information?" Jacob asked, annoyed.

Emily sat down as Jacob stood with his arms crossed, showing a commanding presence. The room felt warm, and Emily couldn't wait to get out of the situation, wanting to put this crazy experience behind her.

Emily slowed her words. "I know these things because I, too, am part of the rebellion and a real patriot. Now, I ask you to please reconsider your son's true love for a wonderful, beautiful person. She is also a real patriot."

Jacob lowered himself to the chair behind his desk. Emily saw defeat in his eyes and suspected that her presence was unsettling for him. She felt sympathy for the man. She leaned forward, putting her hands on the desk.

"Jacob," she said softly.

He looked at her with less contempt this time.

"I understand your loss. I know about your wife, and I'm sorry for the pain you're in. As far as being a patriot, I'll leave you with this. You're helping with a remarkable cause, one your country will appreciate someday. People like Isabel and even the slaves will live free and have all kinds of opportunities. You all will. And one more thing. You, sir, are loved by God, and because of that love you're able to see the good in others." Emily waited a moment to see if she was getting through to Jacob and felt certain she was.

Jacob left his seat and went to the door. "I appreciate your condolence," he said gesturing towards the door for her to leave.

Emily went over and stood next to him without saying a word.

"And you think Isabel is worthy enough for my son to marry?"

"Yes, absolutely," Emily said with confidence. "She is good, good for your son, good for your family and most of all, just like you and Jeremiah, Isabel is on the right side of history."

An hour later Emily strolled along the dirt road back to Captain Miller's house. On the way, she couldn't help but feel sorry for Jacob. She hoped that her knowledge of what he was up to would be enough leverage to persuade him. Emily had the sense that Jacob believed her, and he also was well aware of his son's affections and love for Isabel. He couldn't put his prejudices aside over how his son's standing in the community would be affected by marrying a servant. Lucky Emily had been quick to point out that Jacob's own uncle Vergil had the decency to help out a poor servant and her child, going as far as giving his name to them for protection. Emily was glad she knew the Stanford heritage even though she had to lie to her own six-times, great-grandfather. Lies twisted around the truth. She had to do it; otherwise, she wouldn't even exist, a scary thought she tried to keep out of her mind. She felt confident Jacob was going to talk to his son Jeremiah and knew it would all work out. After all, Emily thought, Isabel and Jeremiah are my five-times great-grandparents.

Emily walked towards the front door of Captain Miller's house when she heard a strange chanting coming from the back of the house. She followed the sound and could see it was coming from an older woman kneeling by the river. The chanting had a musical rhythm with a sad sounding ancient language coming from a woman who was ancient herself. Emily came within two feet of her.

"Are you all right?" Emily asked softly, hoping to not startle the old woman.

She wore feathers hanging over long braids with a headband which had a tribal symbol, indicating she was a Native American. She wore what looked to be a beaver fur coat. The woman looked over her shoulder with her eyes brightening at the sight of Emily, turned her head towards the river, and resumed her chanting with much less sorrow. Emily knelt next to her, mesmerized by the mysterious chant. When finally she made eye contact with Emily, she spoke in English.

"The last of the bloodline must travel far in time telling those affected by the curse that their creator loves them."

Emily felt the blood drain from her face. "I have traveled far to get here. Do you know something about me? Something I need to know?" Emily asked in desperation.

The woman made an effort to stand, and Emily put her hand under her arm to assist her. She immediately felt a strange energy coming from the older woman, who looked to Emily to be in her late nineties, if not older. Emily noticed her small, frail face had leathery skin, and her dark brown eyes were so clear and filled with knowledge. The woman appeared thoughtful as she spoke again.

"Two families are cursed. Only one—the last of the Stanford bloodline—can break the curse cast by Orenda."

"What do you mean? I don't understand," Emily pleaded, but the woman remained silent, looking at Emily as if pleased to be in her presence. "Can you at least tell me your name?"

"Catori, which means Spirit." She put her hand on Emily's cheek. "Your face—a vision of long ago. Hair red as fire, eyes as green as emeralds, a heart thoughtful but sad."

"What vision?" Emily asked. "I don't understand any of this. Who are you? How do you seem to know me, and who is Orenda?"

Catori wrapped her hands around Emily's and squeezed gently. They were warm and somehow comforting. "Orenda, which means Magic Powers," she said, bowing her head in reverence. "She was my oldest friend."

Emily was a little frustrated by not getting the precise answers she hoped for or even ones that made sense to her. Catori turned and walked with careful steps towards Kit, who was waiting discreetly by one of the maple trees. Emily followed.

"You said two families. Who is the other family?" Emily asked.

Catori stopped, glanced at Emily, and then looked towards the house. Emily noticed that her dark brown eyes were focused on Captain Miller, who was standing in the window.

"Miller? Is that the other family?"

Catori gave Emily a regretful look and instead of answering Emily's question she offered haunting words: "A curse is like a stone hitting water as it ripples through time until it meets its end."

"I don't understand. Tell me—what curse?" Emily implored.

Catori pointed in the direction of the river. "The curse on the Magic River."

A voice yelled, interrupting Emily's questioning. Isabel ran towards them, trying to catch her breath as she stopped in front of Emily and Catori.

"If ye would excuse us, Catori," Isabel said, grabbing Emily's arm and escorting her towards the house. Emily looked back, finding Kit helping Catori to walk over to a bench to sit. Emily felt reluctant to leave her conversation with the old woman, desperate to find out more. Isabel's eagerness overshadowed the moment.

"So, did ye get somewhere wi' Mister Stanford?" Isabel asked.

Emily patted Isabel's hand, smiled, and Isabel shrieked, squeezing Emily's arm with excitement. "I can't believe ye did it! So tell me."

Emily and Isabel came around the side of the house, and Emily saw Jeremiah standing by the gate. "Come, I need to say something to both of you," Emily said.

Upon reaching the gate, Emily noticed how Isabel and Jeremiah gazed at each other, both clearly in love.

"Hello, Isabel. You're looking well today," Jeremiah said politely. He then bowed to both women. He looked pleased and gave Emily an extra nod and smiled.

Emily knew Jacob must have spoken to Jeremiah right away, and he wasted no time coming over to see Isabel.

"I thank you, Mistress Emily, for your help, although I don't quite know how you were able to persuade my father so quickly," Jeremiah said.

"Let's just say I have a certain perspective on what lies ahead in the future," Emily said.

Isabel looked slightly confused over the exchange of words between Emily and Jeremiah. "So what is it ye need to say to us, Mistress Emily?" Isabel asked.

Emily took Isabel's hand, placing it on Jeremiah's. Emily could feel that strange energy she felt when helping Catori up from kneeling on the ground a few minutes before.

"First, I'm so happy for the two of you, and second," Emily hesitated, looking at Jeremiah. "Believe me, your father wasn't easily persuaded, but he's a reasonable man and knows the love you have for Isabel." Isabel blushed and looked at Jeremiah with sheep eyes as Emily continued, "and third, I need you both to know one important thing: God loves you, always remember that."

Emily suddenly realized where the urge to tell this particular piece of information came from, knowing it had to be Catori's claims of breaking some strange curse. Emily had said it first to Jacob and now to Isabel and Jeremiah. There was only one question Emily had to ask herself: How many more generations am I supposed to tell?"

Chapter 5

INTERROGATION

THE NEXT DAY WAS BUSY with accomplishing more mundane chores on Captain Miller's list. Isabel remained in the Captain's care for now with no obligations to be a servant any longer. To Isabel's credit, she took on the work of the day without skipping a beat. She and Jeremiah were to be married soon, and Emily was glad she had a hand in making sure it happened.

Emily had a restless night plagued with worries of being stuck in the eighteenth century indefinitely. *Was there someone else I needed to tell about their creator loving them? Could it be Captain Miller?* she wondered. Emily sat in the main room by the big fireplace, churning the fresh cream to make butter. She looked around the room while cranking a lever that turned a barrel position on a bracket. She still couldn't believe where she was or how she got there. She wouldn't have wanted to live in these times, which felt so primitive compared to her own. But here she was, her arm killing her from churning butter for the past thirty minutes. To pass the time, she focused on the painted portrait of the Captain's wife and remembered what Isabel said about the woman: She had drowned in the river two years ago along with her friend. That friend, Emily thought, happened to be her ancestor. Emily wondered if that tragedy had anything to do with the curse. She wanted desperately to talk to Catori again, hoping she would get the chance after helping Isabel or in this case Isabel helping her. Suddenly she heard Isabel running down the stairs interrupting her thoughts.

"The Captain calls for ye. I widnae make him wait," Isabel said.

Emily wondered if the Captain learned of her visit to Jacob Stanford and was concerned about how it looked. The Captain suspected that Jacob was a traitor, and, in a way, Jacob was a traitor or at least to the British army. Emily also knew the Captain didn't trust her either by his reaction to hearing her last name. Emily knew at some point Captain Miller would have questions for her. She put her hand on Isabel's arm for reassurance. "It'll be all right. Don't worry." Although Emily tried calming fears in Isabel, she needed to do the same for herself as well.

She found Captain Miller standing by the window facing the river. The room was pleasant. The walls were covered with bookshelves, which reached to the ceiling. Captain Miller's desk wasn't quite as impressive as Jacob Stanford's but still was beautifully made. The only thing on his desk was a wooden box with a design carved into the top. The room had a military feel, with muskets hanging on racks along with swords displayed in several places throughout the room. A pistol leaned against the brick on a mantel of a small fireplace. Next to the pistol was a miniature painting of a child held by the same beautiful woman in the painting downstairs.

"I saw you speaking with Catori yesterday," Captain Miller said with his back turned, still looking out the window.

Emily took a deep breath to calm herself. "Yes, she's an interesting woman."

"She raised my father since he was five. She was like a grandmother to me even though I could never understand why she spoke so strangely," he said.

Emily could see the Captain's shoulders drop as if defeated over an argument he couldn't win.

"She told me my wife died because of a curse," he turned to look at Emily. "The old Indian woman has been bloody ranting and raving for years."

Emily resented his disrespect for Catori. She had a strong urge to let him know how displeased she felt, but she saw a shadow suddenly came over the Captain's face.

"My dear sweet Mariah drowned in that river, and I was unable to save her. My son Oliver could not get over her death," he said, looking again out the window as if trying to will his wife back from the water.

Emily felt sorry for the Captain, knowing all too well the pain she had felt when she lost Lucas, the same pain she felt every day. The Captain's loss had shown all over his face and most likely affected him the same way.

"I'm so sorry for your loss and your son's heartache," she said stepping forward. "I lost my husband in an accident."

The Captain abruptly turned towards Emily as though he had forgotten his manners. "How inconsiderate of me. I should not have told you. I would not want to cause unwanted distress, Mistress," he said in a strange tone.

Emily shook her head. "No, no, of course, you wouldn't. It seems we both have heartache to deal with."

Emily could feel something was off about Captain Miller's demeanor. She detected a hint of insincerity in his voice when he tried to convey his half-hearted sympathies towards her. The Captain pointed to two chairs with a side table, and they both sat. Emily was able to get a good look at his face from this vantage point, and she was amazed at how much he looked like Rick. Same eyes and thick hair not covered up this time by a ridiculous wig. She missed Rick at that moment, and then Lucas's face popped into her head, causing conflicting feelings inside her. Her thoughts and the assessment over Captain Miller's looks were interrupted by that uneasy tone of voice she sensed from him a minute ago.

"I'm sorry, but I must ask a question which has distressed me," he said.

Emily sat up in the chair, waiting for the questioning she had already expected. He looked at Emily closely, as if studying her face. She watched his gaze traveling down her body and back up again until his eyes met hers. She sensed being sized up for a more personal task and tried desperately to shake off those unwanted thoughts that made her uncomfortable.

"May I be so bold as to ask: How does a beautiful woman such as yourself come to be indentured? Surely your deceased husband's family, and with the Stanford name I might add, would care for you quite nicely without being indentured to anyone."

He continued to stare at Emily, and the uncomfortable feelings increased.

"I'm sure, Captain Miller, my looks and status can't be the only reason you called me in here," she said trying to deflect his question.

He leaned towards Emily, coming within inches of her face. His breath was warm and smelled of cherry tobacco. He was handsome, and she found herself oddly attracted to him. His eyes seemed to read her mind, and she had all to do to keep her thoughts hidden.

"Why would you call on Mister Stanford?" he whispered.

"Because of Isabel and Jeremiah," she answered. Emily explained the young couple's predicament with Jacob Stanford, and how Jacob wanted nothing to do with his son marrying a servant. She also told Captain Miller that her Stanford name could have some influence in changing Jacob's mind about Isabel.

The Captain abruptly strode to his desk making it obvious he did not like her answer. "I thought you said you were no relation to Mister Stanford?" he said with a hint of anger in his voice.

"Well, if I am related, I'm certainly unaware of it," she said feebly.

The Captain lifted the cover of the wooden box on his desk. "Do you recognize these objects," he said, holding up her notebook, pen, and Rick's key.

Shocked, Emily instinctively patted her pocket. She hadn't realized the dress she had worn the day before had been switched somehow. To Emily, all the dresses looked the same.

"You won't find them there," he said smugly. "You see, Kit did the laundry and found them."

Captain Miller now had custody of the three things that had made her feel connected to the twenty-first century. Emily had no explanation for the three items.

"You know what bothers me the most? Why would you be in possession of my key?" he displayed the key. "A key, I might add, that belongs to my house."

Emily stood up, brushing off invisible lint from her skirt nervously. She walked over to the Captain with as much confidence as possible, hoping he would back off as Jacob did the day before. But Captain Miller didn't; he stood looming tall and superior over Emily.

"I found the key on the floor in the entrance way. I tucked it into my pocket and well…forgot about it." Emily said. What a lame excuse, she thought.

"What excuse do you have for this strange device?" He held her pen.

"It's a writing tool and a new invention from where I come from." She could tell immediately the Captain wasn't buying it.

"Where you come from? And where might that be, Madam?"

Before Emily could answer, Captain Miller spoke firmly and with growing accusation. "I'm sorry, but I don't believe you. You showed up yesterday, two days early. You have a suspicious meeting with Jacob Stanford. You possess strange objects, like a notebook filled with descriptions of the bridge, roadways, and houses—something a spy would do." He held up the key and focused on Emily with a look of contempt. "And then there is this— my key! It bloody well doesn't add up."

The air in the room grew hotter, as the two stared at each other waiting for one of them to make the first move. Finally, the Captain walked over to the door, showing Emily out. Every fiber in her body screamed with a mixture of anger, fear, and anxiety. Her heart pounded. She had no idea what he would do to her; she was his servant after all. She made her way to the door without looking at Captain Miller, but before she could leave, he stopped her by grabbing her arm. She was once again within inches of his face and could see by the look in his eyes that it was the Captain this time who seemed oddly attracted to her.

"You need to go to your quarters until I decide what to do with you," he said more calmly this time.

She forcibly pulled her arm away and walked down a short hallway with Captain Miller one step behind. She walked into the room. He seemed reluctant to close the door. His gaze traveled to her breasts and back to her face as he slowly shut the door without a word. She heard the door lock. Emily leaned against the door, wondering how she would ever escape.

Emily paced back and forth, stopping to look out the window in hopes of getting someone's attention. It was a cloudy day and other than the single candle burning on a small stand it had little effect in lighting the room. She kept going over in her mind their conversation that led to her being locked up like a criminal. She knew it was time for her to go. She sensed it. She felt the energy around her. But where will I go? Will I be able to get back to my own time?

She looked out the window again and saw Catori sitting on the bench by the river when it suddenly occurred to Emily. She hadn't told the Captain about his creator loving him. Emily was certain that his wife Mariah was a victim of the curse. Emily would feel awful if she didn't at least tell Captain Miller the one thing that could save him or anyone he chose to be close to in the future. She searched the room for some paper and a quill, finding both on a small desk partially hidden behind long window drapes in the corner of the room. She sat in the chair, dipped the quill into ink, and wrote a note to the Captain.

Dear Captain Miller:

I regret our departure in this way but felt I needed to tell you something important and didn't have the chance with all the suspicion you have about me. I never meant you any harm, nor am I a spy. It pains me over your loss of Mariah. I need to tell you how blessed you are and how much God loves you. Mariah is with our loving God at this very moment. Do not hold anything against Jacob Stanford, for he is a good man, as I know you are. I am well aware that both you and Jacob share the same tragic loss. Now you both are in the midst of a war for independence. Soon, a document will be read in every town and city that will lay out what America will look like going forward for both sides. Remember me when you read this document, for I know with great certainty that these words will live on for many generations to come. I also want you to know, Captain Miller, not only does God love you, but he also wants all of us to know that all men are created equal.

Sincerely,

Emily Stanford

P.S. Please tell your son Oliver that God loves him, too.

Emily folded the note in half and noticed on the desk a wax stick and a gold stamp with the same design that was featured on Captain Miller's box. Although she had never sealed anything with wax before, she had seen it done in a movie once. Emily folded the note once more, taking it and the wax stick over to the candle. Holding the stick over the flame she dripped the melted wax onto the note, sealing it. Emily pressed the gold stamp lightly on the wax and waited for it to dry and then wrote Captain Miller's name on the outside.

"Well, this will have to do," she sighed and placed it on the bed. She nervously paced back and forth again until she heard a gentle tap on the door.

"Mistress Emily? Are ye in there?"

It was Isabel speaking softly on the other side. Emily whispered back, not wanting to cause any attention. "Isabel? The Captain locked me in."

The doorknob rattled and then swung open with Isabel holding Rick's key, which apparently opened every door in the house.

"How in the world did you get the key?" Emily asked, amazed at the sight of Isabel holding it in the palm of her hand.

"No fret yourself none. I ken where Captain Miller keeps most things, and I think ye'd be looking for these I suspect," Isabel said, handing the pen and notebook to Emily.

Emily gave her a big hug in appreciation and became hopeful she would get out of the eighteenth century as soon as she stepped through the front door. "Thank you, Isabel, for trusting me."

"Aye. I widnae open the door if I nae trust ye. Besides with all the help you have given my beloved Jeremiah and me, I ken you're a good person."

Suddenly, Emily heard the sound of rushing water and felt the situation becoming more urgent. She knew it was time to go. She took the note from the bed and handed it to Isabel. "I need you to do one more thing for me: Would you make sure that the Captain gets this?"

Isabel seemed uncertain, but she took the note, nodded her head, and started to walk away. Emily reached out to stop her. "Isabel? I'm glad I got to meet you and Jeremiah. I wish you both a long and happy life." Emily felt her eyes fill with tears, knowing she would never see her five-times great-grandmother again.

"I will miss ye, Mistress Emily. Haste ye back," she said and smiled sweetly.

Emily matched her smile and said, "I wish I could."

Both women nodded in agreement. Isabel disappeared around the corner, leaving Emily standing in the doorway. She could never be part of Isabel or Jeremiah's life, and she knew what she had to do. Emily made her way down the stairs quickly when Captain Miller came swiftly down after her.

"Stop! Stop!" he yelled.

The sound of rushing water grew louder in Emily's ears, and she felt the breeze on her face. She saw a dark-haired woman standing in the mist, which filled the front doorway. Emily vaguely heard the pleas from Captain Miller demanding her to stop. Instead, she ran right through the image of the woman and into the fog.

Emily kept running until she ran straight into Rick's arms. She held on tight, shaking like a leaf.

"Are you all right?" he asked.

Emily couldn't respond at first when suddenly she realized she was back in her own time and being held by a man she hardly knew. She reluctantly pulled away, staring up at Rick.

"I waited over an hour for you to come out of the old house," he said. "I even walked around the house to see if you had gone out back. You were nowhere to be found." She saw Rick narrow his eyes. "Emily? What ghost did you see this time?"

Chapter 6

THE HERO

THE SOUNDS IN THE MAPLE RIDGE DINER were magnified for Emily from the tinkling bell over the door each time someone came in or went out to another louder bell that rang when an order was ready. The sounds of silverware scraping across someone's plate as they ate and the slurp of a person sipping a drink reverberated in her head. Emily rested her head in her arms at the table and then raised her head to see the slurping sound was coming from Rick sipping coffee from a mug.

He put his coffee down, rested his arms on the table, and raised his eyebrows with a question written all over his face. He had the same suspicious look in his eyes towards her as Captain Miller did, but Rick said nothing.

Emily was quick to break the silence between them. "What?" Emily asked, encouraging the verbal interpretation of his question.

"You know, I don't mind a woman running into my arms with such enthusiasm. In fact, it was quite pleasant, if you ask me," he said with that familiar smirk she remembered on his younger self. "What I want to know is: What on God's green earth were you running from?"

Emily collected her thoughts and knew she had to tell someone or go completely insane. "Well, in November when I went into the old school..." She swallowed hard, hoping he wouldn't think she was crazy. "Something strange happened when I was in there."

"Uh-huh. Is that why you had that 'I saw a ghost look' on your face that day? The same look I saw about an hour ago when you seemed to be running for your life."

"Yes, although I didn't see a ghost in either case. I—I went back in time," she said abruptly and cringed from what clearly sounded deranged even to her own ears.

Rick pushed his hair back, pausing for a moment seemingly in thought. Emily saw the baffled look he gave her. "That's quite a tall tale you're telling," he said.

"I completely understand if you don't believe me." Emily shook her head and let out a tiny laugh that revealed how ridiculous she must sound. "Why in the heck would you believe me anyway? You hardly know me. For all you know, I could have just been released from an insane asylum. So, yeah—AKA, nut case."

"Now, I didn't say that. In fact, I'd like to hear more," he said.

Emily was amazed over Rick's willingness to give her the benefit of the doubt. She told him everything and felt relieved, glad she no longer held such a secret. He listened to every little detail with interest. He laughed when she told him about the younger version of himself in first grade and then discovered that neither one had memories of the other in first grade. Rick seemed concerned that she had put herself in a dangerous situation with Jacob Stanford and Captain Miller. It wasn't until she talked about the curse that he had the most questions.

"So, what you're saying is, you have to go back in time to tell these people who are under the curse that their creator loves them? That's it?"

"That's what this Native American woman said anyway," Emily replied.

"Uh-huh. And I'm part of this curse because I'm a Miller?"

"Right. I'm part of the curse, too," she admitted.

Rick held his coffee mug without taking a sip, as if contemplating Emily's bizarre story. The diner was filling up with the supper crowd, and the air was getting stuffy. He put his coffee mug down with his gaze settling on Emily. She felt an attraction towards this unexpected new friend, and she was sure he felt the same from his steady eyes and reassuring smile.

"So, do you believe me?" she asked.

Rick put his hand on top of Emily's, squeezing it slightly. "It sounds like *The Twilight Zone* if you ask me." His tone was lukewarm, leaving Emily unsure of how he felt. "Yes, Emily, I believe you experienced something very unusual." His mouth turned up, and his gaze appeared to be drawn to her lips. "Besides, you seem like a level-headed woman. So yes, I believe you're telling me the truth."

He kept his warm hand on hers. He seemed sincere and open minded, but Emily still wasn't sure if Rick was only trying to make her feel better. In any case, she had to take him at his word just as he was willing to accept hers.

Two days later, Emily sat at her desk at the town office and wrote her article about the old saltbox house titled "The Captain's House." She felt a presence behind her. It was Rick peering over her head.

"Nice title," he said, coming around and sitting next to her.

"Well, what would you have me call it?" Emily asked without expecting an answer.

"Maybe 'Escaping the Clutches of Captain Miller'?" he said in a ghoulish voice.

Emily poked him with her elbow. "Very funny."

"What's funny?" Mark Johnson roared as he marched into the room. He sat at the desk opposite of Emily's and then stuck the unlit cigar back in his mouth. "You got some inspections to take care of Miller. Or are you just going to bother the help all day?"

Rick got up and put his hand on Emily's shoulder. She felt a warm sensation throughout her body that surprised her.

"Call me when you're ready to go back in time," he said. Emily thought he was half-joking, half-serious.

Rick turned to Mark. "Well, I'm off to aggravate the next group of people over their bad roofs and leaky plumbing." He gave a charming wink to Emily and out the door he went.

She looked back at Mark, who had a grin on his face. "What?" Emily asked, shrugging her shoulders.

"Haven't seen him this happy in a long time is all. Don't go by me, but he might be a little smitten."

Emily rolled her eyes. "I don't know. I don't think so. I'm sure he's got better things to do."

"Suit yourself," Mark said while rummaging through papers on his desk. "I still say he seems pretty happy lately."

Emily turned her story in, and the next day it was in circulation throughout Maple Ridge. She stayed as truthful as possible in the article, leaving out the whole curse part and being chased by a British captain.

To get her mind off her strange experience, she decided to visit the Maple Ridge Nursing Home where she had previously worked. Emily wanted to talk to one particular gentleman, Walter Green, who knew some stories about his ancestors. He had shared them with her several times. Most of his stories were from the Civil War era. Walter was also a history teacher back in his day, so Emily and Walter shared the same interest. Emily had known Walter for years, and he seemed to be in and out of her life just at the right times. He was always a kind man and a good friend to her. Recently Walter had moved into the Maple Ridge Nursing Home. He had been very ill in the past year with heart problems, which gave Emily another reason for her visit.

She found Walter in his room squinting through his thick glasses trying to read what looked to be the *Maple Ridge Gazette*.

"Keeping up with the latest I see," Emily said cheerfully.

"Oh! Emily, my favorite nurse. I see my best student is keeping busy in her retirement," Walter said, holding up the paper showing the title of her article, "The Captain's House."

Emily sat next to Walter, hugged him, and could tell he had lost more weight. "Nice to see you too, Walter. How are you feeling today?"

Walter pointed to a small table next to him with several bottles of prescription drugs. "How do you think I feel with all that stuff going in me every day?"

"It's supposed to keep you alive, Walter."

"Yeah, yeah. Being alive at my age is overrated, if you ask me. Anyway, let's talk about you," Walter said, patting the paper in his lap.

Even though she had written the article, she had no desire to talk about it but knew Walter did. He must have seen the uncertainty in her face.

"What's the trouble, darling?"

Emily smiled, dismissing his question. "So, how do you like the historical column so far?"

"I'd say your perspective is quite extraordinary, as if you were right there and experienced it first hand," he said with a sly look as if he knew of her time travel experience.

Emily couldn't tell Walter about how right he was, so instead she kept to more recent news. "I wasn't sure I'd get the job at the town paper with not having any writing experience."

Walter moved forward in his chair, trying to boost himself up with no luck.

"Here, let me help," Emily offered. After she placed a more comfortable pillow behind Walter, he patted Emily's arm.

"We all have a story to tell, darling. You don't need a degree over what's swimming around in your head."

"Thank you, Walter. That's very reassuring."

"Hey! You don't happen to know Rick Miller? He works over there at the town office."

"Er...yes, why?" Emily said, feeling caught off guard by the question.

"He such a great guy and a war hero."

Another piece of information catching Emily off guard. "Really? What do you know about him?" she asked.

"Did you know that Rick is part of our veterans' group in the VA? And did you also know he saved two of his comrades?"

Emily had heard stories of soldiers coming back from war, never wanting to talk about the horrors they experienced. She also knew that some soldiers came home without limbs and with a bad case of PTSD. "So, what happened?" she asked.

"Well, you see, Rick and two other guys were in a convoy, driving a Humvee, kicking up so much dust they couldn't see two feet in front of them. Rick was the gunner looking out for the enemy when an improvised explosive device detonated alongside their vehicle, blowing Rick's hand clean off and wounding the two guys in the front seat."

Emily couldn't imagine being in that situation. Even as a nurse, she questioned whether she could have been that brave. "So, how was Rick able to save his friends with his hand blown off?"

Walter took a deep breath causing him to cough uncontrollably. It took a couple of minutes for him to settle down. He cleared his throat and took a sip of water from a cup Emily had gotten for him.

"You see, Rick took off the belt he was wearing with his one hand and wrapped it around his arm, using that one good hand and his teeth to tighten it enough to stop the bleeding. He then got his two fellow soldiers out and away from the Humvee into a ditch, all while under small arms fire. Rick applied first aid to the men who both got knocked out. One had a huge cut on his head; the other had a broken leg." Walter shook his head, and Emily noticed the amazement on his face as he told her the story. "Minutes after Rick pulled the two guys into the ditch, a rocket-propelled grenade hit the Humvee, blowing up their vehicle along with the one behind them."

It was unsettling to Emily as she wondered how much this harrowing event had affected Rick. He appeared to be put together, confident, even happy. But she hardly knew him or his demons, if there were any.

Walter looked towards the one window in his room. The distant expression on his face told Emily that he was probably imagining the whole horrible picture in his mind. "I knew soldiers like Rick who fought hard and became heroes in WWII, Korea,

Vietnam, and our most recent wars. I have an enormous amount of respect for those men. Guys like Rick, they just don't make them any better than him. He's a real hero. Rick was even awarded the Purple Heart."

"That's an incredible story. Thanks for telling me. He never said anything to me other than he lost his hand in Iraq."

Walter looked over his glasses. "No, a hero never talks."

Emily nodded in agreement. "He really is an amazing man," she added. Her face suddenly felt warm.

Walter laughed slightly, and Emily realized she must be blushing. "What's that look for?" she asked, trying not to be so transparent.

"Seems to me someone I know might just be interested in this home-town hero," Walter said with a sparkle in his eye.

Emily waved one hand, swatting away Walter's words. "Why is everyone so interested in my love life all of a sudden?"

Walter raised his eyebrows in question. "Hmm. Does that mean there is a love life?"

Emily put her arm around Walter's shoulder, squeezing tight, saying, "Just like those heroes who never talk, a woman never tells about her love life either."

Later, Walter and Emily had lunch together in the main dining room. Her former co-workers came by the table asking about her new job at the town office. Some of the other residents were glad to see her, while others didn't remember who she was at all.

Her old place of work was pleasant, with brightly colored walls and beautiful paintings hanging everywhere. Some showed cornfields and farmhouses, others were depictions of what Maple Ridge looked like during the 1940s, 1950s, and 1960s. One painting showed what the town looked like over a hundred fifty years ago. Emily must have looked at that one at least a hundred times, finding it fascinating, since it showed the building that currently housed the nursing home. The building itself was old and had been kept up over the years. At one time, it served as a hospital before the twentieth century and became a nursing home just after the first World War. The outside of the nursing home was beautifully maintained, and the land extended into Stanford Park with a view of the Magic River in the distance, making the grounds around the building look enormous.

Walter ate slowly, unable to swallow very well, and Emily cut his food into tiny pieces. After they both finished, she asked about his ancestors during the Civil War.

"So, for future reference for more articles," Emily began. "I thought I'd take some notes on information about the Civil War stories you've told me about."

Walter looked at the ceiling as if trying to recollect the stories. "Ah, yes, my great-grandfather was just twenty years old back then. Name was Vance Green, which reminds me since we were speaking of Rick," Walter said, giving Emily a side glance. "Did you know that Rick's two-times great-grandfather, a guy named Louis Miller, was Vance's brother-in-law? You see, Vance married Louis's sister Lillian. They went on to have a son named Stuart, who would be my grandfather."

"I suppose that makes you related to Rick," Emily took her notebook from her purse and started writing. "Go on, tell me more," she urged. "This is good stuff."

Chapter 7

IN DESPERATE NEED

IT HAD BEEN THREE MONTHS since Emily's last assignment, and Mark was not happy she hadn't been exploring other locations. She would turn in stories from research found on the Internet, avoiding the possibility of another episode of going back in time. She started an article on Walter's ancestors but never finished. Then one day, she ran across some folklore and legends about Salem witches burned at the stake. Although these stories were fictitious in nature, her further research provided a more accurate account, showing that hanging was the preferred method of execution. She decided to avoid any material on witches that popped up in her research, not wanting to think about the reality of a curse only she could break.

She and Rick talked about the strange time travel a few times on an occasional date, consisting of dinner and walks in the park. She was glad to have Rick's friendship; if nothing else, she could talk to him and him alone about her strange experiences. Their conversations would end abruptly when Emily became upset over the fear of it happening again. Kind, patient Rick would immediately change the subject. In Emily's mind, the same thoughts continued to haunt her. Would the next time be a situation I couldn't handle? But just as quickly she reminded herself that she had dealt with the past two occurrences perfectly fine. All the turmoil inside her was the reason she failed to do the job Mark had asked. If she didn't start taking an interest, she knew her position as a writer for the *Maple Ridge Gazette* would be at risk. Something else kept bothering her: Other people's lives would be at risk if she continued to ignore the curse.

Rick and Emily stared at the old Queen Anne farmhouse that was Emily's next assignment. The home was quaint with a large wrap-around front porch and a gazebo-style roof on the far end, giving the home a magnificent appearance. They stood at the bottom of a broad stairway that approached a sizable oval stained-glass front door. A for-sale sign on the front lawn waved in the breeze. The home had been vacant for quite some time, eventually going into foreclosure.

All Emily knew was that her grandfather once lived there, but that was over sixty years ago. As far as other Stanford ancestors, she knew she had a great-grandfather who had died in World War I but had found little else pertaining to his father before him. However, one ancestor who showed up on the Ancestry.com website stoked her interest: Marcus Stanford, a Civil War colonel and Emily's three-times great-grandfather. The man had two children, but no names were documented on the website or even in the Stanford Library. Unfortunately, she couldn't find much more information on Marcus other than his military rank and place of residence.

For the past sixty years, the home had several owners, and apparently, the last one couldn't pay the mortgage. She knew Jacob's house was much smaller and closer to the central part of town, and back then, this large farmhouse didn't exist in 1776. The home was located on the most northern border of Maple Ridge with open fields and the Magic River well behind a tree line filled with cherry trees in full bloom. Springtime brought out the pink and white colors of the trees, making the house and property look even more enchanting. A large maple tree shaded part of the big yard with the rotted remnants of a swing hanging from one of its thick branches. The beauty of its location would have no effect in taking away Emily's anxiety over what she was about to do.

"My grandfather lived here once. Nine months before I was born, he had planted that big maple tree in the back, the one with the swing hanging from it. It's as if he knew at that very moment, I existed in my mother's womb even before she knew about me." She gave Rick a speculative look. "Or at least that's what mother told me. Anyway, he died a little over a year after I was born—right there, all alone." She pointed to the place on the front porch where a rocker was moving back and forth from the breeze. "As far as my grandmother, I hardly knew her. I have just bits and pieces of memories; I was so young. She died nine years later after my grandfather."

"What about your parents did they—"

"No," Emily interrupted. "They lived on the other side of town, and we moved near Boston when I was seven after my father was drafted into the army."

"Where do they live now?" he asked.

"My dad was killed in Vietnam when I was ten and my mom... she had cancer, died when I was just nineteen," Emily looked at Rick and hoped he couldn't see the tears welling in her eyes. "Been on my own ever since." She took a deep breath and looked away, not wanting to talk about the losses any further.

"Well, sounds like we got that sad story in common," Rick said.

Emily looked at Rick. "What do you mean?"

"My dad. He died in Vietnam, too."

"I'm so sorry. I guess we've both had our share of losses." She turned back, looked at the house, and felt anxious.

"Are you okay?" Rick asked.

"I'm not sure where I'll end up," she said, reaching in her pocket, pulling out a bottle of aspirin, and holding it up. "I know it's silly, but maybe this will help someone, or if nothing else me, in case of a stress headache."

"They won't know what hit them," Rick joked. "They'll think you're an angel from heaven when their pain magically goes away."

Emily put the bottle back in her pocket and looked at the big house again and sighed. She felt Rick put a protective arm around her. Ever since Emily and Rick met last November, they had felt a strong attraction towards each other. Although Rick told her he had no memories of her when he was a child in first grade, there was no denying the connection between them.

"Emily? I want to go with you this time," Rick said.

She looked at him but avoided glancing towards the end of his arm. "You're afraid I would be at a disadvantage in an unknown time," Rick said holding up his arm with the missing hand. "Not to mention that I could find myself in a sticky situation. Am I right?"

"To be honest, Rick, I don't think you could come with me even if you wanted to. And believe me, I want you to be with me, with or without a missing hand."

Rick nodded as if validated by her honesty. "Where do you think you'll end up?" Rick asked.

"Not sure but I did some research, and this home has been here nearly two hundred years. In fact, it was built before the Civil War." She felt a jolt of terror go straight through her and grabbed Rick's arm, grounding herself to the twenty-first century. "I'm scared, but I need to do this." She looked at Rick. "Remember? Only the last of the Stanford blood line will be able to break the curse."

Rick squeezed her hand and faced her with a lopsided grin. He let go of her hand and brushed a piece of hair off her forehead. "I'm going with you," he said, holding her hand again. "And whatever happens—happens."

Emily's eyes filled with tears. "I don't think I can let you do that."

Rick took a step closer to her. She felt a surge of desire as he touched her cheek, and she touched his thick silver hair softly blowing in the breeze. Their warm breath on each other's lips caused them to merge into a gentle kiss, clearly both in need of each other. Emily had conflicting emotions, not wanting to dishonor her deceased husband's memory, yet feeling a strong attraction to a man she had known for only a short time. But there they were, connected by some cosmic chain of events spanning as far back as seven generations for both their families. They continued to reassure each other through their eyes, not wanting to let go when the strange sound of the waterfall came from the house.

"Do you hear that?" Emily asked.

Rick looked at the front door. "Yes," he said and quickly took the key out of his pocket. "Here, take the key in case I don't make it. I'm going with you." He then held tight to Emily's hand. They gave each other one last glance and walked through the large oval door together.

She entered the fog with Rick. Emily felt his tight grip suddenly pull away. She reached for him in the mist only to find a void. Fear gripped her until she saw the same dark-haired stranger with her hand extended, as if expecting her arrival. Her appearance was so clear that Emily noticed a brown heart-shaped mark on her wrist, then the form vanished into thin air seconds later. Emily heard a commotion taking place beyond the mist. A man rushed past her holding a small child and desperately asking for help.

Emily found it more difficult moving towards the room where the man had run with the child. The large hoop skirt she wore knocked over a table in the entranceway. The suffocating corset under the skirt took her breath away, although she tried to ignore the lack of oxygen. She awkwardly entered the large living room filled with Victorian furnishings. A man hovered over a little girl and seemed distraught regarding her condition. He tried to wake her, but the girl was not responsive.

"Please, can you tell me what's wrong with my Sarah?"

Emily once again had to calm herself, doing everything possible to blend in with her surroundings. The Union uniform the man wore told her that it must be the Civil War period.

"I'll do what I can," Emily said.

She looked over the child and could see immediately that the little girl had a bright red rash all over her face, neck, down her shoulders, and arms. Emily was about to pull up the little girl's skirt but hesitated. "May I?" Emily asked.

"Yes. Yes, of course. Please," he said.

Emily removed the girl's stockings. Sure enough, the rash was all over her legs. Her skin felt like sandpaper. Emily placed her hand on the girl's head; little Sarah was burning up with fever. She knew right away it was scarlet fever. She knew the bacterial illness was easily treatable with antibiotics, a category of drugs not yet invented. Death for this child was entirely possible.

"Are you her father?" she asked.

"Yes. I'm sorry. My name is Marcus Stanford, and this is my baby Sarah." He caressed his daughter's head. "I know she has a bad fever. I can tell."

Emily knew who he was and what war he had fought in. What she didn't know were the names of his wife or children. But now through time and space the ghosts of the past revealed themselves in a little girl named Sarah. Emily patted her large skirt looking for an opening that might contain her aspirin bottle. On the side of her dress was a slit, indicating a pocket. Emily reached in and grabbed the bottle, grateful it had traveled through time with her.

"If I can get this down her throat, it will help the fever," she said, holding up the plastic aspirin bottle. Emily noticed the puzzled look on Marcus's face as he stared at the strange-looking bottle. He seemed to dismiss his puzzlement as his focus was on Sarah.

"All I would need is something to crush the pills and some water," Emily said.

"I can get it, Papa." A young boy around the age of twelve stood in the doorway briefly and then rushed from the room.

"That's my son, Sam. He'll get you what you need."

Sam ran back with a wooden pestle for crushing the pills and a wooden bowl. Emily put two aspirins in the bowl and crushed them down to a powder. She then poured the powder into a small amount of water. Emily looked up at the boy. "Sam? Can you get me some very cold cloths, as cold as you can get them?"

"Yes, ma'am," he said, saluting, and off he went.

Marcus held Sarah up as Emily tried working the water in her mouth little by little. Luckily, Sarah was able to swallow it. Sam returned with the cold cloths, and Emily placed them on Sarah's forehead and neck. Sam had brought extra cloths that he placed on his sister's arms.

"That's very good, Sam. You're a good helper," Emily said.

"Just so you know, I'm going to be a doctor someday," he said with confidence in his voice.

Marcus smiled at his son, and Emily was glad that her three-times great-grandfather seemed relieved that Emily was helping his daughter.

"You'll have to excuse my son's enthusiasm over being a doctor. He's barely twelve years old." Marcus gave his son a slightly stern expression. "And I'm sure he will change his mind many times over."

Sam stared at his father with a disgruntled look on his face. "You just wait and see, Papa. I'll show you. Someday I will find the cure for everything." With that, Sam marched out of the room.

"I'm sure he will make a fine doctor someday," Emily encouraged.

"Be that as it may, he will undoubtedly be a soldier like me."

Emily hoped for a sign that Sarah's fever was subsiding. Emily could only wait and see if her rash went away. If that happened, Sarah would be well on her way to recovery. If not, she might not make it, and Emily thought it would be best to keep that knowledge to herself. She wished she had known Sarah's fate. Even if she had known, there was nothing that could be done about it.

Marcus and Emily sat quietly listening to Sarah's breathing when a young black girl rushed in. She looked upset and disheveled with her hair half hanging out of the white ruffled cap on her head. The apron she wore was sopping wet.

"Oh, Mister Marcus, I'd's be getting in cleaning up all that mess over in yon doorway, but I'd's been rightly trying to get Master Sam in that big old tub."

Marcus approached the girl and patted her on the shoulder to calm her. "It's fine, Sassy. I shall see what to do about Sam. You go on and clean up the broken glass."

"Yes-um sir, I'd's surely will," Sassy said and scurried out of the room.

Emily gave Marcus an embarrassed, regretful look. "I'm sorry. Guess I'm clumsy today. That mess is my fault."

Marcus waved a hand as if dismissing her apology. "Not to worry. Sassy will take care of it, and as far as Sam?" He shook his head with an expression of defeat. "I'll tend to him later."

Emily rechecked Sarah and found that the fever had subsided slightly, but the rash showed no signs of improvement. When the aspirin wears off, her fever may not be any better either, she thought.

"How is she?" Marcus asked.

"About the same." Emily watched Sassy talking to herself as she swept the floor, and Emily lifted her chin towards the doorway. "Sassy? That's an interesting name."

Marcus sat down, glancing over at the hyperactive girl. "My wife took her in little over a year ago—just before she died." Marcus's eyes glazed over for a second and then he continued. "Sassy's mother and father were runaway slaves who made it to the North. They died and Sassy was alone. Edith, my wife, found her roaming around town. As far as her name," he paused as Sassy bounded up the staircase, singing a happy tune. "I believe no explanation is needed."

"I'm so sorry for your loss. Your wife sounds like a very caring woman." Emily hesitated. The curse, she remembered suddenly. "Was she sick?"

Marcus rubbed his eyes, showing signs of fatigue, and then nodded. "Consumption."

Emily felt a strange relief to know it was tuberculosis and not the curse that took Edith. "She's with God and he loves her as he loves you, too, Mr. Stanford," she said.

Marcus sat up straighter, looking as though something just registered in his mind. "I'm so sorry. I didn't get your name."

She decided to give only her first name, staying away from any unwanted explanations. "It's Emily."

"Well, Emily, thank you for your kind words and your know-how with Sarah's condition." He paused for a moment to look at his daughter and then turned his attention back to Emily. "I shall be leaving first thing in the morning to be with my regiment, which is why I have called upon you to care for my children."

Suddenly, Emily realized once again she had stepped into some unknown person's shoes. She also worried about the inevitable: What happens to the children when I go back to my own time?

"The children have no other family?" she asked.

"Just my parents who are not well enough to care for them."

"Why don't they stay here with you?" she asked while scanning the room. "It certainly seems big enough."

He huffed out a little laugh. "Yes, but you don't know my father. I assure you I've talk to him numerous times about giving up that God-awful job at the tannery."

Emily was not aware of a tannery in Maple Ridge, and the confusion must have shown on her face.

"It's a factory west of the town, and they live in a small cottage right next to it. You would think with the factory shut down, I could convince them to move but no luck, I'm afraid."

"I'm so sorry for your difficulties. At least you have Sassy to help with everything and me I suppose," Emily said, sounding a little reluctant.

Just then, Marcus looked over and saw Sassy running down the stairs. Marcus raised his eyebrows. "You're right. I do need your services because I have no intention of depending on another child to do the job needed."

As if on cue, Sassy ran in with Sam on her heels. "Try as I may, Mister Marcus, Master Sam ain't want-in taken even a cleaning to his ears."

"I'm not a baby!" Sam yelled, pushing past Sassy. "No girl is going to see me without a stitch of clothes on." He gave Sassy a dirty look.

"All right. All right. That's enough," Marcus scolded. "Sassy, you go on now and start supper and Sam, you get yourself in the tub and clean your ears." Marcus looked over at Emily. "See, this is proof as to why I need you."

Chapter 8

THE SICK AND THE DYING

EMILY LAY IN BED, GLAD TO HAVE THE CORSET OFF and the seemingly endless amount of clothing a woman was expected to wear. She was thankful not to have lived in these times filled with so much uncertainty. Dying was a common occurrence, no matter the age of a person. Death came in so many ways that barely existed in the twenty-first century. Simple illnesses, such as a bad cold, turned into pneumonia; accidents sometimes led to nasty infections. In the nineteenth century, childhood diseases killed young ones; in the twenty-first century, those same diseases were prevented by simple vaccines. Then there was war, a painful reminder that wars were fought somewhere in the world throughout every century.

She thought about Sarah's illness and wished she could do more for her. Marcus had carried Sarah up to her bed, which was across the hall from Emily. I will check on her throughout the night, she decided. She also decided to stop thinking such negative thoughts because they weren't going to help anyone. The bed was comfortable for its time with its giant canopy overhead with curtains attached for privacy but most likely for keeping out the cold. Emily made a mental note to herself before falling asleep. When getting dressed tomorrow loosen the corset.

Emily finally dozed off and slept fitfully until she heard a little girl crying, jolting her right out of bed. The first thing she looked for was a digital clock with illuminated numbers but immediately came to her senses. By the morning light streaming into the room, Emily estimated she had been asleep for several hours. She got up, put on the robe that she found at the foot of the bed, and then made her way across the hall to Sarah's room. Emily could see the little girl was asleep and thought Sarah might have been dreaming when she cried out. The nasty rash still covered Sarah's body, and her fever had returned. Emily crushed two more aspirins and was able to get her to take them. She stood by Sarah's bed, praying the dose would be enough when she noticed a note on the table next to the bed with the name "Miss Emily" on it.

She took the note and sat down in a small chair beside a beautiful dollhouse with all kinds of miniature furniture. I pray Sarah will play with this dollhouse again, Emily thought and felt extremely worried that her prayer might never be answered. She studied the paper the note was written on and admired the beautiful handwriting. She quietly opened the letter, and the first thing she saw was the date, orienting her to the year she was in.

May 8, 1864
Dear Miss Emily,

I regretfully departed you without farewell, for I did not have the heart to wake you. As I informed you in our prior conversation, my duties call me to my regiment as training is near complete. I am also under pressure not to keep the brigadier general waiting. Now we are off to fight for our cause to preserve freedom for all, God willing. I leave my dear children in your care and pray my Sarah fully recovers. Patience will undoubtedly be needed when dealing with Sam, but he is a bright and good boy. Sassy should be very helpful *with the tasks of the household. I imagine patience is also required when it comes to our spirited Sassy as well.*

I shall be gone for a few months and will return hopefully unharmed. If possible, and if it's not too much to ask, would you call on my parents? Between my duties as a colonel and my wife's passing, I'm afraid I am guilty of not attending to my parents as often I should. As I have explained, they live in a small cottage west of town next to the factory. I'm sure they would be so grateful for your and the children's company as soon as Sarah recovers. I have no doubt that Sam will be more than happy to navigate the trip.

With my sincere thanks,
Marcus Stanford
Camp Meigs
Readville, Massachusetts

Emily folded the note and slipped it into the pocket of her robe. She heard a slight rustling sound coming from the doorway and found Sam lingering there with sadness in his eyes.

"Good morning, Sam," Emily said cheerfully.

He didn't answer and walked to his sister's bedside, looking at her and touching the rash on her arm. Sarah whimpered from his touch and called out. "Papa! Papa!" Emily thought she sounded so sick and afraid. Emily rushed to her side: "Sarah, Sarah, can you hear me?"

"She can't hear you," Sam said, feeling her forehead. "She's going to die." His face showed an unusual strength for a twelve-year-old. He looked at Emily. "If she dies, we need to take her to town and bury her next to Mama," Sam said in a matter-of-fact way that suggested he had no doubt in his mind that it would happen.

"You shouldn't talk like that, Sam. Sarah could get well if we don't give up on her."

"No. My friend died of the same thing. He was sick one day and then just like that," Sam snapped his fingers. "He died two days later."

"Well, we're not going to let that happen now, are we?" Emily said with as much confidence as possible.

That afternoon the sun shone through Sarah's window with small amounts of dust and lint dancing off each ray of light. Emily's stomach growled. Her mind was exhausted with worried, and Sarah wasn't getting any better. Her breathing had slowed. The aspirins were no longer working, and the ice-cold cloths caused her to shiver. What am I supposed to do if she dies? Emily thought. She saw Sassy pass by the room carrying an arm load of towels when Emily called to her.

"Yes-um, Miss Emily," Sassy said, turning to the doorway.

Emily walked over to Sassy taking the towels from her. "Let me," Emily offered.

"Oh, Miss Emily that ain't your rightful job."

Emily gave her a reassuring look. "It's fine. You stay with Sarah. I'll put these away and get myself something to eat. I'm starving."

"I'm-a goes and fetch some right nice bread and jelly, cus that ain't your job neither."

"You do know, Sassy, you're not a slave anymore, right?"

"Ain't you never mind. I'd's be more than peachy in getting it, Miss Emily."

Emily appreciated the girl's need to do what came naturally, but she certainly wouldn't treat Sassy like a slave. To Emily, Sassy was a child like Sam. "You would be of more help staying with Sarah. I need a little break anyway, if that's good with you," Emily said, giving Sassy another reason to feel needed.

"Yes-um, Miss Emily, I'd's surely do's my best."

Emily strolled through the long hallway admiring the architecture of the old sprawling home. The staircase was stunning. The wood looked like hickory with a lavish runner made of wool with a black center and white dots. The brown trim edges presented a green leafy pattern matching the giant round rug at the bottom of the stairs. When she reached the bottom, she stood in the entranceway. To her right was the parlor and to the left was a large dining room with a crystal chandelier featuring eight tiny candle holders. Just behind her was a small hallway leading to a white door with clouded glass. That must be the kitchen, she thought. Emily pushed the door open and found Sam sitting at a round table reading a book.

"Oh, there you are," Emily said.

Sam grunted, visibly annoyed with something.

"Troubles—penny for your thoughts—spill the beans," Emily said trying to be silly to lighten the mood as she sat down opposite of Sam.

Sam look up from the book he was holding showing a blank expression. "Spill the beans?" he questioned.

Emily opened her mouth to respond to Sam, but he slammed the book down on the table. "I hate this book. Papa told me I had to read it while he's gone."

Emily tipped the book up and glanced at the title: *All the Branches of the Military*. "Yikes," she said. "Sounds boring."

"He just doesn't listen to me. This is not what I want to read— AT ALL!"

"What is it you want to read, Sam?" she asked.

He pushed the chair back abruptly and darted out of the kitchen. "Sam? Where are you going?" Emily called out. She went to the door just as Sam swung it back open. He was holding another book.

"This is what I want to read," he handed the book to Emily, who scanned the title: *Family Health and Science*. Sam sat back down, sighing.

Emily sat across from Sam and put the book in front of him. She needed a moment to think. She noticed the bread and jelly next to a cutting board along with a knife in the center of the table. She spread the bread with jelly and got an idea.

"Sam. Look at me," Emily said. "I heard someone say once: If every day you can't think of anything else but the thing you love to do, then that's what you should be doing."

Sam seemed confused. "Miss Emily? I don't know what you're talking about."

"What I'm saying, Sam, is this: If every day all you can think about is being a doctor, then you should be a doctor."

Sam's face lit up. He had soft features as a twelve-year-old boy would and thoughtful brown eyes, which showed he had made up his mind what his future would be.

"Yes, that's it. No matter what Papa says, I'm going to be a doctor," he announced, grabbing the book and then tucking it under his arm.

Suddenly, Emily heard a thumping sound followed by crying. She and Sam looked at each other and simultaneously said, "SARAH!" Sassy thumped-down the stairs and then sat abruptly with both hands gripping the railing for support. Emily and Sam met her at the bottom of the step as she breathlessly tried to speak.

"What's wrong? Is Sarah all right?" Emily asked. Sam pushed past Sassy and ran up the stairs.

"Oh, Miss Emily, I'd's done near dozed off when a frightful sound from my dream snap me clean awake. I'd's check on Miss Sarah, and she done not breathe no more."

Emily bolted up the stairs and ran into Sarah's room to find Sam hugging Sarah and repeating "No, no, no" in between sobs.

Emily gently put her hand on Sam's back for comfort. She reached past Sam and felt for a pulse that wasn't there. Sarah was gone. Emily knelt beside Sam, caressing his brown hair.

"Oh, Sam, I'm so sorry, honey." She heard whimpering behind her and saw Sassy with her hand over her mouth with tears rolling down her cheeks. Emily reached out her hand for Sassy, and the girl knelt alongside her and Sam. Emily embraced both children for reassurance.

When Sam glanced at Emily, she saw his big brown eyes were glazed over with tears, and she saw the pain on his face. He sniffled and wiped his tears on his sleeve.

"Sarah's dead," he whimpered and then fell into Emily's arms, releasing a further rush of tears.

She held him and kissed his forehead. "It will be okay, Sam. I'm here now."

Sam rested in Emily's embrace for several minutes. "Miss Emily?" he asked when he was finally calm.

"What is it, Sam?"

"What does 'okay' mean?"

Emily released the sorrowful breath she had been holding in and let out a slight giggle. "It means 'all will be well soon'."

But Emily wasn't so sure, especially when a sudden thought occurred to her: I can't go back now. I can't leave Sam alone. He needs me for however long it takes.

The next day the ride to town was slow going. Emily and Sassy had cleaned Sarah's body, wrapped her in a white sheet, and gently laid her in the horse-drawn carriage. Emily sat upfront while Sam drove for the trip into town.

She had written a letter to Marcus with the grievous news of his beloved daughter Sarah's passing. Sassy was left behind to ensure the letter would be brought into town to be dispatched. Emily had hoped the colonel would receive it amid all the fighting. Emily never had a child but could see how the pain of losing a child far outweighed never having one at all. Loving someone was much more painful, and although she didn't know Sarah well, Emily felt her loss through Sam.

She had seen death before in the nursing home, but those people had already lived their lives. Those deaths were unlike Lucas's death; he had died before his time, and it felt unfair to Emily. Losing Sarah at the young age of six seemed horribly unfair to Emily. She felt sure that Sam thought so, too.

All Emily could do for now was look at the scenery, as they trotted along the bumpy dirt road. Pretty as it was, the landscape left her feeling depressed. Nothing looked the same. So much was different. The old painting of Maple Ridge she had admired so often in the nursing home came to life as they got closer to the town. The dirt road they were on followed the Magic River, and it was a constant reminder of the curse she was supposed to destroy for both her and Rick's family. She had a sudden ping in her stomach thinking about Rick and wished so much he could have made it through time with her. Where was he now? Would she see him again? There was so much uncertainty, yet she had to be strong for Sam and his grandparents. Their home would be the first stop along the way.

They turned west on another long dusty road until they could see the old factory, which stood out like an eyesore in the distance. Emily had never seen the factory before; she knew it had been taken down long before her or her parents were born. For as long as she could remember, this was the location of a strip mall and a supermarket. They pulled up to a small cottage located next door to the factory. These cottages didn't exist anywhere in Maple Ridge in her time either. The home was boxy, plain, with just one floor, two front windows, and a small front porch leading to a half-opened door. Emily saw the concerned look on Sam's face, and they both got off the carriage and stood on the porch.

A slight odor seeped through the door. Emily wasn't sure if it was old food, human waste, or both. She pushed open the door and found a man and a woman asleep in leather chairs with a fire smoldering in the fireplace, indicating they had been asleep for a while.

"Grams? Gramps, are you well? Sam asked when the older couple awoke. They seemed disoriented but appeared to regain their senses when they saw their grandson.

Emily followed the smell to a small opening leading to a narrow back porch. On the floor was a five-gallon tin bucket filled with bloody stools. She covered her nose with her sleeve and shut the door in the hope of lessening the odor.

"And who might this young lass be?" the old man asked.

"This is Miss Emily. She's my friend and is taking care of me," Sam said proudly.

Emily walked over, shook the man's frail hand, and found his wife's condition no better. Emily looked at Sam, and the two exchanged glances that telegraphed the message to not yet reveal the news about Sarah.

"How do you do?" Emily said, hesitating, "and you are…"

"My name is Nelson. This is my wife Elvira," he put his hand over hers.

Elvira said nothing, only showing a weak smile. Emily knelt next to them to assess each one further. "I'm Emily, and I'm here to help." she said. Elvira could only nod her head.

"You will have to excuse my wife. We've not felt well for quite some time and can't seem to get better I'm afraid."

Emily patted Nelson on the knee and went over to grab a footstool by the fireplace bringing it over to sit next to the unwell couple.

"I'll make you some tea, Grams," Sam said, hugging his grandmother. She squeezed his arm in a gesture of thanks.

"I'm going to ask you some personal questions that might help me understand your illness better if you don't mind," Emily explained.

"Of course," Nelson responded.

"Do you both have diarrhea?" she asked with her eye shifting towards the back porch.

"We do," he said, looking regretfully in the same direction.

"How about nausea and stomach cramps?" Emily asked.

"We do."

Emily could tell they were both dehydrated by the uneven complexion, dullness to the skin, and sunken eyes. She also knew dehydration occurs with diarrhea.

"How long have you both been sick, do you think?"

"I'd say, little by little since the tannery factory closed about six months ago," Nelson pointed to the leather chairs he and his wife were sitting in. "These chairs were made there. They gave them to us for free. Imagine that. Elvira was tickled pink, weren't you, dear," Nelson looked at his wife.

"Your son Marcus told me you worked in the factory."

"For many years and only left because of the shutdown, which was quite sudden, I might add."

Emily was becoming suspicious over the reasons why the factor abruptly closed. She heard Sam put down the cups of tea and gave Emily another knowing look. Emily walked over, picked up one of the cups, and smelled it. She wrinkled her nose and put the cup down. Her suspicious were right, and by the look on Sam's face he knew it, too.

"I thought the water smelled strange," Sam whispered, not wanting to get his grandparents upset.

"Sam, where's the well?" she whispered urgently.

"Come, I'll show you."

As they walked towards the side of the house facing the factory, they found the well's location steps away from what appeared to be a dumping ground. The two investigated the contents lying on the ground. Sam picked up disintegrated debris and leftover scraps from animal hides with mold and some grassy stuff that Emily couldn't identify. "Sam! Don't touch them! They're contaminated," Emily said. She looked over at the well and then back at Sam. "And so is your grandparents' well water."

Sam flung the contaminants to the ground, looking for a grassy area to wipe off his hands. "I read about this in that medical book I showed you. My grandparents have the bloody flux!" he said, shivering with disgust.

"Yes, Sam, I'm afraid so. That's why they're sick." Emily said as she pointed back towards the house.

Sam stood unmoved, his face turned pale as he stared down at the polluted ground.

"Come on, Sam. We have to get them out of here and quickly."

Chapter 9

WITH LOSS COMES NEW LIFE

EMILY AND SAM HAD BROKEN THE SAD NEWS to Nelson and Elvira. It was painful for Emily to watch as the older couple clung to Sam and to each other in their moment of grief. Once again she was in the position of finding a solution to another problem. In this case, find a safe place for the very ill couple.

To clear her thoughts and give the grieving family time to process the loss of Sarah, Emily stepped outside where a gentle breeze blew through her red hair. She tucked the disorderly strands behind her ears. She stood at the back of the carriage where typically trunks or luggage would be stored but not today. It contained Sarah's small body wrapped in white sheets. Emily placed her hand on Sarah's lifeless body. The child felt stiff and cold.

Emily's vision became blurry, and she felt a growing lump in her throat when off in the distance, she heard the Trinity Church bells ring. Suddenly Emily knew just what to do. An hour later they were on their way to Trinity Church. When they arrived, Emily spoke to the priest and thankfully he let them all stay in the rectory that night, far from the contaminated water.

The next day Sarah was laid to rest in the Trinity cemetery alongside her mother, Edith. At the grave site, Emily looked over at Nelson and Elvira sitting in the carriage. They were too weak to stand, so they looked on as she and Sam stood by a pine box containing Sarah's remains. All the times Emily had been in the cemetery, she had never seen Edith or Sarah's graves. Her eyes scanned the area, and she noticed a marker showing the letter "S" and a tiny stone that simply said "Edith." Emily concluded that in the future the small stone might have been swallowed up by the earth over time. Other than Emily, Sam, Nelson, and Elvira, no other family members were there to grieve over such a loss. Although Emily was technically family, it was information best kept a secret. Only two other people were present, an undertaker and the priest from Trinity Church. Two men who had dug the grave stood far in the distance with their hats resting over their hearts out of respect for the dead.

Emily felt heartbroken that Marcus couldn't be there for his baby girl's burial. He may not know yet that Sarah is gone, she thought. Emily saw the tears rolling down Sam's cheeks, and she put her arms around his shoulders as they listened to the priest recite Psalm 23, "The Lord is My Shepherd." Sam leaned his head into her, wrapping one arm around her waist. She kissed the top of his head and rubbed his wavy brown hair.

"I'm so sorry, Sam," she whispered in his ear. "God loves you, and he knows how much it hurts."

Emily saw Nelson holding his wife close by his side as they remained seated in the carriage. Elvira wiped away tears with her ruffled hanky. The sorrow was all too real for Emily.

She felt emotion bubbling up inside her, and she thought about the loss of Lucas. She instinctively looked over towards the spot where Lucas would someday be laid to rest. Emily tried distracting her thoughts by admiring the Trinity Church. The brownstone was so beautiful in its day, before the weather had battered it over the past century and a half. It had been a new church two years ago in this time but an old church in hers.

She found herself once again missing Rick and wondered when she would see him again. Thinking of him had comforted her, and if she returned, she would at least have someone to tell her adventures to. Then there was Orenda's curse, which felt unsettling, but what she did have settled in her mind was staying long enough to help her four-times great-grandparents get well again.

* * *

The air of melancholy slowly lifted on the ride back to Sam's home. Nelson and Elvira rode in the backseat of the carriage as Sam and Emily took their rightful places in the driver's seat. She turned around every so often, finding them in better spirits yet still in poor health. They had stayed with the priest for an additional night before their trip back home and with their receiving fresh water and proper nutrition right away, Emily was hopeful that Nelson and Elvira would be well on their way to recovery. Emily, however, wasn't feeling too great from the carriage bouncing and dust kicking up in her face with each passing horse and buggy, causing her to cough.

"May I ask why you didn't want to live with your son?" she asked Nelson when she finally stopping coughing.

He laughed at her question. "I see Marcus has complained about it to you, too."

Emily grinned and then nodded over her shoulder."Yes. I'm afraid so."

"I suppose we felt we need not burden our son with all he has to contend with. Being a colonel is a large responsibility and worrying about his mother or me shouldn't be on his mind."

"Aye, Gramps, I can take care of you and Grams, "Sam suggested.

Nelson reached up and patted Sam on his lower back. "You already have, Sam. If it weren't for you and Miss Emily, we'd be dead from that poisoned water. Your Gram and I had no idea it was contaminated."

"You couldn't smell it, Gramps?" Sam asked, wrinkling his nose.

"Guess our old snouts don't work too well any longer, Sam," Nelson said, putting his finger affectionately on his wife's nose. Elvira smiled, snuggling up closer to her husband. Emily thought the old couple was sweet.

"It was Miss Emily who knew for sure. I just helped," Sam said.

Nelson gave Emily an appreciative smile and mouthed the words "thank you." Then he spoke louder to Sam. "You're a good boy, Sam."

When they arrived at the farmhouse, they saw a black stallion hitched up to the post out front. Sam pulled the carriage alongside the stallion. Emily could see a man sitting at the side of the porch near the gazebo. Upon their arrival he stood. Emily noticed that he was in full military dress with a long blue coat with gold buttons. He carried a gold sword and wore white gloves reaching to his elbows and an impressive Union hat made for an upper-rank officer.

"It's the brigadier general," Nelson said.

"What does he want, Gramps?" Sam asked.

Without answering, Nelson got out of the carriage and helped Elvira to her feet. Sam followed his grandfather's lead and offered his hand to Emily, helping her down from the carriage. The general approached them, looking somber. Emily could see Sassy standing on the porch holding a hanky to her mouth, clearly in distress.

"Hello, Nelson," the general said.

"Ray! What brings you here?" Nelson asked.

The general tipped his hat at Elvira and Emily. "And whom might this lovely lady be?" he asked.

Emily put her hand out to shake his, but he kissed the top of her hand instead. "I'm Emily, Sam's caregiver," she said.

The general looked strangely at Emily as if he knew her somehow. But Emily had no clue who he was until Sam spoke up.

"How come you're here, General Miller?"

Emily's ears perked up when hearing the name Miller. Another one of Rick's ancestors? The same general that Marcus mentioned in his letter? she wondered.

"I am so sorry to hear about your little sister," General Miller said to Sam. Then General Miller looked at Nelson and Elvira and handed them a sealed envelope. Nelson's knees became weak, and

Emily darted over to hold him up. Emily and the general guided Nelson and Elvira to the porch and had them sit down.

"What's going on?" Sam asked, confused.

Emily took Sam's hand, leading him over to his grandparents. "It'll be okay, Sam. Your Gramps will read the letter." Emily already had a sick feeling in her stomach, knowing what was probably in the letter.

"I shall take my leave then," General Miller said formally, bowing to Sam and his grandparents. He then turned towards Emily with a slight nod. "Madam."

Emily bowed her head in response to the general's formal departure. He walked away and unhitched his horse, looking sorrowful as he rode slowly away.

Nelson read the condolence letter out loud with great poise, with only one small tear running down his face. Sam hugged his Grams and Gramps closely. Elvira leaned into Sam's embrace and whimpered quietly as Sassy stood on the other side of the porch listening with a hanky to her nose and sobbing.

To the Stanford family:

I regretfully inform you of the death of your son, your father, and my friend Colonel Marcus Stanford on May 10, 1864. A practice scrimmage took place between regiments, during which the colonel was knocked off his horse and hit his head on a large rock. It pains me personally for he was my friend for many years. I had trained the colonel myself in his command of his regiment. This duty ultimately led to Colonel Stanford's death in this most tragic and unfortunate accident. Colonel Stanford was ready to fight and die alongside his men and would have never backed down from any fierce battle he most surely would have encountered, if not for this terrible misfortune. You can be proud to know that Colonel Marcus Stanford was ready to fight with great honor toward the ongoing battle for freedom and liberty for all men.

    My deepest of sympathies,

    Brigadier General Raymond Miller

The sunrise the next morning warmed the front of the house. Emily stood on the porch feeling the warmth on her face. The pleasant sound of birds singing and nesting nearby felt peaceful given the sad time it had been for Sam and his grandparents. She leaned over the railing and caught a glimpse of someone through the tree line by the river. She walked to the back of the house and headed towards the Magic River.

Cherry trees heavy with white and pink blossoms formed a line alongside the woods with the river just beyond Emily's view. She found Sam sitting on a large log holding a fishing pole. He showed little interest in fishing, and his face seemed to reflect an expression of deep thought for a boy so young. He did, after all, lose both parents and his sister within such a short time, Emily reflected. Her heart went out to her new little friend even though she knew that Sam Stanford was, in fact, her great-great-grandfather. Pushing that reality aside, Emily wanted to talk to her twelve-year-old friend.

"Anything biting this morning?" Emily asked.

Sam shook his head and continued staring out into the water.

"I'm here for you if you want to talk," she said, sitting beside him on the log. They both sat for a while in silence, when finally, Sam looked above.

"This is my favorite spot in the world. I like when the breeze blows through the cherry blossoms." He pointed up, just as a tiny gust of wind blew through the white and pink petals, causing them to fall to the ground. Sam glanced at Emily, grinning slightly from the sight. "It's like sitting under a snow squall blessing the top of your head," he added.

Emily was glad Sam could find some solace in nature. The fishing spot was, in fact, peaceful despite the curse running through the tranquil waters of the Magic River.

Sam turned himself on the log towards Emily. "Did you know there's a legend about the Magic River being cursed?" he said.

A shiver went through her body, and she was shocked at how Sam knew about the curse. "So, where did you hear about this?" she prompted.

"I heard my Papa talking to General Miller one time about some papers the general found in a locked box from one of his ancestors," Sam looked as if trying to come up with the name of the ancestor. "I think he said his name was Captain Douglas Miller, who served in the Revolutionary War."

Emily was instantly interested. She remembered Captain Miller opening a wooden box containing her notebook, pen, and Rick's key but did not know what else was in the box. "What did these papers tell about the curse?" she asked.

"About some old Indian woman's crazy talk and how this captain believed her." Sam shrugged his shoulders. "Guess he wanted everyone else to know it, too."

Emily's mind raced. She wondered what the captain might have seen when she disappeared into thin air right in front of his eyes. Could that have been the reason he started to believe Catori, the Native American woman? She also thought: Is it possible Catori told him about me being a time traveler? Was Catori able to figure out that part on her own? Sam's information about the wooden box only caused more questions with no answers.

Emily could hear a faint voice in the distance, breaking through her thoughts. It was Sassy saying something or rather yelling something incoherent. Emily and Sam stood up and saw Sassy running towards them, pushing a low-hanging tree branch out of the way.

"Miss Emily! Miss Emily! You's right come quick. Mister Louis need you's right quick," she said trying to catch her breath when she reached them.

"Sassy, what in the world are you talking about?" Emily asked.

"Mister Vance's wife in need of doctoring," Sassy said, nodding towards a man running through the same low-hanging branches.

"Are you Mr. Vance?" Emily called to him.

"No. No," he said, swallowing some air as he straightened his coat and hat back into position, finally catching his breath again.

"My name is Louis Miller. My sister Lillian is in need of a doctor. She's about to give birth."

Emily was confused over Sassy's mixed-up information. "If you're Louis, then who is Vance?" Emily asked.

"Vance Green is my sister's husband, the father of the baby."

Suddenly Emily remembered the little notebook she kept where she had written some notes when visiting Walter Green at the nursing home. Vance Green was Walter Green's great-grandfather. Louis Miller was Rick's great-great-grandfather. A jolt went through Emily as she stared at Louis. How is this even possible? she thought.

Emily recognized the English saltbox house they were approaching. It was the same wooden gate apparently re-built by the newness of the wood. The same oak tree was in the front yard but split down the middle with half the tree missing, which was most likely from a storm. Only the remnants of the tree existed in her own time, as a large stump adorned with a potted plant. This was Captain Millers' house, Emily thought. She knew it for sure by the cornerstone that read: "Built 1740"—making the house a hundred and four years older.

Louis escorted Emily and Sam into the house. Sam had insisted on coming; he hadn't witnessed a birth before. Even with Emily discouraging him from coming along, Sam had adamantly insisted.

Lillian was upstairs, where the captain's office used to be. The large bed was located between two windows and the same place

Captain Miller had had his desk. Lillian's bed was surrounded by servants and a man sitting by Lillian's side. By the strain in the man's face, Emily concluded he was Lillian's husband, Vance Green.

"Ah, thank God you're here," Vance said, with relief in his voice. "This is my wife, Lillian." Lillian let out a loud moan, and Vance rubbed her back for comfort.

"This is Miss Emily," Louis said, looking over his shoulder. "Oh, and this is Sam."

Vance's eyebrows raised in surprise. "A child? A child should not be present for such a situation as this," he complained.

Sam pushed forward, weaving past the servants who were beginning to leave the room. "I'm not a child. I'm studying to be a doctor," Sam informed him.

Emily felt proud of Sam's convictions. "I assure you, Mr. Green, Sam has been a wonderful assistant to me thus far," Emily winked at Sam.

Louis put his hand on Vance's shoulder. "Come, my friend, let Miss Emily do her job."

Emily thought Louis sounded a lot like Rick and surmised that Rick would have handled the situation in the same way. Emily gave Vance a reassuring smile and noticed how Vance resembled a younger version of Walter Green. Everything about her experience was either unsettling or completely amazing.

Another thought crossed her mind. She had never been responsible for delivering a baby before. Many doctors or midwives were always available, leaving Emily to watch. She had assisted only once in her training. Emily would have to rely on those old memories and plain old nursing experiences to deliver Lillian's baby safely.

Lillian was no more than eighteen, Emily thought. Sweat poured down Lillian's forehead and a look of terror crossed her face as another pain started.

"Lillian, I'm going to check to see how much longer you have before you can start pushing."

Lillian flinched and put her head back, squeezing her eyes shut from the pain. Emily saw the whole top of the baby's head, which meant that Lillian was at least ten centimeters dilated. Emily looked up at Sam and gave him that knowing look; and he nodded back with no words needed. Emily was proud of Sam and how intuitive he was. By the look on his little boy face, he was now a man who knew it was time for Lillian to give birth.

"Lillian, I can see the head; you're fully dilated."

Sam seemed confused over the term Emily used. "What does 'dilated' mean?" he asked.

"It means she's ready. So, Sam, I want you to get behind Lillian and prop her up by the shoulders in a sitting position. Lillian, I want you to push with the next pain."

In the next instant, Lillian's pain returned.

"Ready, PUSH—PUSH!" Emily yelled.

Lillian gave out the most primal howl Emily had ever heard. After Lillian gave one more big push, the baby popped out. Emily placed the baby onto Lillian's chest. Both Emily and Sam shared the same astonished look after witnessing the miracle before them. Lillian cried at the same time her baby did. Emily put her hand on the baby's back, feeling just as overwhelmed as Lillian. Emily then told the mother and child those echoing words she had repeated before.

"God loves you and your precious baby so much," Emily said.

Sam interrupted: "What is it? What is it?"

Both Emily and Lillian laughed as Emily turned the baby over slightly.

"Oh! It's a boy!" Sam exclaimed, patting Lillian on her shoulder. "Nice work," he added and then ran out of the room to make the announcement.

Chapter 10

SAM'S HOUSE

THAT EVENING EMILY LOOKED OUT of the open window towards the tree line. Sam and his grandparents had turned in early, leaving Emily to herself. She roamed around the bedroom upstairs, unable to sleep. She could hear the Magic River flowing gently in the distance, giving her an uneasy chill of uncertainty. The feeling left her restless, wondering when the wind and water would call her back to her own time.

The day had been hectic and nerve-racking, but still, Emily felt a sense of accomplishment. After the birth of Lillian's baby, she had met the whole family in the main living room. She remembered the room from her appearance in 1776. Everyone stood when she entered the room and congratulated her for her excellent work. Even Brigadier General Miller was there to offer his thanks. She spotted other people she didn't know such as a young man behind the crowd holding hands with a young woman, leaving Emily to wonder if they were related to the Millers somehow. She saw Sam lingering by the entrance appearing annoyed that he was being ignored over his contribution to the happy event. Emily had waved to him to enter the room, ensuring he received the same gratitude the family was offering her. They had asked her to speak, as if she was the guest of honor at a party.

"Thank you for your kind words," she had said, putting Sam in front of her and placing both hands on his shoulders. "I couldn't have done it without my trusted assistant."

The room erupted in applause and then Emily told them the one thing that would break the curse for everyone present in the room. "It's important for me to tell you how blessed you all are and how much God loves each and every one of you."

Emily sat on the bed, remembering the look on Louis Miller's face after she had told the family about the love of God. It was a look of bewilderment and an expression that no one else in the room shared except maybe for the general who had seemed to recognize her from the day he came to the house with the news of Marcus's death. "The general and his son, Louis, know something," Emily said out loud to the empty bedroom. "But what?"

Persistent banging coming from the front door knocked Emily off the edge of the bed. She felt her heart was in her throat. "What in the world?" She hurried down the stairs before anyone was awakened by the sound. She opened the door and found Louis Miller standing there with a fixed look of uncertainty in his eyes.

"Louis? Is everything all right? Is Lillian—"

"She is well," he interrupted.

Emily slowly opened the door further. "Please come in," she said. They made their way to the living room. Louis's expression had the same bewildered look he had had earlier that day, making her nervous. "And the baby?" Emily inquired.

"The baby as well is fine," he said.

"Please sit." Emily pointed to a chair.

Louis remained standing and gave Emily a dazed look as if searching for the right words. "I've told myself this couldn't be real," he finally said. "I had to find out for myself." Louis reached into his pocket and pulled out two envelopes that were yellowed from age. "My father, the general, kept a box with assorted papers, notes, and keepsakes that have been passed down from generation to generation," Louis explained as he approached Emily. "Oddly, there are also letters pertaining to a particular woman."

Emily wasn't sure to whom Louis was referring and couldn't let on that she knew about the box. It was the same box Sam had told her about that morning and the actual box Emily had seen for herself when it was in the possession of Louis's great-great-grandfather, Captain Miller.

Louis took out a letter from one of the envelopes and looked directly into Emily's eyes. "This is from a woman named Emily Stanford."

Emily hadn't told a soul her last name, but Louis seemed to have figured it out.

"This Emily had told my great-great-grandfather that God loves him and how she found it important to let him know that. In her letter she also mentions strange predictions as if the future was known to her," he said suspiciously.

Emily drifted down into the chair, feeling weakness overtaking her legs. She could only feel stunned over the slight accusatory tone in Louis's voice, as he held the very letter she had written to Captain Douglas Miller before she slipped through time. "So, you think this woman has something to do with me?"

Louis sat opposite Emily and handed her the second envelope. "I believe this one would be of great interest to you," he said.

Emily turned over the unsealed envelope, which told her that Louis had likely read the letter. Written on the front in Captain Miller's handwriting was the name "Emily Stanford."

November 24, 1784

Dear Mistress Emily,

It has been eight years since your departure, which had stunned and confused me. You had disappeared before my eyes in a strange mist that was unexplainable.

I was suspicious when you first arrived, especially by your early ar-

rival. I was well aware that a new indentured servant was not expected for several more days. Then the Stanford name gave me more cause for such suspicion. After you were gone, the rightful indentured servant appeared on my doorstep, which validated all my prior suspicions. Still, I have remained puzzled over the mystery of this most beautiful red-headed woman, who refused to wear a cap and let her hair drape down over one shoulder in a long braid, which, may I say, was an usual behavior for a servant.

This had indeed prompted me to ask more questions of Catori, as I have not believed or even paid attention to her incoherent stories over the years. She told me that the Magic River had a curse that only you, Mistress Emily, could break. I still do not understand, but it explained your mysterious departure. You also predicted the arrival of the Declaration of Independence document, and you stated your kind words that God loves my family and me, which breaks this so-called curse, according to Catori. I most sincerely thank you for that. I now trust what you had written in your letter, which gave me a reason to believe an Indian woman, a woman who has been like a grandmother to me. I regret that I thought she was crazy.

I shall hold onto this letter I am writing to you in hopes of the possibility of hearing news of your arrival at a destination where this letter will somehow be delivered to you. It also may be possible that I will no longer live on this earth when such time takes place where you will read my words. So, therefore, I would like to extend my deepest apologies for my disrespect over what undoubtedly must be an extraordinary task given to you

in breaking such an awful curse.
Forever Grateful,
Captain Douglas Miller

Emily set the letter down slowly on her lap, gazing past Louis Miller, as if he wasn't even there. She felt her stomach clench, as the walls closed in on her. She finally made eye contact with him, finding skepticism in his stare.

"Are you this? The woman with red hair braided down one side of her shoulder, because if you're not, Mistress, you undoubtedly fit the description."

Emily instinctively reached up, touching her braid, unable to answer. She vaguely heard the sound of water trickling and the movement of air coming into the room. Emily folded the letter and tucked it into her pocket. The rushing water sound grew louder, and she knew it was time to go.

She gathered her thoughts and stood up wanting to run out the front door when suddenly the thought of Sam came crashing into mind. She desperately wanted to say goodbye to him.

"Excuse me, Louis. I hear Sam calling," was all the excuse needed to get out of her current situation and say goodbye to Sam. She ran past the front door, where a small amount of mist was seeping under the door. Quickly running up the stairs into her bedroom, she grabbed the bottle of aspirin from the nightstand drawer.

Emily tapped gently on the door to Sam's bedroom. "Sam, are you awake?" She opened the door slowly.

Sam rolled over and made a groaning noise, but the only noise Emily worried about was the sounds of rushing water and whipping wind gathering strength. She knelt by his bed, shaking him. "Sam, wake up. It's Emily," she said urgently.

He sat up in bed, rubbing his eyes, as if trying to figure out what the fuss was all about. "Miss Emily, what's wrong? Is someone else sick?"

"No, Sam. I need to tell you something. I'm leaving. I'm so sorry. I have to go."

"Now?"

"Yes, now. Oh, Sam, I'm sorry that I have to leave you so soon."

"But who will take care of me?"

Emily's heart began to break. She loved Sam like he was her own child. "I wish so much that I could stay, Sam, but I can't. It has to be this way."

Tears rolled down Sam's face, and Emily felt tears welling in her eyes.

"Please don't leave me. You have to take care of me," he said desperately.

"Your grandparents are well enough to take care of you now," she said feeling an uncontrollable shiver go through her. "Believe me when I tell you, Sam, I don't want to leave you. I can't explain it, but I must go now."

Sam held out his arms to hug Emily. She felt his body tremble, and he began to cry even more. She reached into her pocket, taking out the bottle of aspirin. "Here, Sam, take this and give it to your grandparents if they're in pain or if someone has a fever." Emily's voice shook as she tried her best to hold back the sobs that were rising in her throat. "It's good for a fever and for God's sake don't show anyone the bottle."

Sam took the bottle and then wiped his tears with the sleeve of his pajamas. "I love you, Miss Emily."

"Oh, Sam." Emily held onto him tightly, kissed his head as she smelled his hair, never wanting to forget either, and then she looked him in the eyes. "Sam, promise me that you will never give up on your dreams of becoming a doctor. Promise me?»

"I promise," he said, sniffling and trying not to cry.

"Be brave, my sweet little friend, okay?" Emily said, showing what she hoped was a brave face of her own.

"Okay," Sam said.

"I love you, Sam. Always remember how much I love you," and

with that, Emily bolted from the room and ran down the stairs.

She stopped to look at Louis standing by the entrance of the living room in shock, apparently still trying to make sense of Emily's existence. "Thank you, Louis, for giving me Captain Miller's letter." She opened the door, allowing the mist to overtake her. Emily could vaguely hear Sam calling to her: "Don't go! Don't leave me!"

From one of her last lucid moments, she saw Sam running into the mist and finding himself standing on the front porch alone. "Miss Emily, where are you?" He couldn't hold back the tears, and then he felt a hand on his shoulder. He turned around, finding Louis Miller with the same staggering look on his face. All Louis could utter was, "My God, so it really is true."

PRESENT DAY

Emily sat on the farmhouse steps with her face covered in her hands. Tears filled the space between her fingers and sadness filled her heart. She suddenly felt a presence and looked up as Rick approached her quietly. He sat next to her on the steps, and she began to feel calm in seeing him.

"Is everything okay? Did someone hurt you?" he asked.

She remained silent as she felt the lump in her throat tighten.

"Did someone chase after you this time?" he said in a soothing voice.

She nodded.

"Okay. Who was it?" he asked.

Emily looked at Rick, and a small tear ran down one cheek. "It was a boy named Sam."

Two days later, Emily stood in the middle of her family room focusing on all the pictures of her and Lucas. Photos of them on the beach in Ocean City's boardwalk, taken by a stranger who was kind enough to stop. Photos from a cruise, taken as they stood in front of a beautiful giant staircase that looked like the one from the *Titanic*. Wedding pictures with their love displayed so clearly by the passionate kiss Lucas gave her when they left the Trinity Church. She walked over, abruptly taking every framed photo off the walls and placing them in a box.

"I can't do this anymore, Lucas. You're gone, and I can't bring you back," she stared into the box.

She sealed the box with tape and placed it in the corner with the others and then looked out the window. "I'm so sorry, Lucas, but it's time for me to move on," she looked at the for-sale sign recently placed on her front lawn.

Emily sat in the chair by the window and daydreamed about Rick. After she returned from 1864, he had sat on the steps of the old farmhouse, holding her as she cried. He wanted to escort her home, but she refused and told him she'd be okay. He had kissed her gently on the lips and then opened the car door. She could see him in the rearview mirror, standing in the road waving as she drove away. Emily knew she was falling in love with Rick, and at some point, she would have to tell him about Lucas. The subject was so painful for Emily it had made her physically sick just thinking about it. Then she thought about Sam. She missed him and wished she could have taken him back to her time.

"I could have been a good mother to you, Sam," she said out loud, only to realize the actual reality of it all. Sam Stanford was her great-great-grandfather. Just then, something occurred to her. Something so wonderful. She looked out the window again at the for-sale sign on her front lawn. The same for-sale sign was also staked in the ground at the old Queen Anne farmhouse.

Emily turned around, scanning the emptiness of the walls and looking at the pile of packed boxes in the corner. And for the first time in so long, she knew for sure what would make her happy.

"That's it! I'm going to buy Sam's house."

Chapter 11

THE WITCHES ARCHIVES

FOUR DAYS HAD GONE BY since returning from 1864. Emily had worked nonstop to get everything packed. She felt lucky to have a buyer for her house already, and all she needed was her bid on Sam's farmhouse to be accepted. She had wasted no time in making an offer on the house, and she prayed it would be accepted.

Emily heard the hissing of the teapot and went to the kitchen to dip one of the last remaining tea bags in the one remaining cup that hadn't been packed. She sat at the kitchen table sipping her tea when she heard a tap on the door. Who could that be way out here so late in the day? she thought. She knew enough to peek through the small window next to the door before opening it to anyone. But it wasn't just anyone: It was Rick. When opening the door, she found herself excited to see him, and by the look on his face, he felt the same.

"Rick, it's you," she said, not moving a muscle. He looked handsome, wearing blue jeans, cowboy boots, a leather coat, and a charming smile that had a way of catching her off guard.

"Hi, Emily. Just thought I'd check on you to see if you're okay after...well, you know."

Emily continued to stare as they both lingered in the doorway when she saw a smirk on his face, indicating he was about to say something humorous.

"Are you going to let me in?" he leaned forward. "Unless you think I might steal all your worldly possessions."

"Oh, sorry, Rick. Of course, come on in," she said feeling foolish.

Rick entered and seemed surprised at the state of the room. "You going somewhere?"

Instead of answering his question, Emily asked a question of her own. "How did you find me?"

Although they had been together in different places, Emily had not told Rick where she lived. She still felt guarded over certain parts of her personal life, mainly the painful loss of her husband. She had gone to Rick's apartment several times. They often found themselves at the diner or the Maple Sugar Barn just outside of town.

"Mark Johnson gave me your address," Rick said as he glanced around the room and at the boxes piled on top of each other in the corner.

Emily nodded. "I see. So, Mark Johnson gave a possible thief my address?"

Rick seemed to appreciate her sense of humor, and he moved closer and took her in his arms in an affectionate embrace. He smelled her neck and hair, and she sensed his desire for her. He kissed her, and she responded by letting him for as long as he wanted. "I've missed you," he said.

"It's been only a few days since the last time you saw me," she reminded him and then touched his face, rubbing her thumb across his lips and causing the urge for both to kiss again. "I missed you, too," she whispered.

Emily's phone rang, interrupting the romantic moment they were sharing. "Sorry, I gotta get this." She reluctantly disappeared into the kitchen and then returned to the family room less than a minute later.

"Good news I hope?" Rick asked.

"They accepted my offer on the old farmhouse," she said and then smiled.

"Wait. What? You bid on that old house—the one that just four days ago spit you out onto the front porch?" Rick raised his voice. "Are you crazy? What if you go back in there, and it takes you away again?"

"Rick, it's okay. The house isn't going to swallow me up again and send me back. I think it's going to be fine," Emily reassured him.

Rick paced back and forth, running his fingers through his hair. He stood firmly in front of Emily. "I don't know, Emily. I worry about you going again, and to be honest..." He looked at Emily breathlessly. "I don't want you to go—anywhere—AT ALL."

"Rick, listen to me. I feel a pull when it comes to that house, Sam's house, like I belong there, as if, I'm supposed to be there."

Rick held her close again, and Emily could sense his obvious fear of losing her. They sat on the couch, still holding each other for a while, not saying a word. He caressed her hair as she did the same to his arm, both comforted by the warmth of their bodies when Emily suddenly remembered something.

"I have something to show you," she said and then walked over to a small desk, opened the drawer, and pulled out the old yellowed envelope. "Here, read this. Your six-times great-grandfather wrote this to me."

"Who's my six-times great-grandfather again?"

"Captain Douglas Miller. Now, just read." She cuddled up to Rick and put her head on his shoulder.

When he finished reading, he looked at Emily with a mischievous grin, "Well, at least Captain Miller appreciated the same beautiful mysterious red-headed woman as I do."

Emily kissed Rick on the cheek. "Why thank you, Mr. Miller, and if you don't mind me saying so, you and Captain Miller share the same looks, which means you both are not bad to look at."

"I never thought of myself as looking like a Revolutionary War captain, but," Rick lifted his chin with a look of dignified satisfaction. "I suppose I could pull it off quite successfully if I do say so myself," he teased.

"And you would be right, sir," Emily agreed. "But nevertheless, we do have something to celebrate." She got up and went into the kitchen, finding in the refrigerator a half bottle of cranberry juice and a small bottle of wine with enough wine left for one glass.

Rick refused Emily's offer of the last bit of wine, settling instead for the cranberry juice. They sat at the kitchen table, clinking their glasses together in celebration of Emily's upcoming move. He reached in his pocket and pulled out an envelope of his own and placed it on the table.

"Another reason for my visit tonight," he said, pushing the envelope in her direction. It was a wedding invitation to Rick from Mr. and Mrs. Collins.

Emily opened the invitation and read that Meghan Collins was to marry Derek Miller. "Derek Miller?" she questioned.

"Yeah. My son."

"You have a son?"

"Sure do and an ex-wife, too," he said reluctantly.

"I didn't know that. So, what happened?"

"What didn't happen. She left me over my drinking, and my son thinks I'm a loser."

"That's not true. I've only known you for a short time, but I know enough about you to know that's simply not true at all."

Rick reached over and squeezed Emily's hand. "Thank you, but I'm afraid it's true. I wasn't exactly the perfect husband or father when I came home from Iraq." Rick again ran his hand through his thick hair, a trait Emily had noticed he did when anxious about something.

"It's okay, Rick. You can tell me; I won't think any less of you, I promise."

Rick glanced at the empty stump where his hand should be. "I came home feeling useless, less of a man. I started drinking too much, drowning out the pain of it all. Pain from losing my hand, pain from losing so many friends, and most of all, pain from not being able to save my friends." He looked into Emily's eyes.

She saw how sad he was speaking of such things. "I'm so sorry, Rick, but it's not your fault. You probably struggled with Post Traumatic Stress Disorder."

Rick got up and looked out the kitchen window into the yard. "It's so dark out there. Kinda how I feel sometimes."

Emily walked over and looked out into the darkness. She lived far enough away from Maple Ridge that its lights were absent in the distance. She put her hand on Rick's arm, showing support.

"I knew a guy that lived on this road once," he finally said in an almost haunting tone. "Nice guy. Used to help me with jobs sometimes. Until one day, he couldn't help me anymore."

Emily wanted to know everything about Rick, his loves, his losses, all the good as well as the bad. She loved him, even though she still felt torn between her love for Lucas and now for Rick. But Lucas was gone and Rick was not. She needed to move on somehow. Emily held him close as he continued to stare out into the darkness. She hoped her embrace would somehow diminish the darkness that seemed to live deep down inside of him.

"I'm afraid to say I don't know too many people on this road," Emily said, "but I want to know more about your son."

He turned, looking a little less sad. "I was thinking. Maybe you can go with me to my son's wedding. For moral support? The wedding's in Salem, Massachusetts. Maybe we can check out the Orenda witch story—what happened to her, find out more about the curse. What do you think?"

Emily grinned and put her finger on her chin as if thinking about his proposition. She gave him a playful, mischievous look. "I'll go anywhere with you as long as you have no intention of stealing all my worldly possessions."

Four months had passed, and it was now September. Some of the leaves had started to change already in the mountains of Massachusetts. She picked Rick up at his small apartment in town, an old house that offered four units. Rick had told Emily his rent was cheap because he offered to fix anything the owner needed. It was an eight-mile ride from Maple Ridge to Salem, and Rick suggested going to the enchanted town first to research their archives before the wedding.

The two had become inseparable since the move into Emily's new house or, in this case, Sam's old house. On the day of the move, Emily and Rick had stood in front of Sam's house with hesitation, waiting for the mist to start seeping out from under the oval stained-glass front door. They saw nothing, didn't hear any water rushing. Emily had held Rick's hand anyway as they both went into the home together. Emily was surprised by how much different it looked since she last saw it in 1864. The previous homeowners had tried to modernize the place with wood paneled walls in some rooms and horribly gaudy wallpaper in others. The beauty of the Victorian faded behind the hideous chaos of color. Regardless, Emily soon became comfortable in her new home with its long Stanford family history.

Emily glanced over at Rick in the passenger seat on the ride to Salem. He was looking on his phone at a website that showed nineteen-century decor.

"You're still trying to come up with some remodeling suggestions for my house?" she asked.

"I have a lot of good ideas for you. I know you want to bring back the original look, but it'll take some doing though," he continued to scroll through all things Victorian.

They reached Salem and drove through the downtown district until they pulled up in front of a Greek Revival-type building that Emily guessed was built as far back as President Andrew Jackson's time. Another time capsule, she thought, and hoped she would stay in the twenty-first century when going in. "We're here," Emily announced and exited the car.

They walked on the red brick sidewalk and found themselves in front of a mahogany double door. Emily looked at Rick and suspected that they were both thinking the same thing.

Rick gave Emily a reassuring smile. "Come on. It'll be fine," he said.

Inside, a woman sat at a reception desk with her head bowed over a folder of papers. Rick cleared his throat to get her attention. "Excuse me. Can you tell us where the office of archives would be?"

The woman looked up over her big red-framed glasses. "Ah,

yes. Welcome to our enchanted little town," she said, standing up.

Emily could smell the woman's strong perfume which battled with the loud colors of the floral dress she wore.

"You see that door? You go through there and take a left. The office you want is at the end of the small hallway," she said and smiled, showing lipstick-stained teeth.

Emily smiled back and then noticed Rick wrinkling his nose from the overwhelming perfume aroma.

"Thank you," Emily said. She grabbed Rick's arm and dragged him towards the door before his quirky sense of humor kicked in over the woman's choice of style and perfume.

"So, what witches' cult do you think she belongs to?" he said in a low voice after they passed through the door.

"Stop!" Emily said, hitting his arm. "I'm sure she's a very nice lady."

"Yeah, well, I don't think she's belongs to Orenda's cult of witches, that's for sure," he joked.

The room looked like a library with bookcases that reached the ceiling. A rolling ladder leaned against one of the bookcases, awaiting a librarian or a patron who wished to get books on the upper shelves. A long table held several computers. Emily noticed that the screen saver on each computer had a witch logo and a caption that read: "Salem, the history of witchcraft and all of its legends."

Emily scrolled through the information of all the accused witches as far back as 1692. "Look at this," Emily said, pointing to the screen. "It's under myths and legends. It said that one of the most notorious accusers in the Witch Trials was a man named Hector Stanford."

"Guess that explains Orenda's beef with the Stanford family," Rick said, rubbing his chin. "As far as the Miller connection? Guess it's still an unsolved mystery."

"I never saw anything on this when researching my ancestors."

"Probably because he's a mythical character, according to this information," Rick concluded.

Emily continued to read. "It goes on to say that Hector Stanford, a prominent figure in Salem, accused several young women he deemed to be witches and was known to have physically abused the women. He had been successful in persuading all those in power to condemn them, and as a result the women were accused as witches."

Emily scrolled down to a section that had more information about the legends as she continued to read. "Over twenty people were accused of witchcraft in May of 1692. Nineteen out of the twenty resulted in hanging. Fourteen woman and five men some being teenagers. It says here that one person was tortured and pressed to death under heavy stones."

The reality of the information struck Emily, and she looked at Rick " Orenda and Catori must have been in their teens when the curse was cast upon our families," Emily concluded.

Rick huffed. "Talk about your out-of-control teenager."

Emily continued to scroll through the information stumbling across more myths and legends, as Rick looked on. "Wait! Wait! Look!" Rick pointed to the name Catori.

"Oh my gosh," Emily whispered. "There's a whole section on here about Catori." She pointed to the text, which they read together:

"Legend has it that when the new Governor stopped the witch trials, the townspeople were still afraid. One young girl in particular that caused great fear was an Native American seer named Catori. The townspeople were aware of Catori and that her tribe was slaughtered under the orders and command of Sherman Miller. The news instilled fear in the people of Salem, thinking a witch who is also a Native American seer would be sure to cause retribution on the innocents in the town."

"Now we know the Miller connection to the curse," Rick said.

"It also says that they let Catori go, banished from the town never to be seen again," Emily added.

Rick took out his phone and opened the calculator app. "Let's say Catori was fourteen in 1692," he said, taping on the numbers. "That would make her ninety-eight years old in 1776."

Emily felt amazed over the validation from actual records of Catori's existence. Although Catori was deemed to be a legend, Emily knew it had to be true having met Catori in person. If Rick's calculations were correct, Catori would have been ninety-eight when Emily saw her last. "It makes sense because she was extremely old and frail when I talked to her."

Rick searched through the website, looking for any other information. The room felt warm with more people filing in, mostly tourists using the computers. Emily couldn't help but wonder how many of those tourists were there merely for entertainment reasons. For her and Rick, their investigation was much more personal.

"I found something," Rick whispered.

Emily peered at the screen. "What is it?"

"It's a list of the names of two hundred people imprisoned for being witches."

They both concentrated on searching for Orenda's name, but no one by that name was listed. "It's just first names and ages that are listed," Emily said.

Rick reached the bottom of the long list and found two girls, one fourteen-year-old named Rebecca and one eighteen-year-old named Sandra. "They would have been in the same age range as Catori, and you did say Catori was best friends with the one who cast the spell."

"Catori did tell me she gave her friend the Native American name Orenda. She also told me that the name meant Magical Powers. The witch who cursed our families could be one of these girls," Emily suggested.

The lines between Rick's eyes became deeper showing he was thinking. "I wonder which one it was, Sandra or Rebecca?" Rick took a deep breath letting it out slowly as he tapped his hand on the table looking irritated. "You think this Sherman Miller was my ancestor?" Rick asked still staring at the computer screen. "Because if he is— what an asshole. It's a good thing he's dead because I'd want to kick his ass then kill him myself."

Emily sat back in the chair, considering how grateful she was, glad not to have gone as far back as 1692. She would have been ill-equipped to handle such harsh circumstances and would likely find herself accused of being a witch herself. "If it makes you feel any better, Rick, the man who helped send the witches to their deaths could have been my ancestor and just as much of an ass-hole."

"Yeah, well, this Stanford bastard would be next on my list of ass kicking. No wonder why the witch put a curse on them."

Emily agreed, adding, "Unfortunately the immature teenage witch didn't think it through. Many innocent people died because of that curse."

"I don't think we'll find any more information here," Rick concluded.

They both stood up and exited the room. Emily sighed, feeling disappointed at not finding a definitive answer about Orenda. The lively receptionist offered to look further for information on Catori, Sandra, and Rebecca, taking Emily's email just in case.

As they stood outside, they both looked back at the old building. Emily's discouragement must have shown on her face, and Rick must have noticed.

"Come on, Emily," he said putting his arm around her waist and pulling her in to himself. "At least we have possible first names for Orenda." He let out a witty snort. "Not to mention one of them was undoubtedly an out-of-control teenager."

Chapter 12

WITCHES IN THE FAMILY

THE BALLROOM WAS LARGE with Victorian style moldings and a grand staircase at the entrance displaying a vintage floral rug runner draped down each step. Two pillars at the bottom of the stairs featured large vases with orange and yellow fall flowers that fit an autumn wedding theme. Before the ceremony, a cocktail hour was held in a room just beyond the ballroom that usually handled small receptions and dinner parties. In the background, a woman vocalist and musicians played old standards from the forties and some soulful blues from the fifties and sixties.

Emily waited for Rick by a table displaying assorted appetizers. She felt out of place, not knowing anyone, and discreetly looked herself over for flaws. Her light-pink chiffon skirt swayed gently with every movement, and her white top had see-through lacy shoulders and sleeves. She wanted to look nice and hoped to make a good impression on Rick's son.

As Emily filled her little appetizer plate with small pieces of cheese, fruit, and crackers, she felt a welcoming presence from behind. Rick stood with a sultry gaze suggesting he had more on his mind than eating appetizers.

"Did I tell you how captivatingly beautiful you look this evening?" Rick said formally.

Emily found herself to be just as captivated with Rick's amazingly handsome face.

"You don't look too bad yourself, Mr. Miller," she offered in the same formal voice.

They gazed at one another until the orchestra began playing "At Last." Rick took the plate of appetizers from Emily's hand and placed it on the table. He took a step back, bowed, and then presented his hand. "May I have this dance?" he said charmingly.

Emily melted into his close embrace, and they swayed back and forth to the lyrics that spoke of love arriving after so long. Rick gazed at her, and Emily could read the profound love in his eyes. Her own eyes filled with tears over the romantic sound and the meaning of the song. He kissed away one tear that had escaped from her eye, and she rested her cheek on the lapel of his tuxedo. She felt his chin rest gently on the top of her head, and he squeezed her tighter. Longing came to both of them, as time had no meaning. The world seemed to stop, if only for a moment.

When the song was over, Emily heard applause and realized they had been the only two dancing on the small cherrywood dance floor. Emily and Rick paused, both unsure how to respond. Rick bowed to the crowd and then presented Emily as if their performance was part of the festivities for the evening. Emily curtsied, holding out her pink chiffon skirt, and grinned until she noticed a woman with a scowl on her face glaring straight at her.

"Oh shit," Rick said, seeing the same woman. "It's my ex-wife."

The woman approached the two, as the crowd returned to murmurs of small talk. She was an attractive woman with dark brown hair done up in a twist and secured with a diamond brooch. She wore a beige gown with sequins throughout and carried herself as if she owned the biggest bank in town.

"Well, well, I see you still have the need to be the center of attention," she said.

Rick deflected the comment. "What can I say when I have the most beautiful woman in the room to dance with." Rick put his arm around Emily's waist, pulling her closer. "I'd say the center of attention is all hers."

"So, who might the little lady be?" said the brown-haired beauty with the evil stare.

Emily didn't like being talked to as if she was some mindless tramp off the street.

"I'm Emily Stanford, Rick's friend," she said, not offering a handshake or any other kind of gesture of friendliness.

"I see," the woman said, looking at Emily as if she was a bug that needed to be squashed.

Rick cleared his throat." Emily, this is my...my—Bernice," Rick choked out.

The two women stared each other down.

"Charmed, I'm sure," Bernice sneered and then walked away.

Emily held onto Rick's arm as they walked away from the awkward situation and found a seat where the ceremony would soon begin.

"What did you ever see in that woman?" Emily whispered to Rick.

"Just so you know, Emily, I wasn't always as smart as I am today," he said with a wink.

The ceremony began with the bride descending the grand staircase in a white strapless gown with a long, lacy, rosebud-printed train. Her father proudly escorted his beautiful daughter down each step slowly towards Derek Miller, waiting at the bottom. Derek resembled a much younger version of Rick with thick dark hair and the same welcoming smile.

Emily kept having flashbacks of her long-ago wedding, remembering how in love she felt seeing Lucas waiting for her by the altar in front of the church. She glanced over at Rick, feeling mixed emotions. I need to tell him soon, she thought. Rick gazed back with his reassuring eyes reaching for her hand and kissing it. Emily leaned slightly closer offering the same reassurance.

The reception was the typical traditional wedding filled with daddy-daughter dance, mother and son dance, garter and bouquet toss along with a whole lot of partying and dancing. At the end of the evening, Emily and Rick gave their cordial greetings to the bride and groom as people were pressing for the attention of the newly married couple. Before Emily knew it, the evening was over. Derek and his bride Meghan lingered with friends outside of the reception venue. The couple were to return to Maple Ridge before departing on their honeymoon the next day.

Emily and Rick took their time strolling along the streets of Salem, making their way back to Emily's car. They stopped in front of an ancient cemetery. The two stood next to an old wrought iron fence, and Emily felt the stillness in the air. "I hate cemeteries," Emily said, peering into the dark towards the silhouette of stones.

"Nah, it's not so bad," Rick said, leaning on the fence. "It's kind of peaceful. Besides, most of those people in there have been dead for three hundred years."

Emily nodded, agreeing with Rick's observations. She looked over to where all the party goers were parked and saw Derek and Meghan getting in their car. They drove past Rick and Emily without so much as a glance.

Emily felt bad for Rick over his strained relationship with his son. She was also beginning to feel guilty with not being honest about Lucas and knew it was time to tell Rick. She kicked the wrought iron fence gently, looking down on the ground. Emily thought it looked obvious that something was on her mind but to his credit, Rick keep quiet, which allowed her to gather enough courage to say whatever needed saying. Emily took a deep breath and, squaring her shoulders, faced Rick.

"I need to tell you something."

"Okay. Is everything all right?"

"Yes, of course, it's—just, well."

Rick took Emily's hand. "It's okay. Whatever it is you need to tell me."

Emily was about to speak but then a sound coming from the direction of the cemetery caught her attention. Emily felt a presence and heard the words "Save them."

"You got that 'I saw a ghost' look on your face again," Rick whispered.

Emily heard it again, only louder: "Save them."

"Did you hear that?" Emily asked.

"No, I didn't. What is it you heard, Emily?"

She then saw the apparition of the dark-haired woman pointing at the road leading back to Maple Ridge. Emily noticed the brown mark shaped like a heart on the woman's wrist. "It's the woman it the mist," Emily said.

Rick glanced in the direction where Emily was looking. "I don't see anyone," he said.

Once again, the ghostly figure spoke: "Save them from the Magic River."

"Did you hear that?" Emily asked.

He looked again into the dark void beyond the gravestones just as a woman's voice yelled, "GO—NOW."

"Now that I heard," Rick said.

Emily was confused, wanting the woman to clarify. "Who do we need to save from the Magic River?" Emily asked the ghost of what appeared to be the same girl that had greeted her when going through time.

The woman's face began to fade when Emily heard her say the name "Derek."

An icy grip shot through Emily. "Oh no, Rick! It's Derek and Meghan. They're going to drown in the Magic River."

After jumping in her car, Emily raced down the road to catch up with Derek and Meghan. So much was going through her mind. "Why didn't I tell them at the wedding that God loves them?" she said to Rick as he desperately tried calling his son on his phone, getting no response.

"It's not your fault, Emily. We barely talked to them."

It took just under ten minutes of driving fast when Emily spotted the directional sign indicating that Maple Ridge was three miles ahead. "I'm praying we get there in time," Emily said.

Rick shook his head, running his hand through his hair. "Yeah, well, I'm praying your brown- haired witch friend uses some of her magic—like maybe emptying out Derek's gas tank."

Emily was amazed at Rick's ability to use his humor to lighten even the most stressful situations. She glanced over at Rick, and although he talked a good game, he was obviously upset.

"I can't lose my son," he said in a low voice.

Emily reached over, squeezing his arm. "Not if I can help it."

Rick leaned closer to the windshield. "There's Derek's car making the turn towards the road alongside the Magic River."

Emily's mind held an image of flashing lights from emergency vehicles, and her husband's dead body being pulled from the river. She shook those awful thoughts, vowing never to let anyone else suffer the same fate.

Emily gunned the car and when she was close to Derek's vehicle, she blew the horn repeatedly. She saw Derek's brake lights go on, so Emily pulled in front of his car, causing Derek's car to swerve. Rick jumped out at the same time Derek did.

"What the hell do you think you're doing?" Derek yelled.

Rick held up his one hand, "Hold on, buddy, let me explain."

Derek walked straight towards his father. "Are you crazy or something, old man? Oh yeah, that's right, maybe you're just drunk again in which case get the hell out of my way."

"Watch your mouth, kid!" Rick said.

Emily got out of the car and darted in front of Rick, holding up both hands. "You should listen to what your father has to say before judging him," she tried to explain.

"I got nothing to say to that old man," Derek barked and started to walk away.

Emily decided to be as blunt as possible. "You were going to die by drowning in the river tonight," she said.

Derek stopped in his tracks and swung around to face Emily.

"Both you and Meghan would have drowned if we didn't stop you from going further down that road," she said, pointing in the direction of where Lucas had perished and where she had laid flowers by the roadside on many occasions.

Meghan opened the car door and got out.

"Get back in the car," Derek yelled at her. She ignored him and walked towards Emily and Rick.

"I told you to get back in the car," Derek yelled.

"You know what, Derek, you should talk with a little more respect to your new bride," Rick said.

"Since when do you, of all people, give out marital advice? All you ever were was a drunken loser who left his wife and son alone."

"Don't talk to your father that way," Emily defended Rick. "You know nothing about what he's gone through."

"Emily, it's okay." Rick interrupted.

But Emily was eager to give Derek a reality check, a history lesson about his father, and information that Rick would never say himself.

"Well?" Derek said. "Why don't you enlighten me, Miss who-ever you are?"

Emily could sense Rick's growing anger. Emily put her hand on Rick's arm to calm him. "I got this," she said and then took two steps closer to Derek.

"Did you know that your father was a war hero? Did your mother ever tell you that? Or did she just let you believe that your father was a drunken loser, as you so easily put it?"

Derek stood frozen in place and looked as if he was trying to avoid eye contact with his father. Meghan came around and stood by her new husband as Emily continued.

"Your dad was in a Humvee with two other guys. They were in convoy with other Humvees behind them when a roadside bomb went off alongside your dad's vehicle, blowing his hand off and wounding the other two guys." Emily took another step towards Derek, speaking softer. "Your dad tied a belt around his arm to stop the bleeding and then pulled out the two guys with him in the vehicle who, by the way, were unconscious, dragging them to a ditch all while under small arms fire. If that weren't enough of a tragedy, other men in that convoy were killed, blown up seconds after your dad saved those two guys." Emily glanced over and saw the look on Rick's face.

"I see you've been talking to Walter," he said with a weary grin.

"Sorry, I hope you don't mind," she said with a crooked smile. She turned her attention back to Derek, softening her expression to a more pleading look. "Don't you see, Derek? Your dad's not the bad guy you think he is."

Rick moved forward, standing close to his son. "You see, son, I was in no condition to be around you. I was pretty messed up for a long time. Then your mother had you believe what she wanted you to believe. So, I left her to raise you," Rick then lifted his arm with the missing hand. "I let her raise you without a damaged father."

Derek wore a look of disbelief. He opened his mouth but looked as if he hardly knew what to say.

Emily took Derek and Meghan's hands. "You both are so lucky to have parents that love you so much. I want you both to know how much God loves you, too. You also need to know Rick and I have no doubt that God will bless your marriage so that it will last a lifetime."

A lingering silence blanketed the road, with only the sound of ice-cold raindrops splashing into the Magic River in the distance.

Rick held out his hand, as Derek seemed reluctant to accept. Emily hugged Meghan and felt a strange connection.

"May I ask you something?" Meghan said.

"Of course," Emily responded.

"What made you think we would die tonight?"

Rick put his arm around Emily's waist. "Emily has premonitions." Emily hoped he wouldn't tell the whole story, and he didn't. Emily noticed a knowing look appear on Meghan's face.

"My grandmother also had premonitions. She used to talk all the time about some curse on the Magic River, but we never believed her," Meghan said.

"Where is your grandmother from?" Emily asked.

Meghan glanced at Derek as if trying to get approval. He

nodded to her. "My mother's family are descendants of Salem witches from as far back as the famous Witch Trials of 1692."

Emily and Rick looked at each other in disbelief.

"What is your mother's family name?" Emily asked.

"Spencer. One of my ancestors supposedly got thrown in jail. I was told her name was Rebecca."

Emily shot a look at Rick, who lifted his eyebrows.

"What?" Derek and Meghan said at the same time.

"All I can say, son, is it's nice to know we now have a witch in the family whose ancestor could very well be Orenda."

Derek and Meghan exchanged puzzled looks. "We don't know what you're talking about," they said.

Emily hugged Derek and then Meghan. "It's okay. We'll explain it some other time. Right now, you have a honeymoon to get to."

Father and son shook hands again awkwardly. "Congratulations, Derek," Rick said. Yet Derek's response was little more than an expression of skepticism. Rick then hugged his new daughter-in-law and kissed her on the cheek.

Emily and Rick were about to get into the car when Emily saw Derek approaching Rick. She could see the hidden tears behind Derek's eyes.

"Hey!"

Rick lifted his chin in Derek's direction. "What is it, son?"

"You should've told me! I didn't know…you should've just told me!"

Rick nodded. Then Derek turned and walked away without another word.

Emily and Rick sat in car watching the newlyweds depart. She turned towards Rick and gently touched his arm. "Give it time, Rick." He looked at her with a weary grin and said nothing.

On the rest of the way home Rick remained quiet. Emily was pleased to see Derek had spoken to Rick. It was at least a start. Now that Derek knows the reason for his father's absences in his life, Emily was hopeful things would be better between them from here on out.

Chapter 13

UNDENIABLE PASSION

IN LATE OCTOBER, MAPLE RIDGE BUSTLED with townspeople getting ready for the annual Octoberfest in Stanford Park Square. Each year the organizers would decide which event in the town's history would be honored at the dedication portion of the festival. This year's pick was to honor all those who were lost in the town of Maple Ridge during the deadly Spanish flu pandemic. Stanford Park Square had two other festivals – one in summer, one in winter – during the year. It was the Octoberfest that seemed to draw a bigger crowd due to the magnificent fall foliage. Throughout the park, vendors sold hotdogs and hamburgers; some sold pizza and sub sandwiches. But most people looked forward to the cider donuts and apple pies.

Emily strolled along the main road alongside the Magic River towards the Shady Brook Bridge that crossed over the river right into the park. She had a meeting scheduled with her boss, Mark Johnson, to discuss some new ideas for the historical column. Emily felt anxious about her next story, and her recent situation of going back in time made her think about quitting the job.

Emily also realized by the grace of God it was up to her to break the awful curse that plagued the Stanford and Miller families. If nothing else, Derek and Meghan's wedding day was proof that the curse continued to have its nasty grip on its victims. It had been over a month since that scary incident. She didn't know the details of how the couple would have ended up in the river and just the thought of it twisted her stomach. One thing Emily did know: there was no doubt in her mind about the dire warning from the ghost of the dark-haired woman. The impending doom was undeniable. Still, the fear of the deadly curse and taking another trip back in time terrified her.

Emily was about to cross the bridge when her phone chimed, showing a text from Mark saying he had returned to the office. "Shit," Emily grumbled to her phone. She looked at the river, then at her phone again, and took a deep breath hoping Mark Johnson's assignment didn't cause another trip through time. "Okay, let's get this over with before I change my mind," she said and walked to the office.

Emily sat at her desk waiting for Mark to come into the room. She was in a foul mood with all the tension ready to grip her at any moment. Then a tapping noise on the smoked glass door made her jump. It sounded as if someone had taken a knife and hit the glass three times.

"Come in!" she yelled, a little annoyed and not wanting to get up. Then again, she heard the tap, tap, tap.

"Ugh, seriously!" Emily got up and flung open the door. "Can't you open the damn door yourself?" She found Rick standing there smiling and holding up his arm with the missing hand. In its place was a prosthetic hook.

"You like it?" he asked playfully.

"You're wearing your hook! That was the strange sound on the door?"

"That be me and my little friend, Mr. Hook," Rick presented his hook. "Hey, I was thinking, maybe I could be Captain Hook for Halloween this year. What do yah think?"

Emily laughed, "Aren't you a little too old for dressing up for Halloween?"

"One is never too old for Halloween," Rick replied. "Besides I think I'd make a very good Captain Hook, if I say so myself."

Emily was happy to see Rick accepting his disability so well. Before, Rick had wanted nothing to do with wearing a hook or anything resembling an artificial hand. She thought the reconciliation between his son might have contributed to Rick's newfound acceptance and good mood.

"Yes, you would make a very nice Captain Hook, and I think it's great you're embracing your inner pirate," Emily added.

Rick wandered around the room, casually looking into the adjacent office with its door partially open. "So, is Mr. Boss Man in?"

"I heard that, Miller," Mark hollered as he suddenly entered the room from his office with a big folder tucked under his arm. "Don't you have something better to do than fraternizing with the help?"

Rick used his hook to offer a salute. "Yes-um, boss. I'm afraid you caught me." Then he walked behind Emily and kissed the top of her head. "I'll see you later, where we can do some more fraternizing."

Mark took the cigar out of his mouth and pointed it at the radiator where the endless heat seemed to come from "And Miller, while you're at it, find a plumber to fix that damn boiler in the basement."

"Oh, Rick," Emily added. "When you do come over to my house later can you help me store some more boxes to the basement?"

"It will be an honor, ma'am," he said, saluting with his raised hook. He then turned towards Mark. "Later, dude." And out the door he went.

"I still don't understand what you see in that guy," Mark said, throwing down the large folder on Emily's desk.

Emily ignored his comment and instead focused on the papers sticking out of the folder. "So, what's all this?" she asked reluctantly.

"It's old information I found on the Spanish flu outbreak in the town. And seeing that the organizers chose this historic event for the dedication portion of the festival this year, I thought an article in the *Gazette* would be fitting," he said, sitting down in front of her desk and pulling out a handkerchief to wipe the sweat off his forehead. "Besides, it's a start among other ideas I had thought of."

Emily hesitated then stood and turned towards the window behind her and opened it a crack. She was stalling, wanting to gather her thoughts. She felt the cool air run up her arms as she tried to control her reluctance over her next assignment. After a couple of deep breaths, she returned to her desk to look inside the folder where she found various brochures, flyers, and old admission tickets to the first festival which took place in October 1920 just six months after the Spanish flu had ended. She looked over at Mark, concerned. "Start? You said to start. What other things do you want me to write about?"

Mark leaned over, pulling a couple of papers from the bottom of the pile and placing them on top. "Something else you might be familiar with, I believe, the Maple Ridge Nursing Home."

Emily sat quietly leaving an uneasy void between her and Mark as she tried fighting off the creeping panic from taking over. She calmed herself with reasonable questions. How much trouble could I get into going to the nursing home? I've been inside that building a million times. She shifted nervously in her chair and saw Mark's eyebrows draw together.

"Is everything all right? he asked. "You look like you've seen a ghost."

Clearly, an expression Emily heard way too often.

"Oh, I'm fine. I suppose I should get started then," Emily grabbed the folder off her desk and headed out the door with no further conversations about ghosts.

Emily took her time walking slowly through Maple Ridge. The streets were filled with pumpkins and corn husks along each storefront. Baskets filled with fresh-picked apples and jars of maple syrup lured customers at several of the produce stands. She sat on a bench across from Owens Drug Store for what seemed like hours, watching all the shoppers go by. Her procrastination was deliberate until she finally stood to walk towards the inevitable—her assignment. Emily found herself standing by the Shady Brook Bridge when she suddenly became overwhelmed. She started to have the same strange feeling of doom that would run through her veins before she slipped through time. She paused, watching the mist come off the river and sweep over the surface of the bridge.

"Not yet," she said to the sinister fog, trying to fight her fears of the unknown. "I need to talk to Rick. The assignment will have to wait.

When Emily arrived home, she saw Rick's truck out front. As she entered the front door, she could hear Rick wrestling with boxes and talking to himself with complaints of un-sealed tops and un-sticky tape. Emily put her keys and phone on the entrance-way table.

"Is everything okay in there?" she asked, coming around the corner.

Rick gave her a side glance. "Does it look like everything is okay?" he said pointing to the ripped box with his hook.

"Sorry. I guess I should have gotten new boxes."

"And new tape," Rick added.

Emily sat down, not saying any more, only half interested in the task at hand, and barely looking at the contents in the box in front of her. Out of the corner of her eye, she could see Rick studying her face.

"Something's wrong. What is it?" he asked.

She did have a lot on her mind, between her new assignment, which could throw her back in time to God only knows where and the fact that she still needed to tell Rick about Lucas.

"Mark gave me an assignment on the Maple Ridge Nursing Home. You don't think..." She hesitated, feeling worn out just thinking about whether or not the witches' curse could have any-thing to do with her upcoming assignment.

"Seem to me you've been in that building hundreds of times with no problems."

"I know. I guess I'm letting my imagination run away with me," she concluded. But she could see by the way Rick lowered his head to look into her eyes that he thought she had more on her mind.

"What else is there, Emily?"

"I've been meaning to tell you something."

She got to her feet, pacing mindlessly back and forth to the front entrance and back into the living room until Rick stood in her path. He put his hand on her shoulder, stopping her right in her tracks.

"Look, Emily," he said, putting two fingers under her chin, lifting it for her to look into his eyes. "You've been trying to tell me something for months. I'd say I'm a pretty patient man, and I also realize that half of what's going on in that pretty little head of yours might not be my business."

Rick touched Emily's cheek softly, which caused her breathing to grow faster and her desire for him more intense, making her forget she needed to come clean about Lucas. Rick leaned in, and instead of his lips touching hers, he whispered in her ear. "Maybe it's time it becomes my business."

Emily felt his gentle kiss on her lips. They looked into each other's eyes as Rick's breathing quickened and his hot breath sparked the undeniable passion they were both unable to stop.

For so long, they had both held back from the complete act of sex, caring for each other with passionate kisses and long embraces. But for Emily, the waiting was over, and Rick's intense gaze suggested the wait was over for him, too.

She pulled him close in a desperate embrace, looking into his blue eyes. "Rick, I want you. I need you," she said desperately.

He grabbed her by the waist, thrusting her against his body as they kissed again, but this time stronger, more feverish with the pent-up desire locked inside out of respect for each other. Swooping her up in his arms, he carried her to the bedroom, laying her on the soft down comforter. He kissed her with a burning passion as he pulled her skirt up. She felt his knees parting her legs and felt the pulsing heat penetrating from his urgent erection as he pressed his full weight on top of her.

The sensation aroused her body's response with the same feverish passion. He reached under her shirt as his mouth traveled from her lips to her breasts. The pressure of his lips moving across her nipples intensified the ache between her legs that yearned to be satisfied. Within moments their naked bodies merged as one. His kisses became more intense as he revealed his craving for her.

They both showed to one another the love and sexual desire they had felt for each other for so long. She wanted all of him, let him take every part of her, and she felt every movement of his body that told her, he had long ached for her, too, which lead them both to a final satisfaction of pleasure and a passion neither one could deny.

Emily lay in bed next to Rick with her head on his chest, listening to every heartbeat. She wanted this moment to last forever. Emily had never been with another man, never given herself to anyone but Lucas. And now, that intimate part of her belonged to Rick. She hoped Lucas would approve, be glad she had found love again. Lucas would have liked Rick, she thought, might even have been good friends. She looked up into Rick's peaceful face; he was sound asleep. Emily still wanted more of what he offered her a few hours ago, a repeat of how he had satisfied all her desires. Instead, she squirmed out of bed naked, grabbing her clothes off the floor quietly so as not to wake Rick. She walked to the entranceway to check her phone. She found a text message from the nursing home regarding Walter, asking her to please come as soon as possible. She put the same clothes back on and wrote a note to Rick:

I didn't want to wake you. The nurse called. I'm going to check on Walter. If you want, you can put the rest of the boxes in the basement. If they're ripped or not taped, it's okay; I'll deal with them later.

Love,

Emily

P.S. I still want more of you later.

The nursing home's parking lot was filled, so Emily decided to park in the town office lot and walk. It was evening, and Emily knew that Walter most likely would need her all night to sit with him. She found herself once again standing by the Shady Brook Bridge. Going back in time kept haunting her but getting to Walter had given her the courage and focus needed. She successfully made it across the bridge with no sign of the mist other than the small amount coming off the water below.

She navigated quickly through the park where the Octoberfest was in full swing with little sideshows of square dancers and small vocal groups singing harmony. One performer had a puppet show going on for the kids. Everything was pleasant; even the brisk air of the autumn night felt good to Emily. For the first time in a long time, she realized that she could finally hold on to some happiness. Her thoughts returned to Rick making love to her, causing an urge to turn around and go back to him. It almost felt like an addiction, a strong passion running through her. It was only the nagging reality of a curse that kept her feelings guarded. *What if this time, I travel far away into the past, never to return?* she thought.

Emily made her way to the entrance of the nursing home. Her eyes focused on the threshold she had stepped over so many times without thought. She took a deep breath, all the while understanding that her next few steps could determine her arrival in another unfamiliar time.

Emily slowly opened the door to the nursing home without incident and felt relieved she was still in the current year. She entered Walter's room and found him hooked up to an IV and oxygen with no discernible movement from his body. Part of her thought he was dead, until she heard him make a small moan. Emily saw Walter's eyes open, settling on her.

"How's our home-town hero?" he asked in a weak, whispery voice.

She drew close to his bed and took his hand in hers, giving Walter a grin that said it all.

"Ah! I see you've engaged in maneuvers with the hero."

Emily let out a tiny, girlish giggle. "Now, Walter, how can you tell such things?" Emily asked.

"The beauty in a woman's face after such a blissful act never lies."

"You must possess special powers with reading faces that I never knew you had," Emily said.

Walter squeezed her hand as he lifted his head slightly. "You have chosen the best," he said, dropping his head onto the pillow.

Emily wasn't ready to lose Walter. He had been her only family for so long. He was like the father she never had a chance to know. Walter had been a friend to her especially after Lucas died, and feeling the pain of another death so close caused her stomach to feel nauseous. Emily knew the signs, especially with Walter's breathing becoming shallow. His skin had a gray tone that often means someone is in the last stages of the dying. Walter began to struggle with his words. He lifted his hand, pointing towards the door to the hallway. "Picture," he said.

Emily looked in the direction of the door, a little confused, finding no picture. "What picture? Do you need to tell me something about a picture?" Emily asked.

Then she heard the clattering of a cart that stopped outside Walters's room. The nurse came in with a fluid bag to replace the almost empty one. "Hi, Emily," the nurse whispered.

"Ashly, how are you?" Emily was glad to see a woman she had worked with for many years.

"Not ready for retirement yet, but believe me, I'm getting close. I envy you. It must be wonderful."

Emily didn't respond to Ashly's comments about her retirement. For Emily, her retirement life had taken too many strange twists and turns. She watched Ashly hang the replacement fluid bag on the hook and noticed that Ashly wasn't giving Walter any of his usual medications. "You've stopped his meds?" Emily asked.

Ashly's expression turned sorrowful, and she put her hand on Emily's arm. "Walter is in hospice now."

Ashly tended to Walter while Emily took that moment to glance out the door, still wondering about the picture Walter had mentioned. "Ashly? Walter was trying to tell me about a picture. Do you know which one he's talking about?"

Ashly pointed to a large picture hanging directly across the hall. "He's probably talking about that one," she said. "It was only a few days ago when Walter was able to get out of bed and use his walker with assistance. I had walked him out into the hallway when he spotted the picture. They had just hung it there a couple days before that. I guess they found it in the basement of the building. Anyway, Walter stood there for the longest time staring at it, studying it, when suddenly he seemed disturbed by it. He mumbled something about his grandparents. The next day he had taken a turn for the worst."

Emily thought she had seen every historical picture throughout the building and was curious about what made this one different from the others. Her thoughts were interrupted by a groan coming from Walter, and she went back to his bedside. "What is it, Walter?" she asked.

He tried lifting his head. "She remembered you."

"I don't understand. Who remembered me?"

"Picture." He dropped his head into the pillow.

While Walter slept, Emily walked into the hallway just outside of Walter's room. The large, framed black-and-white photograph hung in the center of the wall between two other rooms. It showed the nursing home in the days when it was a hospital. She studied it closer: She saw a cavernous room with row upon row of beds with sick patients. In the background of the photo, she spotted a nurse holding blankets. Emily squinted her eyes, focusing intently on the woman's face. The nurse had her surgical mask pulled down to her chin. Suddenly a rush of adrenaline surged through Emily's body. To her disbelief, it was her own face looking back at her from a time that had long passed. She sucked in a breath of air. "Oh! It can't be!"

Chills slithered up her back with a sensation of ice filling her veins. She began to feel a breeze and saw a mist traveling up the hallway. The rushing water sound became stronger. Emily glanced over at Ashly's medication cart. She prayed it would contain an ample supply of the usual antibiotics found in nursing homes to treat bacterial infections. She was in luck. She lunged to grab as many antibiotics as would fit in her pockets. She thought she could see Rick running towards her in slow motion splitting the thick mist in half, yelling "NO! NO!" then he vanished, melting back into the fog.

Chapter 14

THE DISCOVERY

RICK OPENED HIS EYES, FACING THE CLOCK where the numbers blinked on and off. Emily never set the time on this clock, he thought. Another urge came over him that ran down to his lower body that still craved more of her. He reached behind him expecting to caress her naked body, feeling only the sheets. He turned to find her missing and thought he heard the sound of water running and wondered if she was taking a shower.

Rick lay on his back staring at the ceiling. He had slept without dreaming but found himself daydreaming over Emily. The day she came back from 1864 he had been lying in the grass by the river's edge, staring up at the puffy clouds and wondering how much longer Emily would be gone.

Six hours had passed, and from Rick's calculations based on the last time Emily went back in time, one hour meant one day. She had been in another time for six days.

He couldn't stop thinking how much he cared for her. Then his mind conjured up her petite body and long red hair, which gave her a youthful appearance, and thought that if she ended up two hundred years in the past, people might think she was only in her forties. He had tried to go with her that time, but the mist took her away, slipping out of his one hand with ease. He saw the face of the dark-haired woman Emily had mentioned to him previously and the same woman he had heard in the Salem cemetery the day of Derek's wedding. She was just a girl, hardly a woman, and he wondered who she was.

After those six hours had passed, he remembered feeling an alarming chill go through him when he could sense Emily's presence. She was sad, and he felt her despair rip through him. Suddenly, he knew she was close. That had spurred him to walk faster towards the house. As he came around to the front, he found Emily sitting on the steps with her hands covering her face. Just as he could feel her presence, she seemed to be able to feel his as well. She had lifted her head in his direction, and he could see she was on the verge of tears. Tears he now knew were from the loss of a boy named Sam.

Rick touched his lips were she last showed eagerness for him. It had been a long time since anyone came close to wanting him in that way, and the thought of her kiss made him ache for her even more. He sat up in bed and called her name. He hoped she would answer by strolling in the bedroom naked to offer him her beautiful body, and the thought of Emily's touch stirred his insides.

He called her name again, but there was no answer. Rick finally yanked himself away from his daydream and got out of bed. He pulled on his jeans haphazardly, dragging his half-asleep body towards the front entrance. He yawned a couple of times, rubbing the sleep out of his eyes when he noticed a note on the table. Emily's keys and phone were missing. He read the message and chuckled to himself at the last line: "I still want more of you later." Rick put the note down, feeling slightly aroused again at the thought of her. "Believe me, sweet Emily, the feeling is mutual."

Ten minutes later Rick stood in the living room eating a peanut butter and jelly sandwich and staring at the boxes to be brought down to Emily's basement. After finishing his sandwich and downing a glass of milk, he set himself to work. Rick picked up the boxes with ease, wishing he hadn't been so stubborn about wearing his hook. It had made it so much easier to do things. You're such a stupid ass, Miller, he thought as he carried the boxes down the narrow flight of stairs leading to the basement.

The basement was spacious with old-style brick and mortar walls. The ground had been hastily dug compared to what modern-day machinery could do. Rick placed the last box down and noticed one broken open with the tape coming undone. He saw the word "pictures" written on the top and squatted down. He pulled the rest of the loose tape off and opened the box. Inside were pictures of Emily when she was a child, and for the first time, Rick finally had a glimpse of her past. He smiled when he saw a picture of a teenage Emily seated on a horse. She was dressed in cutoff blue jeans, a tank top, a cowboy hat, and boots. "You never told me you could ride a horse."

He placed the photo off to the side, thinking it would be fun to show Emily later. He reached down further, looking for more treasures, when he pulled out a picture that stopped his heart. "What the hell?" he said, not believing his eyes.

He stood up and went over to the basement window for better light. "Holy freaking shit! She was married!" He ran his hand through his hair, not able to comprehend what he was seeing. "Emily was married...to Lucas Easton!"

Rick sat in an old half-broken chair, staring at the couple who seemed so happy and completely in love with each other. Part of him felt betrayed, even jealous. He placed the picture back in the box, not wanting to look any further. "That's what Emily has been trying to tell me all this time?" he said to the hollow spaces of the chilly basement. He couldn't help but stare at the box, trying to decide whether he was mad at her or felt sorry for her. "Why did she keep this from me? Did she think I wouldn't understand?"

His eyes glazed over, barely seeing the brick wall in front of him, unable to concentrate on anything else other than this new revaluation of Emily and Lucas. Rick's eyes began to focus again but not on the box with Emily's secret past but on a strange indentation in the brick wall above the box.

He moved aside several boxes and scraped the wall with his hook, causing chunks of crumbling brick to fall. He could see a seam in the shape of a square and picked at it until it loosened. Finally, a big chunk of brick came out, exposing a wooden box. Rick pulled on the side of the box with his hook to pry it from what looked like a miniature vault. He held it as if a magical genie was about to pop out any minute.

On the top was a family crest that somehow looked familiar to him. He slowly opened the mysterious box that contained old letters and papers. On top of the pile was an old newspaper clipping that crumbled when he attempted to open it. Rick carefully lifted apart the deteriorated paper. It was a newspaper article that caused chills to go down his spine.

He scanned the headline: "Nurse helps the sick as the Spanish flu continues to spread." In the picture was a nurse. Rick looked closely and sure enough it was a woman who was the spitting image of Emily. The deteriorated article from October 1918 slipped from his fingers and floated gently back into the box, as the hair on the back of his neck stood up. "Emily?" he said, trying to understand what he had just discovered. "Could this be where she goes next?"

Rick stood abruptly. An overwhelming sense of urgency ripped through his body as he immediately thought about her new assignment. The nursing home. Then came another chilling thought. No, it's the old hospital.

Rick raced his beat-up old Ford truck down the main street, having difficulty getting through with so many people on the road for Octoberfest. He couldn't go over the Shady Brook Bridge, which allowed only foot traffic during the festival. Instead, he went to another bridge further up the road to get to the Maple Ridge Nursing Home. One question kept nagging at him. Is this when she gets sucked back in time to the year 1918? Will I get there in time before it happens?

He finally pulled in front of the nursing home, shut the engine off, and jumped out of the truck leaving it by the curb. He swung open the nursing home door, ran down a long hallway, and could see Emily filling her pockets with medication from a cart next to Walters's room. What the hell is she doing? His mind had to catch up to what he was seeing. The mist started to engulf Emily, and he yelled, "NO! NO!" as loud as he could to stop her, and with one fell swoop of fog, she was gone.

Rick glanced at the cart, which had scattered pills everywhere.

Nurse Ashly ran up to Rick, gasping at the sight. "What is all this?" she asked, shocked.

Rick knew Emily well and well enough to know she took whatever medication on that cart back to 1918. Rick was almost certain of it and could never reveal the truth. Instead, he came up quickly with a clever idea. "Yeah, some old guy passed by here knocking into the cart," Rick said, pointing down the hallway that contained only a janitor sweeping the floor. "He went that way," Rick gave Ashly his charming smile, which could captivate any woman within five feet of him.

She turned her head towards the janitor, then glanced back at Rick with a suspicious look. "Aren't you Emily's friend?"

"Yup and Walter's."

"Where is Emily?"

"Oh, she just stepped out to answer a few phone calls," he said still putting on the charm.

Ashly looked away with a huff, shook her head as another nurse came around the corner "Hey, Helen, get over here and help me with this mess," she said rudely.

"Nurse Ratchet much?" he said under his breath as he turned towards Walter's room.

Rick walked into the room. He noticed that Walter's breathing was shallow, and his eyes were barely opened. "Hey, buddy, how's it going?" Rick asked.

"Emily's gone," Walter murmured.

"I know, buddy, hopefully she'll be back soon." Rick feared she wouldn't get back in time to say her last goodbyes to the man who had been like a father to her. "Walter? Why didn't Emily tell me about Lucas?"

Walter turned his head and spoke with labored breathing: "A woman's grief...sometimes...is as deep...as the ocean."

Rick nodded. "She could have told me. I would have understood."

Walter coughed, and Rick grabbed the glass of water on the nightstand. "Here, buddy, take a sip."

Walter licked his lips. "She needs you...to bring her back... from such depths of...despair. She cannot...overcome on her own."

Rick kept quiet, seeing how exhausting it was for Walter to talk. Abruptly, Walter grabbed Rick's shirt and seemed desperate to say something else. "Picture."

"Picture?" Rick asked, leaning his ear close to hear his old friend's whispers.

Walter let go of Rick's shirt and pointed towards the door. Rick walked to the hallway and saw the big black-and-white picture on the wall. When looking closer, he noticed it was a replica of the newspaper clipping he had found inside the mysterious box in the basement of Emily's house. Rick peered back into Walter's room, and things were starting to make sense. Rick knew that every time Emily went back in time, it was because she had to save certain people from the witches' curse. This time, though, he wasn't so sure.

He sat by Walter's bedside again. Walter struggled to talk.

"Is there something you need to tell me, Walter?"

Walter gave a slight nod.

"What is it, buddy?"

"My grandmother...almost died...but she didn't." Walter again pointed towards the hallway and dropped his arm, closed his eyes, and mumbled Emily's name.

Rick took a deep breath and stroked Walter's forehead to calm him. Walter knows something, Rick thought. But what does he know, and how did he come to know it? This time something was different. One thing Rick was almost sure of: Emily most likely was the middle of the worst pandemic the world had ever seen. Rick continued stroking Walter's forehead.

"It's okay, buddy. If anyone can save people, Emily can," But Rick had to chase away his own doubts. "Let's just pray she can accomplish it and then come back home to us in one piece," Rick added with a reassuring pat on Walter's arm. But Walter was already fast asleep. "Hang in there, buddy. We'll wait for her together.

Chapter 15

FACT OR FICTION

"GO! GO!" A WOMAN DRESSED IN WHITE with a surgical mask on her face shouted and rushed towards Emily. Emily touched her own face. She was wearing a mask and was dressed in a white nurse's uniform similar to that of the person yelling at her. As the mist completely cleared, she found herself among several nurses, tending to an enormous number of patients. It was as if she had jumped through the photograph she had stood in front of moments before, but now the sounds around her made it real.

"Don't you understand English? I said 'Go!' Get more clean cloths. NOW!" the nurse ordered.

The room smelled of vomit and feces, making Emily gag. She coughed, trying to pull herself together as she took some cotton cloths from a linen cart, placed them in a large pan filled with ice water, and wrung them out. She put one on the forehead of the first person who looked flushed from fever, a young man no older than eighteen. Emily scanned the patients nearest to her and saw that almost everyone was burning up with fever. She quickly grabbed a pan from the floor, catching bloody vomit from the young man she was helping. It took a few minutes to settle him down. She returned the cold compress to his forehead. "You'll be fine. Just rest now," she said, feeling sad for the boy.

The room was overcrowded, which to Emily meant that the conditions were spreading the horrible virus even more. She saw an older gentleman tending to a patient towards the back of the room. He was a short man with thick salt-and-pepper hair. She couldn't see his entire face, but Emily couldn't see anyone's entire face all masked up.

"Excuse me," Emily said to a nurse walking by. "Is that man a doctor?"

The nurse brushed the hair off her sweaty forehead and adjusted her mask. Her eyes showed complete exhaustion. "Yes, ma'am. That's Doc."

Emily repeated the word. "Doc?"

The young nurse laid a cold cloth on the patient next to her. "That's what everyone calls him. I'm not sure anyone truly knows his name. We just call him Doc."

Emily continued to care for the sick as best as she could. She reached in her pocket, feeling the antibiotic pills loosely scattered and then realized she still had her phone. Better keep that out of sight, she thought. Something seemed different this time. The usual path through time had no door to go through, and the dark-haired woman named Orenda hadn't made her typical appearance. But Emily knew precisely where she was and what year. She had studied the Spanish flu of 1918 in nursing school, with history having declared this pandemic the deadliest until 2020. She also knew the antibiotics in her pocket could only help with secondary infections and not the virus itself. She wanted to find a quiet place away from everyone to see how many pills she had and how many people could be helped.

For two hours Emily helped comfort as many of the sick as she could, and then she desperately needed fresh air. As she walked out the back door, the cold air was a great relief from the smell of sickness inside.

She pulled her mask down and walked towards a small set of woods just beyond the hospital's back door for privacy. She sat by a maple tree with its glorious red color illuminated by the full moon that cast a scarlet glow around the tree. She emptied her pockets into a clean linen cloth she had taken from the shelf by the nurse's station and counted each pill. Her heart sunk when she realized how many people could be helped. "Only five people," she said under her breath.

Emily glanced towards the hospital with its hundreds of patients slowly dying. All she could feel at that moment was total defeat. How do I choose who lives or dies? she thought. The depressing thoughts were interrupted by a banging sound coming from the woods behind her.

She stood up, looking into the darkness where the sound of a hammer hitting wood drifted through the trees. A well-worn path was lit up by the full moon, and she followed it when a man appeared out of nowhere, startling Emily.

"You shouldn't be here," he said in a familiar voice.

Emily looked into the man's face and felt as if she would fall over on the spot. Her mind raced, and the shock was almost more than she could handle. She felt faint, and her breathing became shallow. All she could say was "Lucas?" Then she felt lightheaded. The next thing she felt was a slight breeze that blew through the wooded area, carrying the scent of freshly cut lumber to her nose. Her eyes had trouble focusing and she grabbed onto the nearest tree to steady herself. She continued to stare at the man in front of her. "Lucas? Is that you?"

He grabbed her arm so she wouldn't fall and gently set her down. He squatted down to her level and touched her forehead. "You don't have a fever at least," he said in a caring tone.

"Lucas? How are you here?" she said.

The man stood up, taking two steps back. "First of all, ma'am. I'm not Lucas. My name is Alex."

Emily's thoughts became more coherent. "Alex? Alex Easton?" she said, sounding annoying even to herself.

Emily had researched some of the Easton family's ancestry but hadn't spent much time on it. However, she did remember an Alex Easton who had lost his wife from cancer and thankfully not from the deadly curse. Alex was also Lucas's great-grandfather. This man was all Lucas, right down to his build, hair color, and that extremely handsome face her aching heart yearned to see again. Even William Easton back in 1776 hadn't possessed the striking resemblance to Lucas that Alex did. Emily attempted to get up when Alex took her arm and helped her to her feet. "I'm so sorry," Emily said. "It's just that you look so much like a man I knew."

Alex smiled and nodded. "Let me guess: Lucas?"

Emily did everything in her power to separate fact—Alex was not Lucas—from fiction—letting herself imagine that he was. As much as it pained her, she had to face facts: Lucas was gone, and she would never see him again.

"So, what is it that you do out here in the woods?" Emily asked.

Alex put out his hand to help Emily steady herself. "Come, I'll show you," he said.

They continued down the narrow path to an opening where two tents sat in the middle of a clearing with a logging road on the other side and an inviting campfire burning near the two tents. Large numbers of coffins lined up off to one side and small cots were on the other. Emily was astonished over the sight. "You made all these?" she asked, pointing towards the army of coffins.

Alex nodded with regret in his eyes. "Unfortunately, yes. With so many people dying, I can hardly keep up with the demand." He then backed away from Emily as if he remembered something awful.

Emily could see the tension in his face. "Are you okay?" she asked.

"You shouldn't be here. I've done everything in my power to take precautions to not get the sickness."

Then it dawned on Emily what his concerns were. "It's fine. I'm not contagious," she assured him.

"Regardless, I have more than myself to think about," Alex gestured towards one of the tents.

Emily looked in the direction of the tent, saw the half-opened flap, and another realization entered her mind. "A child?"

"My son," Alex clarified.

"Son?"

"Yes, Billy. He's twelve years old."

Emily lowered herself slowly, sitting on a tree stump by the campfire. She was struggling to absorb all of this new information and pondering over Lucas's ancestors' names. Alex—great-grandfather, Billy—grandfather.

Alex sat on a log opposite Emily. "You can see why I worry then," he said.

"Yes, of course. I can't explain it, but I can't give this virus to you or your son."

Emily couldn't tell him that she was from the future and because of that she likely had some antibodies left in her system from years of receiving the flu shot. Besides, she thought, putting Alex at ease from his fear and anxiety would be for the best at this time.

"Virus?" Alex asked, puzzled.

"Sickness, I mean," Emily said.

The two sat quietly, gazing at the fire. Emily wanted to stay frozen in time, remain in the presence of her lost love in this man named Alex. When he died, Lucas had been older than Alex, sixty-two to be exact. Alex looked to be the same age as Lucas even though he was probably in his forties. If Emily had no more sanity nor common sense left, sitting by this warm campfire with forty-year-old Lucas could become her reality without effort. But she wasn't crazy and was well aware of her situation. The fact was she couldn't stay. Instead, Emily stood, brushing sawdust that clung to the back of her white uniform. "I should go, I'm sure they're looking for me by now."

Alex got up and walked with her towards the direction of the path. "Shall I walk you out, ma'am?"

"Please, call me Emily, and no, I can find my way," she said reluctantly. It would be best if I leave now before I do go crazy, is what she really wanted to say.

She started down the path turning once more to see Alex waving. She gave a little wave back. "Take care of Billy," she said, then looked away with tears rolling down her cheeks as she followed the moonlit path back to reality.

Chapter 16

THE DOC

WHEN EMILY RETURNED TO THE HOSPITAL, she found the first patient she had tended to, the eighteen-year-old boy, tossing and turning in pain and coughing with no relief. He was worse off than before. Grabbing a small pill container from the medicine shelf, she poured a glass of water and then dragged a small chair next to the suffering teen. Emily placed her hand again on his forehead. This is bad, she thought, and then took out one of the pills from her pocket. "Here, take this," she said, helping him sip the water to get the pill down. Each patient had a chart hanging at the foot of their bed. Emily leaned over, pulling the chart off the hook, and wrote a notation on the chart to give the boy one pill three times a day for ten days. Emily divided out enough, placing them in the pill container, and writing his name with the dosage on the top. "Lucky you, young man. At least you have half a chance now," Emily whispered.

"What are you giving this child?" a man's voice said abruptly from behind Emily.

She stood, holding the boy's chart and the small pill container. She found the famous Doc with his fingers tapping the side of someone else's chart that he held close to his chest. He narrowed his eyes over the mask. "You're new here, aren't you?" he asked.

Emily followed his gaze that focused on the bottle she was holding. "Ah, yes, I am," she replied.

He took the pill container from her hand and glanced at the top. "What are these?" he asked.

Emily lifted the boy's chart in Doc's direction. "It's a medication that will help his condition. I was documenting his chart," she said with no excuse other than the truth.

"Next time you feel the need to medicate one of my patients, you'll have to go through me first." The Doc's disapproval continued to show in his suspicious eyes. "I could use your help over here," he said.

Emily followed Doc to a group of men. Emily saw that their skin had turned blue everywhere on their bodies.

"Seeing as you know better than I do with your mysterious medications you feel free to give to my patients, maybe you could explain this strange cast to their skin," Doc said.

Emily stood her ground pushing past Doc and lifting the hand of one of the men in the group. "Extreme lack of oxygen by the looks of the nails and the blue tone to the skin." Emily then saw dried blood in the nose of one of the men. "Sinus, ear, and throat infection," she said, pointing to another man with the dried blood showing in each area.

Doc came around to where Emily was standing to get a closer look. She couldn't tell whether he was surprised or impressed over her knowledge of the men's condition.

Emily turned, lifting her chin towards the larger room. "Way too dry and stuffy in here, and in my opinion, with the overcrowding, this room is a gigantic petri dish," Emily concluded.

Doc scanned the room. "You're right. There are too many people in here," he said, with his eyes now showing approval. Doc returned the container of pills to Emily. "You'll get your chance to explain this later, and you better have a good explanation. Now, go put these away in cabinet in the nurse's station."

Just then Doc exclaimed: "Jesus, Mary, and Joseph! What the hell are you doing here?" Startled, Emily followed Doc's gaze to a man approaching them with a camera.

Doc headed towards the photographer, giving Emily time to pull down her mask and rest it on her chin for much-needed air. She picked up a pile of blankets, giving her an excuse to walk away from a suspicious Doc, when a bright flash from the man's camera blinded her. The next thing she saw was Doc grabbing for the man's camera.

"You stupid bonehead!" he yelled, pushing the man towards the door. "Get the hell out before I get stuck taking care of your sorry ass!"

Emily pulled her mask back up and walked over to a nurse staring at the chart of the boy to whom Emily had administered the antibiotics. The nurse looked confused. Emily put the blankets down at the foot of the boy's cot and handed the container of pills to her. "I don't understand," she said to Emily.

"It's going to be fine, trust me. If you keep to the dosage I wrote on the chart, he'll hopefully be as good as new in two weeks."

The nurse nodded, taking the container and hopefully Emily's word for it.

"Well, now, that's quite a statement," Doc said from three cots away. "I thought I told you to put those pills in the cabinet and while you're at it get me my stethoscope in my medical bag."

The other nurse timidly gave the bottle back to Emily and walked away. Emily knew at some point she would have to tell Doc about the antibiotics and hoped he would believe her. She walked upfront where all the other supplies were stored. If Emily didn't know any better, she could swear that the Doc was intentionally giving her minor tasks, so she wouldn't be handing out strange pills to anyone else. She could see a large leather bag overflowing with supplies and, upon further inspection, didn't see Doc's stethoscope. She dug through the contents, moving aside elastic bandages, gauze dressings, and surgical scissors when she felt the stethoscope on the bottom. As she grabbed it, out came an old plastic bottle dropping to the floor. Emily picked it up, knowing right away where she saw it last. "Oh my God! Sam?" she said, turning to see Doc coming towards her.

He stood in front of Emily, blinking slowly while his feet were anchored to the floor as she held what was his only connection to her. Emily slowly pulled her mask down to her chin. "Sam!" she said in a whispery voice. "Is it really you?"

Tears welled up in Sam's eyes, flowing over the top of his surgical mask as he pulled it down, revealing the complete look of astonishment on his face. "Miss Emily?" he said, sounding like the twelve-year-old boy calling for her as she slipped through time. "Miss Emily!" he repeated as he embraced Emily with the same love she remembered when she had left him so long ago.

The two old friends held tight to one another. "Oh, Sam, I've missed you so much." Emily saw that some of the other nurses noticed the strange exchange between them.

Sam took Emily's arm. "Come this way. We need to talk," he said, escorting his long-lost Miss Emily out the back door.

She found herself back under the blazing red maple tree with Sam by her side this time. "How in the world is this possible? You... you don't look a day older than the last time I saw you," Sam said.

"It's a long story," Emily replied.

Sam nodded and paced back and forth. Emily could tell he was thinking. He stood still with his hand on his chin. "I saw you disappearing in some strange mist. What was that all about?"

Emily decided to tell Sam the whole truth but knew it would take too long. Neither one had that luxury with all the sick needing their attention. "I traveled through time from the twenty-first century. I'm sorry, Sam, but for now you have to believe me. I promise to tell you everything if we can get a long enough break," she said.

Sam stood still and said nothing. Then he finally hugged Emily and looked into her eyes. "I believe you, Miss Emily."

Two more hours went by. Emily and Sam worked side by side, helping relieve the pain and cool the temperatures of high fevers, with no good results. Emily could see how exhausted Sam was. He sat down every few minutes, wiping his eyes and cooling off his forehead with the cold compresses. She suggested rest, but Sam had a determination that wouldn't allow him to quit. Finally, another doctor came on the scene, and Sam agreed to go home for the remainder of the night.

"Do you have anywhere to stay?" Sam asked Emily "Never mind, of course, you wouldn't. You're from the twenty-first century."

Emily smiled at his attempt at humor. He put his arm around Emily's shoulder. "You're coming home with me. You need sleep as well."

Emily sighed, nodding in agreement. She was feeling exhausted and putting her feet up somewhere other than the nurse's station sounded refreshing to her.

Emily was in *The Twilight Zone* again as she stood on the front steps of the old farmhouse. She walked through Sam's front door half expecting to see Rick greeting her with humorous comments about something or other. The Victorian feel of Sam's house had not changed much since 1864. Emily made a mental note to take some pictures discreetly with her phone before leaving.

She sat in the parlor by the fireplace while Sam added a piece of wood to the burning logs. He poured a dram of whiskey in each of two small glasses, handing one to Emily. "Drink," he said. "It'll do you good." Then Sam sat in the chair next to her.

"Since when are you a whiskey drinker?" she asked.

"Since fifty patients die every day lately," Sam said, gulping down the whiskey in one swallow.

Emily drank her whiskey down in one gulp, almost gagging as it rolled down her throat. She put the glass down with a thump on the small table between them. "If it makes you feel any better, Sam," she said coughing. "That's the first time I ever had whiskey."

"I can see that," Sam said, grinning. He then wiped his eyes with the back of his sleeve, clearing the sweat rolling down the sides of his face that showed lines of fatigue and regret.

"Are you okay, Sam?"

"Okay," he said as his face brightened. "I remember the first time I heard that word." His face became more somber. He glanced at Emily, and she knew he could see her concern for him. Sam gave her a reassuring tap on her hand. "Oh, don't worry. I'm well enough, just tired."

The two old friends sat quietly listening to the fire crackling. Emily closed her eyes as she began to feel the exhaustion taking over. Then she felt a gentle touch on her arm.

"Emily, this sickness. What in God's name are we dealing with here?"

Emily opened her eyes and turned her head towards Sam. "It's called the Spanish flu, but it's actually a deadly virus."

"Deadly? How deadly?"

Emily sat and organized her thoughts, deciding the best way to tell Sam the horrible truth. But the truth was all she had. "It kills six hundred seventy-five thousand people just in the United States."

Sam leaned back in the chair, clearly trying to absorb the enormity of it all. "Is it contained within the US?"

"No, it was estimated that fifty to a hundred million people died worldwide."

Sam stood up, taking slow steps towards the fireplace putting his hand on the mantel for support. "My God!" was all he said.

Emily stood next to him, putting her hand on his shoulder. "I think there are some things we could do to help mitigate the virus from spreading," she offered.

Sam patted the hand Emily had placed on his shoulder. He nodded and sat back down in silence.

"Sam?" she called to him, worried. Emily reached into her pockets and emptied the antibiotics onto the small table next to their whiskey glasses.

"What's all this?" Sam asked.

"They're called antibiotics, something not discovered yet. They don't do anything to combat the virus itself, but they could treat the bacterial pneumonia, a secondary infection that killed most of those infected."

Sam picked up one of the pills studying it and then gave Emily a side glance. "So, these are what you were so hell bent on handing out. When did they discover this?" he asked.

"Around the end of the 1920's," Emily said, sitting down. "The first antibiotic was penicillin, and it was perfected over time. Believe it or not, it started with mold that accidentally contaminated some cultures being studied in a lab."

"How fascinating," Sam said, putting the pill down. "How many people will this amount help?"

Emily hesitated, not wanting to give Sam the bad news. She picked up three pills holding them in the palm of her hand and sighed. "Only five, and as you already know, I took the liberty of starting one patient on a dose of three a day for ten days."

Emily could tell by the look on Sam's face that he was doing the same calculations in his head she had done earlier. "Four more to go," Sam concluded.

They both gave each other a knowing nod that said: How do we choose who lives or who dies?

"I suppose we can talk about this tomorrow," Sam said, walking over to get his leather doctor bag and taking out the plastic aspirin bottle that Emily had given him long ago. He took a pen from his shirt pocket and wrote something on the bottle. "For now," he said holding up the bottle so she could see what he wrote. "Let's keep them safe in my 'Lucky' bottle."

Over the next two hours, Emily and Sam talked about everything. She held nothing back, telling him about the Native American seer, the witches' curse, and all the time periods she had found herself in. She saw the relief on Sam's face when she explained her disappearance through the fog, not to be seen again until fifty years later. She told him about Lucas and how he died. How she never had any children and how she felt a motherly heartbreak when she left him behind abruptly in 1864. Emily contemplated whether or not to show Sam pictures from the future but trusted him enough to know he would never say anything to anyone. He had wanted to know everything about her, and because she shared so much unusual information, she thought the photos could help him absorb that information more easily. But getting past the idea of twenty-first century technology could be shocking to Sam. She took her chances anyway. Emily sat straight in the chair facing Sam and took a deep breath.

"I want to show you something you'll fine very strange," she said, warning him.

"How strange can it be after everything you just told me?"

"It will be strange for anyone living in 1918," she said pulling her phone from her pocket.

Sam's eyes got as big as dinner plates. "What in God's name is that thing?" he asked as Emily turned her phone on, startling him with an illumined light that casted a peculiar glow onto Emily's face. "Is it a light bulb?" he asked.

"Not exactly."

"Then what is it?"

"It's a phone. Like the ones you hand crank today, but this is advanced technology."

She handed it to Sam, and he gingerly held the thin glowing invention almost as if it would explode at any moment. Emily decided to show him pictures instead of explaining something far beyond Sam's comprehension. She also was well aware that the Internet hadn't been invented yet. Luckily, the phone had enough battery life so she could show him pictures that hadn't been stored in the cloud yet. She scrolled until she found a photo of her and Lucas on vacation. Sam tried his hand at scrolling through pictures, leaving Emily impressed about how easily he managed what to him was a mystifying object. He was like a kid in a candy store in awe at the modern-day sights within each photo. "Who is this man?" he asked, turning the phone for Emily to see.

"That's my friend Rick at his son's wedding. Someone at the wedding took that picture and sent it to Rick."

"Friend, Emily?" he asked, raising his eyebrows.

Emily shrugged her shoulders and hoped her sheep eyes wouldn't give her away.

"That's some friend," Sam grinned. He held the phone closer, squinting his eyes for a better look. "Who, I might add, has you in a pretty tight embrace with less than an inch between locking lips."

The picture of her and Rick triggered memories of him next to her peacefully asleep, after they had made love for the first time. But then her thoughts jumped to Rick running towards her just before she went through time. That's when she realized it was the last time she had seen him. Emily suddenly missed his arms around her, and she hugged herself, looking into the empty corner of the room.

"I'm sorry, Emily. I didn't mean to be indecent with my comment," Sam said.

Emily regained her composure and glanced at Sam with a slanted smile. "Just memories is all."

Sam continued to scroll through the photos. "This is my house," he said, pointing to the image.

"Oh, I didn't tell you, but I brought your house in the future. It was in foreclosure," Emily explained.

Sam nodded. "At least it's back in the family." He handed the phone back to Emily, took out his handkerchief, and wiped his forehead where beads of sweat poured down his face every twenty minutes.

"Are you sure you're okay?" Emily asked. Again, Sam waved away the question with his hand.

Chapter 17

THE LUCKY FIVE

MUFFLED VOICES CAME IN AND OUT of Emily's consciousness. She opened her eyes to see what or who was making the sound.

"You need to wake up now, Miss Emily," a young boy said, hovering over her face.

"Sam? Is that you?" she asked. The child's face came into focus.

"No, silly, that's my grandpa. My name is Thomas."

Emily raised herself on her elbows and glanced around the room and then at the boy. "Thomas?" He looked so much like the twelve-year-old Sam, only a little younger.

"My grandpa told me to wake you. Breakfast is ready," he said and then strolled towards the bedroom door and paused. "Oh, there's a clean uniform for you on the dresser."

Emily jumped up out of bed in a panic. "Where's the dirty uniform?"

"Just over there in the clothes bin. See yah at breakfast," Thomas chirped and then skipped out the door.

Emily rushed over, digging through the dirty clothes, and found her phone. "That was close," she said. She sat on the big canopy bed with memories of sleeping in the same room back in 1864. In her time, Rick had gutted this room. It seemed nice to see the bedroom in its original form. That was a goal Emily had in mind for restoring Sam's house in her time. She had to keep her wits about her and the fact that she had been transported to 1918.

She could hear Sam still coughing and worried he might have contracted the deadly virus. She decided he would be one of the five to receive the antibiotics. Emily came down the stairs to find Sam, nearly out of breath, coming up from the basement. She gave him a concerned look that he dismissed by waving his hand towards the kitchen.

There Thomas had already started eating his eggs and bacon. Emily wasn't going to discuss Sam's condition around the boy, knowing that conversation could wait until later. Instead, she put on a pleasant face and offered them a good morning greeting. Sam pulled out a chair for her. "Thank you," she said, sitting next to Thomas. The morning newspaper was on the table, and the front page was missing an article that someone had cut out. She wondered what the article was about.

"Coffee?" Sam offered.

"Yes, please. I'd love a cup." Emily grinned at Thomas with his head sunk into his plate of eggs. "You must be very hungry," she said to him.

Sam looked at his grandson and tapped the back of his head. "Where are your manners? And say hello to our guest."

Thomas popped his head up with a piece of egg hanging from the side of his mouth. Emily discreetly pointed to the side of her mouth, indicating he was dribbling eggs. Thomas wiped off his mouth. "I already introduced myself when I woke Miss Emily," Thomas said.

She liked hearing Thomas call her Miss Emily, reminding her of how much she missed Sam's young face and voice. "I found Thomas to be every bit of a gentleman when waking me this morning." Emily winked at Thomas adding to the boy's defense. Emily read the look of gratitude that Thomas showed her.

A knock on the door made Thomas jump up hastily, wiping his mouth with his napkin this time. "It's Miss Lily, my teacher," he said to Emily as he went to let her in.

Emily glanced over at Sam. "Teacher?"

"Yes, Miss Lily comes three time a week," he said, waving to the woman as she and Thomas went off to another room for his schooling. "Besides, I'd like to keep him home for a while until this whole sickness goes away."

Emily put her coffee down and leaned forward. "Sam? We need to get some of those people out into the open air and under tents somehow."

"I'm not sure where we can get that many tents," Sam said.

Emily thought for a moment when an idea popped into her head. "I think I know who to ask," she said, picking up her coffee for another much needed sip.

"There is something I need to ask you," Sam said.

"Okay, what is it?"

"At some point you'll need to go back to your own time."

She set her coffee down and gave Sam a skeptical look. "It does seem like that. Well, at least when I have accomplished what I was sent to do. Before it was telling certain people that their creator loved them but now...I don't know."

Sam walked over to the kitchen window. Emily sensed he had something on his mind. "What is it, Sam?"

"I suppose you couldn't carry something back with you." He turned around facing Emily. "I mean, other than what you can carry in your pocket, that is."

"Why? Do you want me to bring something back?" she asked.

Sam picked up the breakfast dishes and placed them in the sink. "Never mind. It's nothing really."

Just as he said that, Miss Lily walked into the kitchen with a pleasant "I hope I'm not interrupting." Emily noticed that Sam's face lit up at the sight of her.

"Not at all, Lily," he said, pulling a chair out for her to sit.

"Oh, no, I've got to get back to Thomas. I just came for a cup of coffee."

"Yes, of course. One coffee coming up." Sam sprang into action.

Emily stood and held out her hand. "I'm Emily, Sam's—"

"Head nurse," Sam said over his shoulder.

The women shook hands, and Emily was hit with a sudden shot of electricity that ran up her arm. She let go and by the look on Lily's face, Emily could tell that the same jolt went through her arm, too. "Do I know you from somewhere?" Lily asked.

Emily glanced at Sam, hoping to get a clue about how to answer. He shrugged his shoulders and gave her a puzzled look. "I don't think so," Emily answered.

Sam handed Lily her cup of coffee, breaking the awkward moment. Lily turned towards the kitchen door and glanced over at Emily. "Nice to meet you, Emily," she said and walked out before Emily could say anymore.

"What was that all about?" Sam asked.

Emily kept staring at the door. "I'm not sure, Sam, but there something about her that seems magical."

A few hours later, Emily and Sam were busy at the hospital, taking over for the night doctor and night nursing staff. They were joined by the day nursing staff. Emily saw another young teen struggling to breathe. The girl had been crying in between breaths, begging for help. Emily took a stethoscope from the nurses' station to check on the girl's condition, stepping over discarded towels and half-filled buckets of vomit. She sat beside the patient, gently rubbing her arm to calm her fears. "What's your name, honey?" Emily asked.

"Marlene," she whispered through tears and labored breaths. Emily helped Marlene to sit up. She placed the stethoscope on the girl's back and listened to the awful crackling and bubbling sounds as the young girl attempted to inhale and exhale. Emily knew it was pneumonia and that Marlene would die soon without immediate intervention. Emily looked across the room at Sam, who nodded his approval. She took the old plastic bottle from Sam's leather bag and counted out what was needed, charting and labeling a new container for the struggling girl.

When Emily finished, she went over to Sam, who was sitting on an empty cot holding his head in his hands. "I'm not going to ask you if you're feeling okay again." Emily said.

Sam glanced up at her. "I appreciate that." He looked towards the young girl.

Emily followed his glance. "I guess we've chosen our second lucky patient," she said.

Sam lifted his chin towards the first boy, who was sitting up and recovering. "And we now know your medicines are truly working."

The large hospital room began to quiet down, giving Emily the opportunity to seek out the man who might know where to get tents. She walked out the front door and took several breaths of fresh, crisp air. She shoved the stethoscope into her pocket along with the nasty mask she'd been wearing for far too long and removed the white head covering, letting cold air reach through every part of her head.

Massachusetts in October was always the most beautiful time of the year, Emily thought. The sunlight flickered through the trees, showing off the dazzling fall foliage that was now at its peak. Emily wandered through the dirt parking area where a mixture of Ford Model T cars stood side by side along with horse-drawn wagons on the other side tethered to hitching posts. Everything was different; even the nicely paved parking lot she had pulled into every day for so many years did not yet exist. She had to remind herself of her temporary situation and focus on the plan of making things better while she was in 1918. This area would be the perfect place for the tents, if we're lucky enough to get them, she thought.

Emily took another long breath of fresh air, tilting her head back so she could absorb the energy of the warm sun. The blue sky with its puffy white clouds was a welcome break from the stale air and looming death inside the hospital walls. She cleared her mind for the next task, which was to find the man with the tents.

As she walked, Emily heard sounds coming from one of the horse-drawn wagons hitched to one of the posts and followed the distressing cry. She found a woman in labor, lying in the back of a wagon and holding her swollen belly. Emily approached the wagon, asking the woman "Can I help?"

"Please do not bring me inside," the woman pleaded. "I fear for my baby."

"You need help," Emily said.

"No, no, please. I'm afraid my baby will get the sickness. My husband, Stuart, is in there deathly sick," the woman said. "He was so bad off I had to drive him to the hospital myself. Then I began to feel the baby coming. I kept it from Stuart, didn't want him to worry. When we arrived, they took my husband in, and soon after my pains became so fierce, I was unable drive myself back. I didn't know where else to go."

Emily looked around, knowing that going into the cesspool of coughing, fever, and vomit wasn't an option. "Come with me." Emily helped the woman up. "I know where it's safe."

The two women made their way through the narrow trail in the woods behind the hospital, leading to an opening where Alex and his son, Billy, were busy working on new caskets. "Alex, we need your help," Emily declared.

Alex ran over, putting his arms around the woman, guiding her inside his tent, and placing her on a cot. "Billy, get some water and a couple blankets," he said to his son, who jumped at his father's command.

"She's in labor and afraid of going to the hospital for obvious reasons," Emily said.

"I get that," Alex replied.

The woman screamed again in pain. Beads of sweat broke out on her forehead with each contraction.

"Listen to me," Emily said, getting the woman to focus her attention on something other than the contraction. "What is your name?"

"Lucy."

"Lucy, the next time you have a pain I want you to breathe in and out slowly. Then when the pain becomes really bad, I want you to blow out short breaths." Emily gave Lucy a reassuring pat on the arm. "Don't worry. I'll help you through it."

Lucy took Emily's hand. "What's your name?"

"Emily."

"Thank you so much, Emily. You're an angel."

Emily smiled and squeezed Lucy's hand. When Emily glanced over at Alex, she could see only Lucas. Sad thoughts crept back in her mind: She and Lucas could never bear children. She would never be a mother. She shook those hurtful thoughts away and focused on Lucy, who cried out with another contraction. Abruptly, Alex left the tent.

The contractions came and went, and within an hour, Lucy gave birth to a baby girl. Emily cleaned the newborn and then handed the mother her beautiful baby. The infant was a joy to behold, in contrast to the death and despair just beyond the tree line. Emily brought some water to Lucy along with a few crackers that Alex had offered.

"What is her name?" Emily asked.

A thoughtful look came over Lucy's face. She seemed to ponder Emily's question and then touched the face of her new child. "Her name is Laura. Laura Ann Green."

Emily's mind stopped and then began to spin. Walter had mentioned his grandmother, Lucy, a few times and how she cared for him since birth because his unwed teenage mother died having him. Such things were scandals in those days. She looked at the newborn and realized that baby Laura was, in fact, Walter's birth mother. The child now cradled in her mother's arms will live only seventeen short years, Emily thought. Knowing the future felt like another curse, causing sadness to creep back into Emily's heart. She sat at the bedside admiring the sight of mother and child bonding together so beautifully when she saw beads of sweat coming from Lucy's forehead. That was strange, Emily thought. She felt Lucy's forehead and detected a fever. If Emily's suspicions were true, the sweat that had poured off from Lucy during her contractions had more to do with the deadly virus and not Lucy's labor pains. She then took out her stethoscope and heard all the signs of pneumonia.

Emily walked over and stood by the entrance to the tent. She felt the weakness of shock in her legs and held onto the flap of the tent for support. Walter's words of his grandmother taking care of him seeped into Emily's mind. The thought made her feel sick, and she knew she needed to save the woman who would look after Walter. She informed Lucy that she would return to check on her and the baby soon.

She stood outside of Alex's tent, completely stunned over this strange responsibility over who lives and who dies. She knew for sure that she couldn't let them die. "Three," she said out loud. "The third person chosen so far, out of the lucky five."

"Are mother and child well?" Alex asked, startling Emily.

Emily yanked his arm and led him away from the tent. "Alex, I think Lucy may have the sickness," she said, glancing towards the tent. "You need to stay away. Maybe sleep in Billy's tent for now."

Alex crossed his arms in front of his chest and stared at the ground. He made a line in the dirt with his boot. Then his gaze rested on Emily. "We must do what needs to be done," he agreed.

"I'm so sorry. Believe me when I tell you, I had no idea she was sick. Perhaps it's because she was in labor that I missed the signs."

"You did the right thing. Don't worry yourself." Alex said.

Emily turned to leave and remembered she needed to ask Alex something. "Is it possible to find more tents like the ones you're using here, only bigger for the hospital?"

"Of course, and you'll need some able-bodied men to put them up."

Emily nodded in appreciation and then walked towards the path.

Alex called to her, "You'll be back then?"

"Yes, Alex, I'll be back and with medicines that will help."

Chapter 18

THE DILEMMA

THE LARGE HOSPITAL ROOM with most of the sick was busy again when Emily returned. She noticed that Sam was doing his best to hang in there by sitting every chance he could to catch his breath. Emily sought out the old aspirin bottle with enough antibiotics for three more people. She found the bottle with the word "Lucky" written on it, counted out the dosage into a container, and wrote Lucy's name on it. She placed the bottle back in Sam's bag for the last two people. If Emily had any say in the matter, one of those people would be Sam.

"I see you've found the next lucky person," Sam said from behind Emily.

Emily lifted her chin at Sam, indicating a direction further away from the present location. "I have a mother and a newborn in Alex's tent in the woods," she whispered.

"Are these medicines good to take for someone in her condition?"

"Yes, it's fine. The antibodies go through the mother's milk protecting the baby and will get rid of the infectious pneumonia for the mother."

Sam sat down, taking his usual hanky out to clear away the sweat on his brow. Emily knew that Sam would never accept any antibiotics for himself and thought of crushing the pills, sneaking them into a glass of water. She also realized that Sam was too clever to be fooled and would know immediately what she was up to. Emily tried her best to pick the next most vulnerable patients, putting aside the urge to help Sam, at least for now.

"Why don't you rest a bit, Sam, and I'll get you some water," she offered.

Sam said nothing. Emily was glad he had allowed her to take care of him for the moment. She grabbed a paper cup, filled it with cold water, and was tempted to crush the pills into it when suddenly she felt a presence behind her. She turned: "Sam! You know, just once, can't you let me help you?"

"Nope." He grinned, grabbed the cup, lifted his mask, and gulped down the water.

Emily took the empty cup from Sam and tossed it into the trashcan, knocking a clipboard off the counter. "What's this?" she asked, picking up the clipboard.

"It's the death list, to keep track and notify the families." Sam took the list and was about to put it in the drawer when Emily stopped him.

"Wait. Can you look up a name for me? The last name is Green. First name is Stuart." Emily wondered if Lucy Green's husband might be on the list.

Sam looked through the pages all in alphabetical order. He glanced up, showing worry lines above his eyebrows and how the virus was beginning to take control. "There is a Stuart Green, and sorry to say he made it onto the list."

"Are there any other Greens on the list alive or dead?"

Sam checked the other list of patients with the names beginning with "G" that had been admitted with the sickness and luckily for them still alive. "No, no one here by the name of Green other than the one who passed."

Emily was beginning to feel uneasy as she looked at Sam. "Walter had told me his grandfather's name was Stuart."

"Who's Walter?"

"Oh, sorry, Sam, he's a man I know from the future." Then something else occurred to Emily.

"Is there a date of birth for him?" she asked.

Instead of looking for himself, Sam handed her the clipboard. "No, only their ages."

She ran her finger down the page, finding Stuart's name and

noting that his age was fifty-four. She did the math in her head, subtracting fifty-four from the year 1918.

"I can't believe it," she said looking into Sam's eyes. "Sam, do you remember helping me when Lillian Green gave birth to a baby boy back in 1864?"

Sam leaned over and saw Stuart's age. "Are you telling me that Stuart Green, who just died, was that baby?"

"I'm not positive but his age and last name certainly match up."

She already knew that Lillian Green had been a Miller and was one of Rick's ancestors. She was married to Vance Green, who was Walter's great-grandfather, and Lillian had given birth to a baby boy, the same baby boy she and Sam assisted in bringing into the world back in 1864. Could Stuart Green be that baby boy? Emily wondered. She remembered that Walter had bragged one day about being related to Rick Miller, the hero, and told Emily about his and Rick's connection through their ancestors. I'm back in *The Twilight Zone* again, Emily thought.

Just then Sam started coughing and struggling for breath, yet he managed to get out a few words.

"Now I'm beginning...," Sam coughed, "to understand how you feel...," coughing again, "with the time travel stuff." Sam leaned forward as he continued to cough repeatedly.

Emily helped him to sit and caressed his shoulder without saying a word. It was all too much for her; the horrible thoughts came rushing in. Sam might die. How will I be able to stop it? He will never let me help him. She felt completely helpless, defeated by a rampant virus. The only control she had now was finding the right words for a soon-to-be-grieving mother and her baby.

It was late afternoon by the time Emily returned to Alex's campsite. All she could see were two tents, a stack of cots, a wagon filled with coffins ready to be delivered, and a smoldering fire in the center of the open area. Lifting the flap of Alex's tent, she saw mother and child sleeping peacefully. When Lucy began to stir, Emily went in.

"Ah, you are back," she said, coughing immediately upon speaking.

Emily gave a pleasant smile as she took out the medication from the container with Lucy's name on it. "Yes, I brought you medicine for the sickness. You should be as good as new in no time."

Lucy barely lifted her hand in a weary wave of thank you. She was getting worse, and Emily had no time to waste. After giving Lucy her first dose, Emily placed a cool cloth on her head. Lucy wasn't a young mother, Emily noticed, estimating her age to be at least forty, young enough to conceive a child. Emily had hoped Lucy's mature age would give her the advantage to accept her husband's death but found that thought to be ridiculous. Emily still hadn't fully gotten over her own husband's death and having Alex just a few feet away had been a constant reminder of the heartache. Maybe if nothing else, we have this one tragedy in common, she thought. Emily sat straight in the chair, trying her best not to show the sadness which occupied her heart and soul most of the time. But Emily had failed to hide her somber mood from Lucy.

"You have bad news?" Lucy asked.

Emily held Lucy's hand and forced out the words: "It's Stuart."

Lucy put her hand up to her mouth; tiny whimpers escaped between her fingers.

Emily leaned forward. "He died this morning. I'm so sorry." Emily couldn't help her own tears from rolling down her cheeks, and the two women embraced, sharing each other's pain and loss.

There was nothing more to do for Lucy and her baby. Emily spent over an hour comforting the new mother and now the recent widow. She gave Lucy instructions on how to take her medication, kissed little Laura on the cheek, and walked out of the tent knowing she might never see them again.

No one was around in the clearing, causing Emily to worry that something might have happened to Alex or Billy. She called for them while making her way to the other tent, but no answer came from behind the canvas or from any other direction. Lifting the flap of the tent, she saw Billy rolled up in a pile of blankets, shivering.

"Billy?" She rushed into the tent and placed her hand on his head, which was hot with fever. Pulling the blankets down, she lifted his shirt and placed the cold chest piece of her stethoscope against Billy's clammy back, causing him to flinch. She heard the same familiar sounds, which revealed the same awful conclusion. "Billy? It's Emily. Don't worry. I'm going to take you back to the hospital with me." He groaned, saying nothing.

She lifted the tent flap and looked down the logging road in one direction and the narrow path in the other. She heard a rustling of leaves underfoot as Alex emerged from the path. He waved happily and approached Emily. "I've secured the tents along with six men to put them up for your hospital in the morning."

Emily didn't know how to manage so many emotions. Happy about the tents, sad for Lucy with the loss of her husband, the countless people suffering from this virus, and now Billy being its latest victim. All emotions could easily cause her to go out of her mind at any moment. She stood frozen in place, lost for words, but she knew that Alex could see the look of worry on her face.

"What is it?" Alex asked.

Emily gazed up into the ghost of Lucas, trying to separate the real from not so real.

"Emily?" he said, holding both her arms slightly and shaking her from her trance. The grip sent a shockwave through her veins, jolting everything back to the real. "It's Billy," she blurted out.

Alex immediately pushed Emily aside, but she pulled on his arm. "No! Don't go in there! You'll get sick!"

Alex backed off, looking bewildered as to what to do next. He stared down at Emily for an answer but by the look on his face he already knew. "How bad is it?"

"Not bad if I can give him the same medicine I just gave to Lucy," she said, gesturing towards the other tent.

His eyes pleaded. "Then you will save my son?"

Emily took Alex's hands, gently squeezing them while willing herself to remain in the real. "I will take him with me. Burn all the blankets Billy was wrapped up in and then come back to the tree line at the back of the hospital. I'll leave you fresh sheets and blankets with extra supplies for Lucy and the baby."

Alex cupped Emily's cheeks with the palms of his hands, kissing her forehead in appreciation. For Emily, all the pain of loss turned into enormous desire, and it took every fiber of her being to fight off what she truly wanted in that very moment—to remain forever in the not so real.

Billy held onto Emily's waist, as the two struggled to reach the hospital. They made it to the hospital's back entrance, and she sat Billy down on the step. She ran in to get a cot, ironically one built by Billy's own hands. Emily placed the cot under the large overhang of the building, laying Billy down, wrapping blankets over him. She wanted to keep him in the open air until his father and his friends set up the tents in the morning. "I'll be right back, Billy. Don't worry; you'll be just fine," she said, rubbing his head.

The hot and stuffy hospital room gave no signs of getting any better. The aspirin bottle in Sam's bag contained the last two precious dosages. Emily saw Sam sitting on a cot with his head down. He's not getting any better, she thought, holding the "Lucky" aspirin bottle in her hands, hoping it would live up to its name. One course of antibiotics for Billy and the last for Sam, she decided.

"What in the name of Lord Jesus himself is in that bottle?" a voice behind Emily said. Emily flinched. "I swear both you and Doc hover over that strange thing like it was the last secret on earth."

Emily swiveled around to find one of the older nurses with her arms crossed, tapping one foot, and displaying a face of someone who had just finished sucking on a lemon. Emily thought the woman was near to her age, but the harsh lifestyle of these times with little modern conveniences and lack of good medicines made the disgruntled nurse look years older. Emily held the bottle like a kid who got caught with a hand in the cookie jar. She had to think of a clever way of explaining the unexplained to the curious nurse.

"It's experimental and enough for five people. Doc has been doing research and decided to see whether or not it would help in such horrible condition as this," Emily said with a straight face. The lie sounded so real she almost believed it herself. The nurse looked baffled.

"I see. In that case, I shall speak to the Doc," she said and strutted off towards Sam. Emily followed, hoping to give facial expressions and nods to Sam, encouraging him to go along with the explanation she had given to the nurse. As Emily and the other nurse approached Sam, he staggered to his feet and collapsed on the floor right beside the cot.

"SAM!" Emily yelled, elbowing her way passed the nosy nurse. "Sam? Can you hear me?" Emily asked. She and the nurse got him to the cot, and Sam lay down, grabbing Emily's sleeve without opening his eyes. "They say the hearing is the last to go," he joked, then coughed uncontrollably.

Emily wiped his head and face with a cool cloth the other nurse had given her before she left to tend to her patients. "Very funny, Sam, but I'm not about to let you go to wherever you think you're going," Emily said.

He peeked out of one eye, took her hand, giving it a commanding squeeze. "Take care of the young, not me, do you understand?"

She did understand and all too well. He squeezed her hand harder. "Emily, promise me."

But Emily couldn't possibly make such a promise and offered Sam a small bit of good news. "If it makes you feel any better, I'm giving the fourth course of antibiotics to Alex's son, Billy."

"Good girl," Sam said with a weak smile.

"Please, Sam, let me give you the last?" Emily begged.

Sam pulled on Emily's sleeve again, lifting his head off the pillow. "NO!" he shouted, coughing and spitting up mucus.

Emily wiped his mouth with the cloth she was holding and saw how exhausted Sam was. He drifted off to sleep, leaving her with the pending agony of loss drifting through an already broken heart. She pulled herself together and tended to Billy and the hundreds of other people suffering. Emily was haunted as she held the aspirin bottle in her hand with Sam's life-saving medication.

Suppose I don't save Sam, then who? she thought. Who in God's name deserves it more the Sam?

Chapter 19

PAINFUL DEPARTURE

NIGHTFALL CAME WITH NEW NURSES and a doctor filing in the door. Emily had no intention of leaving Sam, even though she had been encouraged to go home. But home wasn't in this time or place; home to her was with Sam.

She lay down on a cot near the front entrance with the door half-opened to invite the cool air and dismiss the stench. She took off the mask and rubbed her face and eyes to relieve the tension building on her temples. Not a headache yet, but one would soon come with all the pressure of the current situation. She was grateful aspirin had been invented, at least.

Emily closed her eyes, giving in to her body's need for sleep. Blurred images crept behind her eyelids of the seer Catori sitting so still conjuring up the dark-haired Orenda. Another woman lay dead in the arms of the young seer. A soldier's sword had slashed the woman's throat. Blood ran down the girl's hands and dripped off the tips of her fingers. Catori screamed, but no sound came out of her mouth. Just then, Emily was jolted out of her strange dream by a woman shaking her awake. It was Lily, Thomas's teacher.

Lily sat Thomas at the foot of the cot Emily had been sleeping on. "Emily, it's Thomas. He's burning up."

Quickly, Emily felt Thomas's forehead as he moaned in pain. "Here, Thomas, lie down," Emily said placing him on her cot. "Does your head hurt?" Emily asked. He nodded, and Emily saw tears in his eyes.

She checked for congestion in his lungs and heard a bit of pneumonia beginning. Emily then nodded to Lily indicating he, too, had the sickness. "It's going to get better, Thomas, I promise,"

Emily assured him. It was now clear to Emily about Sam's situation. Thomas would need the last course of antibiotics, and Sam's chances to live just got a whole lot worse.

Lily suggested she return home and wait for word on Thomas's condition. Emily could see the fatigue on Lily's face and hoped she, too, wouldn't fall ill to the grip of the virus. "Yes, Lily, that's a good idea. And thank you for looking after Thomas," Emily said.

Lily nodded. "Sam?" she asked.

Emily lifted her chin towards the back of the room where Sam lay. "He's—" Emily's words came to a halt.

Lily placed her hand on her chest and shook her head slowly as if in denial. The two women looked down at Thomas, and Emily could see that Lily was thinking the same thing: Thomas might lose his grandfather.

"I'll return in the morning to check on them," Lily said.

Emily watched her move slowly towards the door with her shoulder hunched in defeat.

Emily had three nurses help move Thomas outside in the open air where Billy was, as she administered the medication to Thomas. She explained to the nurses that Thomas would be the last to receive the experimental drug.

As Emily sat on a wooden box between Billy and Thomas, it felt so surreal to her. Billy was Lucas's grandfather, and Thomas was hers. Emily had no memories of her grandfather, who had died when she was just a baby. She had fragments of memory showing a bearded face, which would flash across her mind. She had wondered if this bearded man was her grandfather. Maybe it was a dream she might have had as a child. But now, she would know her grandfather as an eight-year-old boy, sick and dependent on her to save him. She touched Thomas's soft cheek, not the rough texture of an older, bearded man. A man who could be her grandfather or a dream.

Throughout the night, Emily checked on Sam as the pneumonia took over his lungs. She had fallen asleep in the chair by his cot where she dreamed images of mist, water, wind, and strange faces of people from another time. She felt a hand on her shoulder.

"Thomas is asking for you," the young doctor said.

Emily touched Sam's arm.

"I will keep an eye on the Doc," the young doctor said.

Thomas was sitting up, still coughing and spitting on the ground alongside his cot. "How are you doing?" Emily asked.

"Better, I think," he said. "My grandpa? Where is my grandpa?"

The question made Emily's stomach turn. She had to tell Thomas the truth. "I'm afraid he's sick."

Emily reached for Thomas's hand. "Like you are. Only you're getting better...your grandpa is not."

"Is he going to die?"

Emily sat on the wooden box next to Thomas as she caressed his hand. "I don't know for sure, but I think so." The anguish of even saying those words caused a surge of nausea to rip through her stomach.

Thomas let go of Emily's hand and lay back down, turning his head away from her. She could hear the tiny sniffling and wanted to hold him in her arms to make the pain go away. "Thomas? I'm here for you, honey," Emily said, trying to console the boy with her soft touch.

Suddenly Thomas turned and reached for Emily. His embrace told her they had both felt the same sadness over the looming demise of their loved one. Then a thought registered in Emily's mind: the curse that had plagued her family. She looked into Thomas's teary eyes. His sandy brown hair reminded her of twelve-year-old Sam. Another little boy she had comforted when he lost his sister and then his father. This time it was Thomas who was losing someone so dear.

"There is one thing you need to remember, Thomas," she said firmly. "God loves you so much, and you know who else loves you?"

Thomas shook his head and wiped his nose. "No, who?"

"Your grandpa," and with that, the two hugged again until Thomas fell asleep in her arms.

* * *

Emily sat on the front steps of the hospital watching the sunrise above the red maple trees, which seemed almost like heaven to her. That feeling didn't last, as the horses and wagons poured in with the sick at the same time wagon loads carrying the dead poured out. She saw Alex in the distance with his men putting up several tents across the parking area.

One wagon pulled in front where Emily was sitting as she saw Lily step down. The teacher was attractive, in her sixties, with large brown eyes and brown hair with streaks of gray. Her hair was gathered up in a small bun on the back of her head. "How are the boys?" she asked.

Emily patted the step beside her, and Lily sat down. "Sam is still alive, and Thomas seems to be recovering."

Lily let out a long breath of relief. "Thank God," she said.

The women were quiet for several minutes, watching the big tents go up. Emily gave Lily a curious side look. "How long have you known Sam?" Emily asked.

"Oh, a long time. I was great friends with his wife for many years." Lily talked about the friendship between her and Sam's wife. Her face glowed when telling Emily about her two granddaughters and how she regretfully doesn't see them as often as she would like. But Lily mainly talked with affection about Sam, which caused Emily to conclude that Lily's feelings towards Sam were more than she was letting on. The two women continued to sit enjoying the cool, fresh air when Emily saw Lily nodding with a look of decision. "I've decided something and wanted to let you know what that was," Lily stated.

"Oh, what's that?" Emily asked.

"IF...," she hesitated, clearly sad over her thoughts. "And only *if* mind you, Sam doesn't make it, I want to take care of Thomas."

Emily considered her proposal, thinking how nice it was of Lily to take on an eight-year-old child at this time in her life. "Does Sam know you feel that way?"

"Yes, we've talked about it briefly once, and seeing I've been friends with his wife and him for so many years well, Sam thought it made sense."

Emily nodded and smiled at Lily. "I'm sure Thomas would also be comforted by that arrangement."

"May I tell you something?" Lily offered with a curious expression on her face.

Emily nodded. "Of course."

"You have a unique purpose that will make a profound difference," Lily said.

Emily was confused over her statement. "I don't understand. What do you mean?"

Lily placed her hand on Emily's arm with the same electric charge from before, but this time Emily didn't pull away. "Just know that your journey does not end here," she said mysteriously.

Emily looked at Lily with puzzlement. She was bewildered over Lily's strange words and magical touch. She knew there was something different about Lily.

Emily heard the hammering and her attention was drawn towards Alex, as he maneuvered the big poles up and pulled the ropes back, staking them to the ground. Emily noticed Alex leaning over, holding his stomach in what looked like a spasm of pain. Emily stood up and stepped down.

"I'd like to ask you more about what you just told me, but I think I'm needed," Emily said not taking her eyes off Alex. "I'll be right back," she said without looking back at Lily.

She rushed across the dirt parking lot. When she saw Alex fall to his knees, Emily sprinted past the wagons and men and reached Alex within seconds. "Are you okay, Alex?"

"No. Something's wrong," he said, wincing in pain.

Emily checked for all the same signs, and sure enough, they were all there. She helped him across the parking lot to the steps of the hospital. Lily grabbed his other arm, and the women brought him to an empty cot right next to Sam.

"It's best we keep Alex and Sam inside. There's no need for the boys to see them so sick. And Lily, you need to leave before you get sick," Emily insisted.

Lily's feet didn't move. Emily saw her look of terror at the dreadful sight of Sam. "LILY!" Emily yelled, "GO!"

Lily left quickly. Emily was horrified over Alex. Oh no, how will I help Alex survive this? she thought. Emily finally got him settled with some pain medication. He drifted off peacefully, so she turned towards the cot next to him to check on Sam. She placed another cold cloth on Sam's head as he shivered. She pulled the blanket to his chin and felt an overwhelming sadness drifting into her heart. "Oh, Sam, please don't die on me," she whispered.

Emily sat with the two men for a little while when she began to feel completely helpless. She got up and made her way passed the other patients, with so many of them crying, coughing, and calling out in anguish. She started to feel spent, no more to give, wanting to give up, and decided to step out front to escape. There she found Lily still sitting on the steps. Emily pulled on her mask with force, yanking it off and throwing it on the ground. "I would love to burn this damn thing," Emily yelled.

Lily's face showed deep circles under her eyes. "Sam? Mr. Easton?"

Emily sat down in defeat, putting her face in her hands. "Still alive," she said. "I can't do this anymore," she felt Lily's hand on her shoulder; this time, it was warm, without shock.

"I know you're doing everything you can; it's all any of us can do," Lily said.

Emily glanced over at Lily when a thought occurred to her. A devastating possibility that sent spikes of pain to her chest. "Do you...do you think you could take in another boy?" Emily asked.

"What do you mean?"

"Mr. Easton's son, Billy," Emily said.

"The boy has no mother?" Lily asked.

"No, she passed on."

She saw Lily trying to absorb the new information. Lily looked back through the glass door, fogged over with death and destruction, and glanced at Emily with a reassuring expression. "Of course. But let's hope it does not come to that."

A little while later, Emily dozed in and out as she sat between Sam and Alex. A faint voice fluttered through her mind. She saw Rick standing by the edge of Magic River, waving, beckoning for her to come. He smiled and blew her a kiss that touched her lips. I'm waiting for you. Come on, let's go, he said, waving in the direction of the river. Suddenly, Rick fell over the edge. She ran to him, but she couldn't reach him in time. He disappeared into the mist, swallowed up by the water. Emily jumped into the water, but instead of hitting the water she was jolted out of her bizarre dream into a cold sweat.

"A bad one?" she heard someone say. Alex lay awake; his eyes focused on her. He took a shallow breath, still holding his stomach.

"Alex? I'm so sorry," Emily said, leaning close enough to feel the heat coming off his face.

A hint of a weak smile came across his blue lips. "For what?" he whispered.

Emily got down on her knees and held Alex's hand, which was also burning up with fever. "I'm afraid I caused you and Billy to get sick."

"No. No," he said in a low weak voice. Emily, not true."

Alex's skin had that awful shade of blue. A tiny tear formed in the corner of his eye. He squeezed Emily's hand. His grip was weak, and she rubbed his fingers.

Alex struggled to speak. "Take...care of Billy," he exhaled. He smiled faintly, and his gaze penetrated Emily's soul. "Thank you for...saving Billy." His words lingered in the air as he closed his eyes and took his last breath.

"Alex! Alex!" Emily yelled, trying to shake him back to life, but there was no response—just, nothing. Emily burst into tears. "Alex! No! No!"

She felt herself on the verge of insanity. The young doctor appeared, leaned over Alex, and checked for a pulse. He placed his hand on Emily's shoulder and squatted down to her level. "I'm so sorry," she thought he said, but yet, she heard nothing. She saw the doctor's lips moving with no sound. As he left her, everything moved in slow motion. She felt her body shifting and saw Sam looking at her. He was trying to tell her something.

"I...love...you," his lips formed.

Emily held onto the sliver of sanity she had left and took Sam's hand. "Not you too, Sam," she said, hardly able to speak herself.

The room closed in with just the two of them now. There were no doctors or nurses, no dying people, not even Alex's lifeless body. Emily couldn't stop the flood of tears. She felt herself consumed with grief that pierced her soul into nothingness. But then she heard Sam call her name. "Yes, Sam, I'm here."

"Box...basement," he said. "Thomas..,box, basement." His words drifted off.

Emily didn't know what his words meant. Still she managed a weak smile and touched Sam's cheek. "Sam? I love you, Sam."

Sam smiled but not at Emily. He seemed to be smiling at someone over her shoulder. "Sarah." He spoke with surprise in his voice. Sam reached out, calling for Sarah again. Then his eyes shifted to Emily. They were soft with an inner glow. "I have to go now, Miss Emily." His voice was strangely strong, as if he knew his words would be his last. "You were like a mother to me when I needed one the most." He then closed his eyes and left his battered and sick body behind.

Emily wobbled to her feet. She couldn't feel her legs. She couldn't feel her arms. Emily was depleted, in shock. Moments later, everything went black.

Chapter 20

THE CURSE

BLACKNESS, SOBS, THE SOUNDS OF CLANKING chain links, slits of light beaming through small cracks above with smells of blood and vomit. Where am I? Emily felt pain from something around her wrists. She tried pulling, causing cuts as if from a dull knife. Then she heard two young women talking in what sounded like Old English. "Thee has pain beyond measure," a young woman moaned in despair.

Then Emily heard another more familiar accent, which she had heard so long ago from an old Native American woman; this time, the voice was young. "Must not weep so loud," she said.

Emily's eyes began to adjust, finding two young women sitting side by side. One pregnant and actively in labor, the other a Native American, consoling her friend. Emily looked down at her wrists and identified the source of her pain. What the hell! Are these shackles?

"Is I who will curse thy accusers. Love shall die forever for thy accusers' descendants," the pregnant woman declared to her friend. The pregnant woman screamed in agony.

Emily desperately pulled on her shackles to reach her. "I can help you manage the pain," Emily said.

The pregnant, dark haired young woman's penetrating eyes glanced at Emily with suspicion.

"Thou shall not declare such things," she responded.

The Native American woman inched her way towards Emily. "Help with words," she pleaded.

Emily looked closer at the young woman speaking. She was beautiful with olive skin and dark eyes, which begged the question that suddenly popped into Emily's head. "What is your name?"

"Catori," she replied.

Emily was shocked, even more so when she realized that Catori seemed to recognize her. "You have great sorrow," Catori said. "Lost mother, father, best friend, child, lover."

"How do you know this?" Emily asked.

"I see woman with hair bright as flames, cursed with loss, end of bloodline, one love gone another enters with the blood of the seer," Catori proclaimed.

Emily felt as though she had lost her mind. So traumatized by Alex and Sam's deaths, she was convinced she had no sense of reality. She looked at Catori, knowing she possessed extraordinary powers as a seer, someone with visions of the future. Suddenly, Emily became aware that she had gone back in time three hundred thirty years to the very place where this whole nightmare had begun. The staggering reality hit her: She was in a time of peril and in a place she dreaded. She was in a prison with all the accused witches and a place that would cause certain death for her. These horrifying thoughts were interrupted by another agonizing scream. Emily shifted herself as close as possible to the young woman in labor.

"Listen to me. Breathe in and out slowly. It will help relax you and then breathe short breaths like this." Emily demonstrated the breathing method. "Now, do just what I did and when the pain starts again, it should be more bearable and help you get through the worse of it," Emily instructed.

Within moments the contraction began again. Emily noticed that the young woman was in more control this time. When the contraction let up, she looked at Emily with suspicion. "How does thou possess such powers?" she asked.

"What is your name?" Emily asked, hoping to steer away from any suspicion over whether or not she had powers.

"Sandra," she said. Suddenly, Sandra gasped as blood and water trickled from between her legs.

"Sandra? What you're seeing is normal," Emily reassured her.

Emily was frustrated with not being able to help or even reach Sandra to assist her. All she could do was talk her through it. "When you get another pain then push hard," Emily told her.

Another voice came from the shadows. "How does thee possess such knowing?" the voice asked.

Emily peered into the dark corner where another woman emerged. She had light-brown curly hair beneath a white head covering and looked slightly older than the others. "Art thou a witch?" the young woman asked.

"No, I'm not a witch."

"Then thy red locks upon thy head give thee the power of knowing?" she asked.

"No, I don't have any powers," Emily answered. Just then, Sandra pushed hard, letting out a howl so loud Emily was sure it could be heard for miles.

With that final contraction, the baby emerged, crying, with Sandra desperately trying to grab onto the child. The shackles prevented her from holding the newborn. Sandra moaned, and Emily saw the anguish on her face from being unable to cradle her newborn. The sight was overwhelming as Emily helplessly watched Sandra pull the shackles, tearing the skin on her wrist to get to her baby. Emily pulled on her own shackles in frustration and with no results.

The door abruptly swung open with shrieks of terror from the darkened room in which she was trapped. A grubby-looking man with a long, filthy beard held a leather strap and loomed over Sandra. A small, older woman peered out from behind him looking just as grimy. He picked up the baby by its feet. "Good. A boy," he sneered, handing the child over to the old woman as if it were a sack of potatoes.

Sandra cried out for her baby, and the man whipped her with his leather strap. "Silence!" he roared, taking a skeleton key out of his pocket and shuffling over to Catori. Without touching her as if he was in fear of contamination, he unlocked Catori's shackles. "Indian witch, out!" he roared again.

Catori looked at Emily and placed her hand on Emily's shoulder. "Curse remains for many moons till the one shall come whose blood ends thy curse upon thee."

With those haunting words lingering in Emily's mind, she saw Catori disappear through the welcoming light of the doorway.

The repulsive man gave Emily a menacing sneer. He grabbed Emily's chain, dragged her slightly across the dirt floor, and unlocked the shackles, freeing her. The man squeezed her arm so hard it felt as if it would break. His foul breath smelled from his rotting teeth as he hovered over her. "Red-haired wench, go!" He didn't seem to have the same fear with her as he did with Catori.

Emily looked down, now free of her shackles, and was able to get a better view of Sandra. She could see Sandra was drifting in and out of consciousness from the loss of blood. She urgently wanted to help and tried to yank her arm away from the nasty prison guard, but he tightened his grip. If she wasn't able to help her now, Sandra would die for sure.

"Get out!" he yelled.

"No, wait! What about her? She'll die," Emily pleaded.

"Good! The witch can go back to hell. Look!" he growled, pointing to Sandra's wrist. "She possesses the devil's mark."

Emily looked closely, and there it was. On the back of Sandra's wrist was the brown mark in the shape of a heart. It was the same mark she had seen on the dark-haired woman in the mist. Sandra opened her eyes, and her glare reflected the vengeance and hate she directed towards the man who gripped Emily's arm. Sandra verbalized her scornful defiance. "Might the blood of Satan run through thy veins," she said to him.

The guard pushed Emily, her knees hit the dirt in front of Sandra as he immediately retreated and stumbled over the chain he was holding. The look of horror overshadowed his face as he abruptly left, slamming the door. Emily could hear the sound of the skeleton key turning the lock.

A fog began to surround Sandra, creeping towards Emily,

when Sandra spoke. "Thou art not from here; thou traveled far."

Emily felt a heaviness throughout her body. It was becoming difficult to focus, but she had enough sanity to ask: "You know who I am?"

"Thy ancestor, Hector Stanford, and my accuser tortured me. Stripped me of clothing, whipped me, said I had the mark of darkness. Told the people: 'Thou shalt not suffer a witch to live.' Was then I put a curse upon thy family. Then I cast the same curse upon the murderous soldier, Miller, who killed the family of my friend, Catori. All who are descendants of these two families shall suffer the heartache and death of those they love by the misty waters of the Magic River. The curse shall remain until the last of the Stanford bloodline ceases to exist."

Sandra's breathing slowed, and she began to have trouble speaking. Emily crawled towards her, but Sandra shook her head for Emily to stop. She looked directly into Emily's eyes. A look that shot straight through her like an arrow. "Thou will be cursed until none is left," she proclaimed.

Emily realized Sandra was telling the truth; her story was not a legend. Emily knew the curse ended with her, the last of the Stanford bloodline. It wasn't until that very moment that the painful truth came crashing through her mind and soul. Something she never realized before: She would have to die for it all to end.

Emily looked into the eyes of the dying young woman and watched helplessly. She covered her face in her hands. The dark walls started closing in on Emily, leaving her in despair, abandoned, and with no hope of ever escaping. Emily knew there was no way out. Lucas died because of this curse and then she vowed: I won't let anyone else suffer the same fate. "It's me you have cursed," Emily said. "I am the last one, and this must stop with me."

Sounds of short, shallow breaths came from Sandra, the Salem witch, whose tribal name was Orenda, A name given to her by her dearest friend, Catori. She looked up to see Sandra struggling to breathe. Emily began to feel a cold breeze seep through her skin.

The prison cell filled with a dreary fog as Sandra's gaze set frozen on Emily. It was then that Sandra took her last breath and drifted away into the mist.

Emily curled into a fetal position on the cold dirt floor. She held her hands over her face. The overwhelming despair engulfed her. She, too, wanted to die and spare the man she now loved from certain death. She could hear the quiet cries from the accused witches behind her when suddenly the cries were replaced by the sound of rushing water and then silence.

Chapter 21

THE RETURN

Maple Ridge Nursing Home
PRESENT DAY

WALTER WAS RESTLESS, MUMBLING INCOHERENTLY. Rick sat at his bedside, remaining quiet, trying to make sense of his words. The hospice nurse tiptoed in with a folder of papers and a laptop. Rick ignored the woman's presence and continued stroking Walter's head. "I'm still here, buddy," Rick said with a catch in his throat.

The hospice nurse shook her head slowly, indicating to Rick, that within hours, Walter Green would be dead. Rick tried to keep Walter alive long enough so he could say goodbye to Emily. He kept talking and telling him silly jokes, with Walter barely responding.

The nurse sat in another chair off to the side of the room and opened her folder, writing things down. Rick could hear the irritating sound of her pen scribbling across the paper and then soon after the tapping of her laptop keys. Rick couldn't contain his annoyance any longer. "If you got anything to say, then why don't you just say it?" he said.

The woman stopped typing, closed her laptop, and placed it on the chair. She handed a small brochure to Rick. "This will explain the process," she said.

She picked up her belongings and stood by the door, ready to leave, when she turned to look at Rick. "If you have any questions or need someone to talk to, my number is on the front." She then left the room.

Rick stared at the brochure. "Don't they make these things for people who are going on vacation?" he said, talking out loud to himself.

"Yes, a permanent one," came a clear answer from Walter.

"Hey, how yah doing, buddy?" Rick was glad Walter was able to respond to his sarcastic remarks over the brochure.

"Thank you...for playing catch with me," Walter said.

Rick put an affectionate hand over Walter's forehead. "Hey, buddy, I'm not sure when we ever played catch, but I sure would have if I had the chance."

Walter's mouth turned up slightly. "You will."

Hopes were fading quickly for Walter. He was beginning to lose all sense of reality. Rick thought Walter was hallucinating. Maybe he was remembering something from his childhood. Rick never knew anything about Walter's family; if Walter did have a Dad, Rick was sure he would have played catch with him long ago. Then Walter began repeating Emily's name over and over, mumbling off into a deep sleep again.

A little while later, Rick stepped out into the hallway to stretch his legs by pacing back and forth in front of the large, framed black-and-white photograph. He had stopped every so often looking at the picture and wishing he could teleport himself back in time to be with Emily. He wondered how she would deal with a pandemic armed with only the small amount of antibiotics she had stuffed so swiftly into her pockets. He missed Emily terribly and could still feel her touch on his skin, still tasted the sweetness of her kiss. He ached for Emily, wanted to tell her it was okay she had kept her secret from him and that he understood. Rick stared at the picture, touching the woman's image, which was so small in a room filled with so many dying people. He spoke softly to the faded image of Emily. "Will I ever see you again?"

Rick returned to Walter's bedside and leaned back in the chair, stretching his legs out with his arms crossed in front of his chest, nodding off. He could still hear Walter making gurgling sounds, and Rick knew Walter's time was near. He forced himself to keep his eyes open and to remain on the alert for Emily's return. He closed his eyes and did the calculations in his head. One hour meant one day. Emily's been gone for three hours. "Three days," Rick sighed.

He began to hear a strange whimpering coming from the hallway. He slowly made his way towards the sound and found Emily curled up in a ball on the floor. "Emily? Emily! He knelt next to her. "Are you okay?"

She didn't move nor make any attempt to move. Rick placed his hand gently on her back, and she shivered to his touch, causing her to flinch. He saw that her eyes were glazed over and looked past him as if he wasn't there.

"Emily? It's me, Rick. You're back in your own time now," he said, trying not to touch her when everything inside him wanted to take her in his arms and never let go.

She finally looked at Rick, saying one name. "Walter?"

Rick could see something was different about Emily. She seemed to dismiss him, and he wondered if she remembered him at all. He attempted to put his hand on her arm, but she flinched again, and Rick could see a severe bruise and strange cuts around her wrists. "What the hell happened to you?"

She ignored his question. "How is Walter?"

Rick decided not to probe into her recent experience and instead offered her a shred of good news. "He's still alive."

Chapter 22

DEADLY CONSEQUENCES

EMILY ROSE AND WALKED to Walter's bedside, putting her hand gently on his cheek. "Walter? It's Emily."

His eyes opened with tears swimming and seeping down to the pillow. "Emily? My darling Emily," he said.

"I'm back. I met your grandmother and your mom," she said.

Walter struggled to breathe. He reached out to Emily. "When I was a little boy...she told me that you were an angel from heaven... just before she died. Emily, our angel...were her last words." Walter seemed desperate to tell her something else.

She leaned down with her ear next to Walter's lips. "What is it, Walter?"

"Your father was...like a brother to me."

"You knew my father?"

"I promised him I...would protect you...if anything should happen to him."

"Why didn't you ever tell me this?"

"He remembers you, too, from so long ago."

Emily was trying to make sense of Walter's words. She wondered if he was hallucinating. Lack of oxygen would do that. Still, the thought of Walter knowing her father was a shocking revelation. Emily wanted to find out more, but Walter was no longer there. His eyes were frozen in a blank stare. The same stare she saw just moments ago from Sandra. Now, it was Walter. He was gone, had drifted away towards the place where Lucy and Laura were waiting.

Rick reached past Emily, closing Walter's eyes. "He's gone, Emily," Rick said with a soothing voice.

Rick touched her arm, and she pulled away; agony had reached far beyond her strength to handle, but she knew what she had to do.

Emily saw the sorrow in Rick's eyes from her reaction to him. She wanted to jump into his arms, hold him forever, feel his touch again, make love into the night, and wash all the pain away. But the consequence of that love would be deadly. "I'm sorry Rick, I can't," she said, shaking her head. "I just can't. I've...I've got to go."

Emily ran out the door. She felt Rick grab her before she got to the entrance. "Emily, what are you talking about? I don't understand," he said.

"I can't do this," she cried. "First, it was my mother, my father, Sam, Alex, Walter, and worst of all, Lucas. I'm not going to let anyone else die because of me." She opened the front door to the nursing home and sprinted down the steps.

"Emily!" Rick yelled. "I know about Lucas."

Emily stood still for a moment, not looking back at Rick. "It doesn't matter. No one else has to die." Emily moved away slowly.

"You're not making any sense. What the hell happened to you back there, Emily?"

She stopped in her tracks and this time turned around. "I am the curse," she stared at Rick and yelled it louder. "Don't you see! I AM THE CURSE!" She turned and ran towards the park. Rick hollered her name several times, but his voice became fainter the deeper into the park she got.

People were getting ready for a new day of festivities. She aimlessly bumped into a woman holding an arm full of souvenirs and then a man with a box of kids' toys, scattering them on the ground with the man uttering a curse word that she barely heard. She went over the Shady Brook Bridge, stopped in the middle, and stared out over the mist floating up from the Magic River. The cold breeze stung her puffy, red eyes and a gut-wrenching pain of hopelessness consumed her. Everyone she had ever loved was dead, except for Rick.

"I'm not going to let you have Rick," she said to the river below. "Do you hear me? It all stops with me." All she could feel was rage.

"Why? WHY?" she screamed, letting out the anger that spilled out and tumbled down to the dark, misty water. "TAKE ME? WHY DON'T YOU TAKE ME?" But no answer came from the silent river.

Three days went by, but for Emily the hours blended, giving her no sense of time. Sorrow drifted through the dark rooms of the farmhouse. "Sam's house," she whispered, wishing Sam would answer somehow. She wanted to give up, disappear into nothing. The thought of Rick anchored her to the ground but tormented her because of her need for him. How will I survive without him now? she thought. It would have been better to have never met him. It would have been easy to live in seclusion. Her depression was deep, bordering on madness, a place only Rick could rescue her from but at what cost? The cost of his life.

The next day Emily lay on her couch by the front window with it slightly cracked open to allow the fresh air to seep in. She heard Rick on the porch but remained still, as he seemed to be hesitating to knock on the door. In the corner of her eye, she could see him peeking through the window. She knew Rick well enough to know that he was trying to give her space from whatever trauma he must have thought she had gone through. She saw the look on his face when he had seen the bruises and cuts that were wrapped around her wrists. Emily was certain that Rick would come to the conclusion that something devastating had happened and a trauma known only to her. She could almost hear him, thinking of the best way to get her to talk to him. It was then that Rick began to tell the story of his own loss as he sat in the chair next to the window.

"Emily? Emily? I know you can hear me."

She saw him look in and she moved slightly; she was sure he knew she was not sleeping.

"I know you went through something extremely difficult. Believe me I've been there. Maybe not in the same way but I get it.

You feel like your head will explode any minute over the loss."

He peeked in the window again, and she shifted her body to hear him better. Emily could tell that Rick wasn't about to give up. "I'm not going anywhere, Emily. I'll wait however long it takes."

Silence fell between them. She started to cry softly and thought he could hear her sniffling.

"We got separated from the rest of the convoy that day," Rick said, re-counting his experience in Iraq. "We were like sitting ducks; then the explosion happened with everything going black. I was certain it was over. I was ready to die. I wanted to die. The pain was unimaginable. But when the smoke cleared, I saw the two guys I was with. They were still alive but in pretty bad shape. I knew I couldn't die just yet. After getting them into the ditch, I kept watching the other Humvee, not certain if the crew was dead, even though the likelihood of them surviving was dismal."

Rick shifted himself in the chair as if uneasy verbalizing the event, something she knew he had avoided at all cost.

"So, I got them out, dragged their dead bodies into the ditch alongside the two wounded soldiers. Whether dead or alive, they were going home no matter what. I wasn't about to let those sand maggots have a chance to loot those dead soldiers' bodies, nor was I going to let them get blown up into a million pieces either. Turns out, I was right, because those bastards finished off those Humvees by blowing them up with an RPG. Minutes later the rest of the convoy caught up and took out the enemy."

Emily saw Rick run his hand through his hair. Most likely disgusted, she thought, and mostly with himself.

"We should've never gotten separated from the rest of the convoy. We should've waited for the rest of them to catch up. But no, I insisted we keep going without any backup. Maybe it's my fault, or maybe it's the fault of any of the six of us. Either way, those guys listened to me. I screwed up and soldiers died." Rick sighed.

Emily lifted her head and saw a look on Rick face that told her he was visualizing that tragic day.

"I never told Walter that part of the story," he said. "I never told anyone, except now, you."

Rick got up and stood on the edge of the front steps. He looked towards the window. She put her head deep into the pillow so he couldn't hear her cry. He had to know, she thought, that she could hear every word he had said to her But it was what Rick said next that shook her from the very depth of her soul where the love she had for him lived.

"There's a soldier's creed: Never leave a fallen comrade behind." Rick turned and took a step down. He hesitated and then looked over his shoulder. "Just like those soldiers, I'm not about to leave you behind either, Emily."

Chapter 23

THE DIARY

THE WINDS OF LATE NOVEMBER blew dry leaves over the last of the green grass. Emily pulled on her muck boots, wrapped a knitted scarf around her neck, and put on a long wool coat. She walked the property, still hearing echoes from the past, finding the loudest ones coming from the river's edge.

She made her way through the leafless trees and stood by Sam's fishing spot where she could see him smiling, bragging about his catch. "I miss you, Sam," she said towards the old log where he once sat. If she tried hard enough, she could almost hear him say: "I miss you, too, Miss Emily."

She sat awhile on the log, not the same log but one like it that she had placed there. She looked out over the fog-covered Magic River, recalling a conversation with twelve-year-old Sam about papers found in a locked box. The writings were about an old Native American woman's crazy talk that Captain Miller came to believe as true, Sam had said. Emily also remembered Louis Miller handing her an old yellowed envelope from Captain Miller with her name on it that came from the same box. Suddenly, she remembered something else. Emily jumped up, feeling as though a lightning bolt had struck her mind. She remembered Sam's dying words: "Box—in basement."

Walking fast through the yard, she reached the house, swung the back door open to the small mudroom, hastily took off her coat, scarf, and boots, and darted to the door leading to the basement. Just as she turned the doorknob, she heard a knock on the front door. From her vantage point, she could see a small figure peering through the oval stained-glass door. The person knocked again, and Emily was torn between running to the basement or answering the door.

"Emily? It's Meghan," said a soft, sweet voice.

It took a second for Emily to process the name. Meghan? Rick's new daughter-in-law? She walked to the door, catching her reflection in the mirror hanging by the front entrance. She touched her hair which was sticking out everywhere and tried matting it down with her hands. Not much I can do about it now, she thought. Emily opened the door to find Derek's beautiful bride looking as if she was having difficulty forcing a smile.

"Hello, Meghan. Sorry I'm such a horrid sight," Emily said as she continued to straighten out her hair unsuccessfully.

"I'm sorry, Emily. If this is a bad time, I can come back," Meghan said.

Emily opened the door wider, gesturing for her to come in.

"I suppose no time is a good time for me lately. Please come in," Emily said. "In fact, I'm glad for the company."

Meghan looked around, and Emily could see she had rested her gaze on the drawn curtains, which must have made the room look dark and dreary to Meghan.

"Would you like a cup of tea?" Emily asked.

Meghan's face relaxed a bit, and she smiled. "Yes, thank you. That would be nice."

The two women went to the kitchen where it was brighter, and Emily put the tea kettle on the stove. "Is there any particular kind of tea you like? I have regular, decaf, and I have several different kinds of flavors."

Meghan sat down at the table, putting her oversized purse on the chair next to her. "Regular is fine," she said pleasantly.

Emily sat across from Meghan. She was a dark-haired beauty, just like Sandra, the dark-haired beauty who had died in front of Emily, an image she constantly had to chase away. "So, what brings you here today?" Emily asked.

"Rick has told us everything: the witch's curse, the time travel—everything."

"I see. And…?»

"And all your losses especially your husband," Meghan said, sliding her hand on the table towards Emily without touching her.

The tea kettle whistled, interrupting the painful thoughts the conversation had sparked. Emily poured the tea in silence and then sat down to inform Meghan of the one missing piece from the story Rick most likely left out. "Did you know, Meghan, that I'm the only one who can stop the curse from continuing? And did you know that being with Rick may very well cause his death?"

"I'm not so sure that will happen," Meghan replied.

"What makes you so sure?" Emily asked suspiciously.

Meghan reached for her purse, pulling out an ancient book and placing it on the table. "Because of this," Meghan said, sliding the book towards Emily.

Emily looked at the cover and one word of the title chilled her: *Witches'*. The book looked old and fragile, and Emily wanted nothing to do with anything coming from some strange time.

"You don't need to be afraid, Emily," Meghan said. "It's a diary written by my three-times great- grandmother. It's been handed down from generation to generation. My grandmother told me many stories of the witches in my family."

Emily narrowed her eyes. "Witches? You mean like your ancestor Rebecca?"

"Yes, good witches, mostly clairvoyants, healing the sick with their special potions and yes, having an ancestor who was in prison during the Salem Witch Trials."

Emily looked closer at the book titled *Diary of the Witches' Testimonies*. She opened it to the inside page. "I see it's been published."

"Yes, a long time ago. Anyway, I just thought reading it would help, and I think you will be familiar with some of the stories," Meghan offered.

Emily couldn't imagine what the book could offer her but accepted Meghan's suggestion to read it. "Thank you, Meghan. I'll check it out later," Emily said and then decided to change the subject. So, how's married life?"

Meghan blushed, picking up her cup of tea and taking a sip which hid her red cheeks. "We are very much in love and happy," she said, then glanced down at her Apple watch. "Oh. It's getting late. I have a meeting in twenty minutes."

"Rick told me about your work. How is your interior decorating business going?"

Meghan stood up, swinging the strap of her purse over her shoulder. "Great! It's amazing how many people need help decorating their homes." She looked around at all the unfinished work in Emily's house. "I can help you with yours if you want," she offered.

"Sure, that would be nice."

"Do you have any ideas? Maybe styles you've been thinking about?" Meghan asked.

Emily smiled for the first time in a long time. She thought a lot about making her home Sam's home again. Rick had his own ideas about the house. They were different than Emily's ideas, but that was because she had seen firsthand what the farmhouse looked like when it was Sam's house. It hurt her to think that Rick's ideas wouldn't matter anymore. She picked up her phone from the kitchen table, scrolled through some pictures, and then turned to Meghan. "You're not going to believe where I took these pictures," Emily said, handing the phone to Meghan.

Meghan's eyes lit up with a small dimple forming on her cheek, making her look like a child opening a Christmas present for the first time. "The detail," she said, astonished. "Where were these taken?"

Emily stood up and nodded in the direction of the living room, and Meghan followed. Emily pointed at the old fireplace. Meghan again looked at the picture and saw the same fireplace surrounded by Victorian-style furnishings and decor. She jolted her head up, and Emily saw the shock on her face. "You took this when you went back in time?" Meghan asked.

"I did. All of those pictures of every room in this house came from the year 1918."

"Sam's house, right?"

"That's right."

After looking at the unusual pictures, Meghan handed the phone back to Emily. The two women looked at each other with appreciation.

"Thank you, Meghan, for stopping by."

"Do you think you can text me those pictures?" Meghan opened the front door, ready to leave. "I'll see what I can do about recreating your home to resemble its former glory."

"Yes," Emily said. She felt a calm, cheerful grin cross her face.

"One more thing," Meghan said, her expression turning sad, "Rick does love you very much."

Emily touched Meghan's arm with appreciation. "I know."

After Meghan left, Emily hurried to the basement. She scanned each area of the musty space and saw where Rick had stored her boxes. A brick was missing in the wall above one of the boxes. She studied the hole with interest placing her hand inside what appeared to be a perfectly square opening and wondering why stone dust and pieces of rock were scattered about on the floor. She continued investigating every inch of the basement, returning to where the stone must have fallen out of the wall. The box below the hole contained her pictures from the past. That's when she noticed the image of her and Lucas lying on top of the box. She picked it up, thinking she would never look at this one again. Then it became clear that this was what Rick must have seen. He must have asked Walter about Lucas after seeing this picture, she concluded. One thing she knew for sure: No wooden box was down here.

What could Sam have meant by urgently telling me such a thing on his death bed? she wondered. The thought of Sam dying came tumbling back into her consciousness, and she pushed it away quickly by looking further in the box with all the pictures. She felt a small book at the bottom and tugged it out from the pile of other little photo albums. Emily could tell the book was old by its yellowed edges and black-and-white pictures from long ago. It looked as though some books had been hastily thrown together. The one in her hand had the year 1925 written on the back. She flipped through the hundred-year-old images when suddenly, three faces caught her attention. Standing by a sign that said "Maple Sugar Barn" was Thomas, Billy, and Lily. Thomas's teacher had her arms around the two young men, and they all looked so happy. Emily turned the photo over, and goosebumps ran up her arms. The handwriting identified those pictures as Thomas Stanford, Billy Easton, and Lily Spencer.

"Lily Spencer? I didn't know she was a Spencer. Wait a minute. I just saw that name somewhere."

She hashed out fragments of memories from the past and from recent events of her own time. Suddenly, it was as if the flood of recall hit her with all the pieces of brick that were scattered on the floor. She ran up the stairs into the kitchen, where the book Meghan gave her sat in the middle of the table like a centerpiece. She picked up the book and opened it to the publication page and saw the name of another ghost from the past: "Written by Lily Spencer."

Chapter 24

TIME FOR CHIVALRY

THE MAPLE SUGAR BARN BUZZED with holiday cheer. Fresh-cut Christmas trees of all shapes and sizes leaned along a fence. A cable above the trees had bright white lights that illuminated the whole tree lot. The Christmas season was in full force. The smell of spruce and balsam took over the usual sweet smell of maple syrup but couldn't entirely drown out the apple pie aroma drifting through the air from the Maple Sugar Barn just feet away from the Thirsty Moose Tavern where Rick was sitting at the bar.

The barstools and tables were filled with lunchtime locals and tourists looking for a bit of the country Christmas atmosphere. Rick leaned his elbows on the counter with his shoulders hunched, staring into his drink, thinking about Emily. He gazed up at the bottles of whiskey, vodka, and all the assorted alcoholic beverages. He looked again at his half-filled glass, taking a sip and pushing all the addictive emotions away by conjuring up Emily's face in his mind.

"This stool taken?" a familiar voice said behind him.

Rick looked over his shoulder to find his son, Derek, lingering by an empty stool. "Take a load off, son," Rick offered, patting the stool. Rick noticed the concerned look on his son's face, as Derek looked at the glass in front of his father.

Rick gestured for Hank, the man who owned the establishment to come over. Hank was seventy-five, short, bald, and sporting a veteran's cap that read: "Army Vietnam 1971 to 1977." "Hey there. What can I get you?" Hank asked.

"I guess I'll have what he's having," Derek said, pointing to Rick's glass.

"Coming right up, young man," Hank said. Hank plunked down a glass in front of Derek, reached under the counter, flicked open a can, and poured ginger ale into the glass. Derek watched as the soda bubbled to the top of the rim. He glanced over at his father.

Rick gave Derek a weary smirk. "Sorry to disappoint you."

Derek let out a faint laugh and nodded in approval. "I'm proud of you, Dad," he said, patting his father's back.

Hank leaned over the bar, interrupting the conversation. "Hey, we look out for each other around here, you know. Watch each other's backs. Ain't that right, Rick?" Hank poured the last few drops of ginger ale into Rick's glass.

"I'd say you're right good at it too, Hank," Rick said and then glanced at Derek.

"So, how did you know I'd be here?" Rick asked.

"It was easy. When I checked the diner, Molly the waitress informed me that if you weren't there for lunch that you would likely be here."

"Good old Molly," Rick snorted. "I swear she knows everybody's movements within a hundred square miles."

Derek took a sip of his ginger ale and swiveled on his stool towards Rick. "Meghan and I are concerned over you and Emily."

Rick slurped the last of his drink and nodded to Derek. "That make three of us," he said. Rick ran his fingers through his hair, feeling frustrated. "I don't know, Derek. I thought giving her time to get over whatever the hell happened to her in God only knows what time period she found herself in would have helped. I think I have a lot of patience, but she sure has a way of testing it."

"I thought you said she might have gone back to 1918," Derek said.

"I'm not exactly sure, but I guess when I saw her in the old newspaper clipping..." Rick hesitated. "I just don't know. I'm just putting two and two together. I suppose she could've ended up anywhere. She said something about Sam dying and a guy name Alex dying, whoever the heck he is. It seems like she blames herself for their deaths along with her parents' deaths and especially her husband's death, and then…" Rick hesitated again, pointing to his wrists. "She comes back with cuts around her wrists and a nasty bruise on her arm. Makes me wonder: Who the hell did that to her?" Rick turned to look straight into his son's eyes. "Something happened to make her think this whole curse thing was completely her fault."

Derek leaned close to Rick and whispered: "Meghan thinks there could be an answer to that very question in an old diary her grandmother gave her."

"Diary?"

"Yeah. You know how Meghan told you guys that one of her ancestors got thrown into prison for being a witch?"

Rick thought for a moment. "Rebecca?"

"Right. And in that diary, well it's actually a published book her three-times great-grandmother wrote. Anyway, Meghan read a story about Rebecca's time in prison, something about a strange woman who appeared out of nowhere and how this stranger helped one of the prisoners by talking her through childbirth. These witches thought this strange woman possessed special powers."

Rick felt confident this story had to be accurate; it sounded exactly like something Emily would do. "So, you two think the mysterious woman could have been Emily?" Rick asked in a low voice.

"Meghan thinks so," Derek said.

Rick now understood where Emily's fears were coming from. She must have experienced harsh conditions in an ancient time. "This means she could have gone through two time periods," Rick concluded. "Possibly 1918 from the newspaper clipping and maybe at the time of the Salem Witch Trials. But it still doesn't answer the one question that aggravates the holy hell out of me: Who was the bastard that hurt Emily?"

"Well, back then it could have been anyone who abused Emily, unlike today," Derek said, lifting his chin toward a table of young women laughing and having fun. "Woman were treated like shit back then, and today they wouldn't put up with it."

Rick glanced over at the young women, wishing he could make Emily laugh like that again. "I'm pretty sure Emily wouldn't have put up with it and probably fought back, almost getting herself killed." Rick banged his fist on the bar. "I hate it. I hate that I couldn't be there with her through all this and worst of all is not knowing if she will ever be the same again."

The two sat silently for a couple of minutes when Derek said: "Well, the only hope I can offer you, Dad, is to give Emily some time to read the diary and hopefully she'll come around."

Rick once again ran his hand through his thick hair. "When did Meghan give the diary to her?"

"This morning. Why?"

Rick put his elbows back on the bar, looked to his right, and then down the bar at Hank, retelling the same old jokes to a couple of guys who had probably heard them a hundred times. Then he glanced at the young women sitting at the table, flirting with a group of young guys at the table next to them. He remembered himself at that age: young, confident, and always getting the girl of his choice with no effort. He turned looking at his empty glass and then looked at Derek. Rick came to the only conclusion.

"I'm not going to lose her. I think it's time I take the old-fashioned approach, a good dose of chivalry to win over Emily's affection," Rick reached into his pocket, threw a few bucks on the bar, and then stood up. He glanced at Derek and lifted his chin towards the door. "Come on. Let's get out of here."

The two walked towards Rick's truck. A stiff breeze carried tiny snowflakes that stuck to their coats.

"Really, Dad? You still drive that old piece of crap?" Derek said and then laughed.

"Hey! Watch what you say in front of the old girl. She's a classic and still has some giddy-up left in her, I might add." Rick opened the truck door with a hard yank. He sat on the edge of the seat, hesitating.

"What is it, Dad?"

"It's not just Meghan's book that could have answers. There's also an old box I found in Emily's basement that could have some answers, too."

"How so?" Derek asked.

"From the old letters—all addressed to Emily."

"Who are these letters from?" Derek asked.

"One guy in particular: Captain Miller."

Chapter 25

THE LETTERS

Diary of the Witches' Testimonies

Thee has had much confusion and mortal pain in such dark spaces. Will thy presences save us all from certain death with thy strange talk and release the bondage brought upon us? Or has the true witch who gives birth in the musty filth of darkness, cast away the presences of the stranger with the bright flaming hair?

Source: A letter written by Rebecca Spencer

ON THE FIRST COLD DAY OF DECEMBER, Emily lay in bed submerged in deep thoughts, yearning for Rick with every ounce of desire that flowed through her body. She placed her hand on the empty sheet beside her and wanted to cry, but the overwhelming tiredness stopped the tears. Emily could easily forget her loneliness over Rick by lying down in the same place where he had made love to her. If she tried hard enough, she could feel his presence beside her. She fell into a deep sleep with no signs of Rick in her dreams. Only ghostly faces from the past entered her subconscious mind—those of Lily Spencer and Lily's ancestor, Rebecca. Emily could see the look on Rebecca's face, questioning who Emily was. Then Rebecca disappeared among the movements of bodies, the sounds of shackles, and tiny sobs from the dark corners.

When Emily woke two hours later, the diary was still open on her chest. She had been reading the first couple of lines in the book when she drifted off from exhaustion. Sitting up on the side of the bed, she tried to get her thoughts together and began to understand why Meghan wanted her to read the book.

Meghan's three-times great-grandmother, Lily, must have transcribed portions of Rebecca's letters about her time as a prisoner. Accounts described a stranger with red hair. Rebecca was referring to Emily in that dark, awful place. Emily was sure of it. Although many other sounds echoed in the darkness, Emily had focused on Sandra and Catori. According to Meghan, Lily Spencer had documented many stories told through the centuries of all the Spencer witches, and Emily would make sure she would read every one of them.

She walked to the bathroom to run water over her face and heard a knock at the front door. As she approached the door, she heard a truck pull away. That's strange, she thought. Peeking through the stained glass, she saw something on the porch. When she opened the door, she saw a florist box. Emily brought the box in where it was warm, found a dozen roses and a note that read: "I will forever wait to see your smile again. Love, Rick." Once again, Emily began to cry.

For the next three weeks, Rick left assorted gifts on Emily's front porch such as books to read, prepared food from the Maple Ridge Diner, and copies of the weekly *Maple Ridge Gazette* with no historical column, Emily noticed. Emily had called Mark Johnson and told him she was dealing with some personal issues that would have to be resolved. She was glad he never questioned her.

With each offering, Rick had left a single red rose. On a snowy day, Emily looked out the window and found Rick shoveling and clearing the driveway. Emily was beginning to soften but also knew she had to do more research on this awful curse. She found Lily Spencer's diary a treasure trove of information but still couldn't shake the feeling something more was missing. It wasn't until the day before Christmas Eve when that would all change.

Most of the second floor of Emily's house needed cleaning

and renovation. She had no interest in tackling all the work and had lived on the first floor for the past several weeks, sleeping in the bedroom across the hall from the basement door.

Emily decided it was time to clean out one of the rooms she'd been wanting to make into an office. She liked the idea of having a workspace at home if she were to write some of her own stories and experiences and, she hoped, write for the historical column, that is, if she still had a job. Meghan was as good as her word and had helped Emily with the design of the new office. She had called several times with great ideas, and Emily loved the conversations with her new friend.

The room was crammed with shelves filled with books and stacks of papers left by previous owners. Emily scanned the room and felt overwhelmed with the mess. Got to start somewhere, I guess, she thought. A small desk with a leather chair sat oddly in the center of the room. Half of its top was covered with papers, old books, folders, coffee-stained Styrofoam cups, and assorted colorful crayons left behind, presumably by a child. A wooden box also sat on the desk, and on Emily's closer inspection, the sight of the familiar box caused a sharp, cold chill to shoot right through her.

"Oh, my God! This must be the box Sam was trying to tell me about."

She knew this box, had seen it before when the wood was new, unlike the cracked, worn box in front of her. The wooden box displayed a family crest on the lid, identifying it as the same wooden box. "How in the world did you get here?" she asked the old relic.

She remembered the last time she saw it. Captain Miller had taken out three items that belonged to her: the notebook, pen, and Rick's key. That was just before Captain Miller chased her out the front door and into the mist of time and space.

She slowly opened the lid and found an envelope with "To Emily From Thomas" written in a bold hand. Emily gazed at Thomas's handwriting. She had never seen her grandfather's handwriting before yet smiled at the memories of Lily hauling young Thomas off to another room to learn his reading, writing, and arithmetic. A newspaper clipping beneath the letter was identical to the nursing home photograph of a nurse standing in the background with so many of the sick and dying.

Emily had a flashback to the day she sat in Sam's kitchen and saw the newspaper on the table with a section cut out of the front page. Emily held the old clipping, which was brittle from age, placing it gently aside, and then gently glided Thomas's letter out of the envelope, and read the message.

Dear Miss Emily,

I wrote this letter knowing the truth of who you are yet felt the need to still call you "Miss Emily." The morning I first met you, my grandpa, Sam Stanford, showed me this wooden box filled with letters from the Miller family. A Mr. Louis Miller, who had taken my grandpa under his wing after his grandparents passed away, became very ill himself and eventually died. Before Louis died, he gave this box to my grandpa. Much of what's in this box pertains to you. Grandpa told me you would own this house someday in the future and wanted to hide the box in a small vault in the basement covered with a stone matching all the others and where he was sure you would find it. If you are reading this letter, it means you have successfully found the box. My grandpa's cremated ashes were given to my adoptive mother, Lily Spencer, for safe keeping. When I was old enough, she gave his urn of ashes to me to do what I saw fit. I had them buried alongside his sister Sarah's grave in the Trinity Church Cemetery. But before my grandpa's ashes went into the ground, I poured out a small portion into the bottle he had labeled "Lucky." He told me it was an aspirin bottle you had given him when he was twelve years old.

Emily dropped the letter in her lap and caught sight of the aspirin bottle tucked away at the bottom of the box covered with several other letters. She held the bottle in her hand and felt the weight of it. Her finger traced the word "Lucky" written on the bottle in Sam's handwriting. Emily opened the top to find all that was left of Sam. She touched the ashes with reverence. "Oh, Sam. How could this be possible? You were so alive to me." She wanted to cry, but once again, the loss was too painful even to try. She closed the top, placed it on the desk, and then continued to read Thomas's letter.

If you read this letter in the future, you might have just left the year 1918, and Sam's death would be fresh in your heart. Hopefully, having his ashes will help in the mourning process. I also know you are indeed my granddaughter. My grandpa told me everything early that morning when you were upstairs still sleeping. He swore me to secrecy, a secret I kept my entire life and one I never even told your father about. I am a forty-eight-year-old man now, who is dying of cancer. I'm afraid I don't have much longer, for there is no cure for the cancer I have. I'm forever grateful I had gotten to see your beautiful face and the red hair you inherited from your grandmother. When your mother placed you in my arms not even an hour after you were born and said, "Baby Emily," my heart burst with joy.

My grandpa told me that morning so long ago that he loved you when he was just a little boy and then again when he was an old man. The same goes for me. When I was a boy, I saw your kind face and felt the loving comfort you gave me when I was sick with the Spanish flu. And then again, as a beautiful newborn baby. I know that your adventures of helping people will not be over. You will come to rescue us once more with all of us in need of your *special powers. If I could leave you with just one message it would be this: Let go of all the past hurt and grief of your loss of Lucas and hold onto the love that stands before you. I am forever grateful that I have known you, and my only regret is that I never got to see you again as a grown woman. I never got to say goodbye.*

With great love and appreciation,

Your loving grandfather, Thomas Stanford

Emily looked at the date of the letter: December 24, 1958, five mouth before her grandfather's death. The ghosts from the past were talking to her once again.

She held Sam's bottle, thinking Thomas was right: She still mourned Sam. In fact, she grieved for so many. She placed Thomas's letter and Sam's bottle back in the box to bring it downstairs when she heard a commotion outside and then a knock on the door. She went to the window and looked down to see Rick walking to his truck. He seemed to sit behind the wheel for a minute or two before starting his truck. He then sped off.

Emily carried the old box down to the living room, putting it on the coffee table, and then went to the door. When she opened it, she found a fresh-cut Christmas tree leaning against the house and a watering stand to go with it. Near the other side of the door was a box of ornaments, Christmas lights, and a single red rose sitting on top of the ornament box with a card. Emily read the card's message: "Give yourself a little Christmas cheer, and I will see you soon. Merry Christmas. Love, Rick."

Emily dragged the tree into the living room and placed it in the bay window. The tree was about as tall as Emily, and the watering stand added at least three more inches to the tree. She sat on the couch feeling a mixture of happiness and sadness at the same time. "Oh, Rick. If you only knew how much I missed you," she said out loud with only the tree to hear her. "Well, let's see what we can do here." She picked up the strand of Christmas lights.

For the rest of the day, Emily decorated the tree and then stood back to get an overall view of her decorating skills. "Mmm, not bad," she said, crossing her arms and putting one hand under her chin in thought. "There's only one thing missing." Off she went to the basement, coming back with the old picture of Thomas, Billy, and Lily Spencer, setting it on a branch. She picked up the old wooden box placing it with great respect under the Christmas tree. "There, my first Christmas present."

The next day, Christmas Eve, Emily's sound sleep was disturbed by a loud noise coming from outside. She glanced down and was surprised to find herself lying on the couch, where she had remained all night. She rubbed her sleepy eyes and then got up to look out the window. She saw that five inches of fresh snow blanketed her front yard. The noise in question was a snowplow going by and pushing a pile of snow into Emily's driveway. She yawned and stretched as she made her way to the bathroom for a much-needed shower.

After her shower and a breakfast of two boiled eggs, a piece of toast, and coffee, she was good to go. Lily's book still sat on her kitchen table. She flipped through some pages when the name of a chapter, "The Indian Seer," jumped out at her. Emily hadn't read that far in the book; she had focused on reading only the stories of the Spencer witches so far. This must be about Catori, she thought. She began reading and an unusual part caught Emily's eye.

The Indian seer found herself in Maple Ridge begging for food. Most people ignored her, passing the girl off as a beggar, which she seemed to be by all indications. A man passed by her on the road one day and was taken by her beauty. He recognized the girl and offered his help, but she was fearful, wanting nothing to do with him. The man was persistent yet kind with concern for the

Indian seer and finally convinced the girl to go with him into his buggy. The story has it that she lived her whole life with this man's family and that she died at an old age. These questions remain: Was this the same Indian seer who was banished from the Salem prison? The same dark place Rebecca Spencer had endured? Was this the same woman cast out, deemed too dangerous to deal with by the people of Salem? Was this the Indian seer, Catori?

Emily put the book down and thought hard about what Captain Miller had told her about Catori. She had raised his father from the age of five because his grandmother had died, leaving his grandfather alone to raise his son. Catori remained in the Miller family and became like a grandmother to Captain Miller. Emily was fascinated by how resourceful Lily must have been to uncover all those stories. Then Emily thought of the wooden box sitting underneath the Christmas tree still filled with unopened letters.

She poured herself another cup of coffee and sat on the couch staring at the top of the box under the tree. Taking out her phone, she looked up family crests, putting the name Miller in the search box. Sure enough, the crest on the box matched the Miller family crest. She read that the symbol of the wolf signifies perseverance and that the medieval steel armor represents the military.

Emily took the box out from under the tree, setting it on the coffee table. The crest was worn and faded from time; she could see three wolf heads and the steel armor upon further inspection. The meaning of the crest made sense to Emily. Given what she knew of the Miller family's past and present, Rick had been one of those men who has persevered through losing a hand, fighting his way back from PTSD, and drinking. She felt an enormous amount of pride and respect for Rick. Emily admired his maneuvers and tactics with gifts, roses, and the certainty he would not give up on her no matter what.

She again looked at the box, opening it, digging through notes and letters, finding a letter sealed with its melted wax untouched. On the front of the letter, she noticed that it was addressed to

her: "To Mistress Emily Stanford from Captain Douglas Miller."
She broke the ancient seal and discovered a three-page letter. She
admired the beautiful handwriting with its oval and slanted letters
and how the quill sloped downward, causing shaded strokes that
connected all the letters, an art that has long since passed.

April 30, 1795

My Dearest Emily,

I hope you don't mind me calling
you dearest, for it is how I've thought
of you over the years. I wrote a previous
letter soon after your mysterious departure, and now I find myself advanced
in age with fewer years ahead. With
the passage of time, I dare say, being
completely honest with you about who
I am is of the utmost importance.

My grandfather, Quincy Miller,
did something so horrific when he was
a young soldier of seventeen. At the
command of his older brother, Sherman Miller, he and a group of colonial
soldiers went into an Indian village to
kill the head chiefs of the tribe over a
land rights dispute. In the process, my

grandfather, Quincy Miller, mistakenly slashed the throat of an Indian woman. This act left Quincy horrified over what he had done. The woman's daughter held her dead mother in despair as my grandfather retreated.

Three years later, my grandfather found this same young girl wandering the streets of Maple Ridge. Concerned for her welfare, he convinced her to seek shelter in his home, and she agreed. Both being so young, Quincy in need of forgiveness and the attractive young girl in need of shelter and care, it was inevitable that they would fall in love. That love resulted in a child, who became my father, George Miller.

Emily looked up at the old box with the Miller crest. Shock ran straight through her as she realized that Rick was a descendent of Catori, the Native American seer, and that Lily Spencer's book confirmed the story. Emily glanced at the letter trying to focus on the rest of the words blurred by the tears forming in her eyes. She blinked a couple of times and wiped her eyes with her sleeve as she continued to read.

The sad reality of their love for each other resulted in a mixed relationship that would not be accepted, causing peril for not only Catori's life but also for Quincy's standing as a military officer. He then married another as if covering up a mistake, and Catori kept their secret even though it had broken her heart. This arranged marriage between Quincy and this other woman lasted only five years when a drowning accident took this woman's life in the Magic River. The same fate as my sweet Mariah. From what my grandmother had disclosed to me, I now know it was the curse.

Before Catori died at the age of one hundred, she had one last vision to tell me. It was of you, Emily, a time traveler who falls in love with one of our Miller decedents, a man named Richard Miller. My grandmother told me that your binding love for each other will have great power over any curse. I suspect this Richard Miller to be a good man, and I hold nothing but the utmost respect pertaining to you, my dearest Emily. You needed to know the truth of it, and I'm sorry I waited this long to disclose such a secret hidden for so long.

I pray this letter finds you somehow. My grandmother, Catori, had told me to write this letter and that you would indeed read it someday in another time far from this one, and I have every reason to believe her. All I could ever ask for in the future would be your happiness. Please give my regards to my descendent, Richard Miller, for he is a fortunate man to have captured your love.

Sincerely yours,
Captain Douglas Miller

Emily's eyes flooded with tears. Her heart pounded, and she put her hand up to her mouth to manage the surge of overwhelming relief. All along she had thought the curse would cause Rick's death. That she needed to stay away to save his life. Now, another message from the ghosts of the past changed her perspective. Catori had had a vision of a distant future which showed Emily and Rick together. This was the realization of the final piece of the puzzle. She stood up, staggering around the room, holding onto the startling truth of all those bottled-up feelings suppressed by her fears.

The sound of the old grandfather clock chiming noontime hit her with another reality. She knew what day it was, which haunted her, pierced her heart with pain. Noontime, the same time the police came to her door on another Christmas Eve, giving her the tragic news of Lucas's death. She glanced at the antique clock looming in the corner of the room and counting down to the horrible hour. At that moment, she decided there was only one thing left to do.

Chapter 26

MISSING

RICK SAT IN HIS TRUCK by Emily's house, going over what he would say to her. He had waited long enough and needed answers, a shred of understanding over her fears and what had happened to her in the past. The snow had been falling hard all morning, just in time for Christmas Eve and Santa's return. "Glad this Santa got his errands done early because this really sucks," he said, watching the snow build up on his windshield. Earlier that day, he had bought a special Christmas gift for Emily. He touched the gift tucked away in a small box on the front seat. He could see the Christmas tree lights were on in the bay windows and noticed tire tracks going from the side of the house near the garage to the road. He grabbed the gift off the seat, tucked it under his wool coat, and jerked open the truck door.

When he arrived on the porch, he stomped the snow off his boots, brushed off his coat, and stood tall, rapping on the door, this time with more force and this time without walking away. The latch popped open. A sudden spike of concern went through Rick. "Emily?" he called. The snow had accumulated to at least seven inches, which muffled the sound, the same dead silence that came from beyond Emily's front door. He grabbed the knob, pushing the door further open.

"Emily? Emily?" He looked at the doorknob and latch. "Better adjust that for her later." He glanced into the living room and saw the wooden box on the coffee table. "Guess she found it," he said out loud.

Rick could see that Emily had decorated the tree beautifully with all the ornaments he had given her. He pulled off his boots and went over to the tree to get a better look. A picture of two young men and an older woman sat nicely on a branch directly in front, and he took it off to get a better look. Three people were standing in front of the Maple Sugar Barn with 1925 written on the white edge of the picture. Turning it over, he saw their names: Thomas Stanford, Billy Easton, and Lily Spencer. Rick recognized the last names Stanford and Easton but couldn't place Spencer.

Rick thought hard: How do I know that name? Then it hit him that Meghan's family on her mother's side are Spencers. "And possible witches," he said under his breath.

He placed the picture back on the branch of honor and then noticed the diary Derek had told him about, *Diary of the Witches' Testimonies*, next to the old wooden box. He picked the book up, flipped through the pages, and then turned it over and saw the author's name. "Yup, all witches. Hah, guess I was right."

He looked again at the lid to the old box, studying the crest on the top. "Miller," he said, recognizing his family crest. Then Rick noticed a letter on the coffee table he had seen when he found the box in the basement. It was a letter from Captain Miller, only now, the seal had been broken.

He made his way to the kitchen. Roses he had given her sat on the table in a vase with an aspirin bottle next to the vase with the word "Lucky" written on it. When Rick picked it up, he felt the heaviness to it. "Hmm, strange," he said, a little confused knowing the last time he saw the bottle it was in the wooden box.

He had been shocked by the newspaper clipping and all the letters addressed to Emily, which had distracted him from giving much thought to the bottle. He put the bottle down next to the roses, returned to the entrance hall, and looked up the staircase. "Emily?" He again received no answer.

On one side of the hallway was the basement door, and on the other was a small bedroom. He leaned on the door frame to the bedroom where he and Emily shared their last intimate moments together. The memory gave him a surge of desire. He had waited, pushed his feelings aside. He wanted to be with her, touch her again, make love to her. He missed Emily and had done everything he could to give her the space she needed, but he also knew it was time for them to talk, figure things out, make sense of all she had gone through. They both needed to help each other through their fears and losses.

Rick glanced at the entrance table where Emily always put her car keys and saw that they were missing. Rick concluded that between the car keys and the tire tracks going to the road, Emily wasn't home. Maybe she went shopping, he thought. Not likely in this weather, he decided. Rick put his boots back on, patted his coat where the Christmas gift was, and then looked around at the empty entrance.

"Where in the world did you go?" he wondered. "Okay, Emily," he said, "I'll find you, so we can straighten this whole thing out." He closed the door, pulling it hard for the latch to catch and locked it this time.

Chapter 27

THE WHITE ROSE

THE MAGIC RIVER HAD A SADNESS TO IT, Emily considered. The mist flowed stubbornly up through the fresh snowfall. It all matched her mood perfectly. Emily had not spent a lot of time in the old part of the Trinity Cemetery, but here she was on Christmas Eve, finding herself standing among the ghosts of the past she had known and loved. They seemed to appear in her dreams, a diary, and an old wooden box. How would anyone understand her unique circumstances? She wiped away the snow from the gravestone of Captain Douglas Miller. Born March 25, 1729—Died April 27, 1795. He had passed three days after writing the three-page letter to Emily that she had read less than two hours ago.

"Hello, Captain Miller. I got your letter," she said, kneeling in the snow. Tears filled her eyes. "Thank you for making sure I knew the truth about your grandmother, Catori." Emily wiped the tears with her glove and slumped back on her heels with her head down. "In a way, I felt something for you, too." She lifted her gaze towards the writing on the stone. "Strange, I know. Perhaps it's your remarkable resemblance to your descendent." She touched the Captain's name again. "You would have loved Rick. He's...he's like you, strong, handsome...brave," she sniffled. "I know you're with your beloved Mariah now...I wish," Emily's chin trembled as she tried holding back the tears. "I wish I could have saved her, too," she said, putting her gloved hands over her face. The wind blew the snow around her in a swirling motion. Looking up, she kissed her glove, placing her hand on the stone, "Goodbye, Captain Miller. It was such a pleasure to have known you."

Emily trudged through the accumulating snow and saw a tall stone that had towered over all the others for over two hundred fifty years. The names of all the military from the last two and a half centuries filled every inch of its surface. Names such as Jacob Stanford, Marcus Stanford, Raymond Miller, Douglas Miller, Louis Miller, Vance Green, Stuart Green, and a new name recently added. Just beyond the knoll was a grave barely two months old. She made her way over and knelt seeing Walter Green's name. She leaned forward, touching his name engraved next to the names of his mother and grandmother, Laura and Lucy Green.

"I'm sorry I didn't make it to your funeral, Walter." She then looked to the snowy sky with the wind whipping in her face and blowing the tears off her cheeks. "At least I was able to be there when you left us," she said, glancing back down to the stone. "Thank you for being there for me. Tell my dad that I wish I could have had more years with him. I suppose if he was like a brother to you, he would surely have been there to greet you in heaven. Rest well, my old friend. Say hi to Lucy and Laura for me."

Emily stood slowly. She straightened the American flag staked in the ground half buried in the snow near Walter's headstone. The flag had been twisted into a knot and was now whipping in the biting wind. She raised her right hand to her forehead in a salute. "I love you, Walter. Thank you for your service, my friend."

Emily walked further and stopped. Her feet seemed frozen to the ground on an unknown person's resting place. Emily's gaze followed a path she had taken one hundred fifty-eight years ago. The memory haunted her: men guiding the ropes that cradled Sarah's casket as it was lowered into the ground and then hearing the heartbreaking cry of twelve-year-old Sam, over the loss of his sister. Emily wasn't ready to say farewell when she still had a part of Sam left: his ashes in an old plastic bottle. The force of the wind pushed hard against Emily's back, shoving her towards her last goodbye.

Wind gusts and biting snow pellets hit the side of Emily's face, as she stood on the hallowed ground that contained the remains of the love of her life. She dropped to her knees in despair and leaned forward, plunging both hands into the deep snow in front of Lucas's stone. "Oh, Lucas, my darling."

She cried harder than she ever did before, her howling sorrow carried off by the winter gale. All her anguish released into a flood of tears that melted the snow where they fell. "I know it's truly time for me to say goodbye. I love you, Lucas. I miss you so much," she sobbed.

The pain and loss ran through her body, and she couldn't control her emotions. She covered her face in shame. "It's my fault you're gone. Why didn't I stop you that night? I...I wish had known about that awful curse then I could have saved you. I could've at least stopped you. I should've stopped you but...I didn't. I'm so sorry," Emily cried out, collapsing in her pool of tears. The wind's icy grip penetrated through her coat. She began to shiver when suddenly she felt a presence near her.

"It's not your fault, Emily," a voice said from behind her. "It's my fault Lucas is dead."

A hand reached out to her. She grabbed the hand that pulled her to her feet, as if it were a lifeline pulling her back from the depths of despair. "Rick?"

He wiped her tears with his fingers. "I was the one who called Lucas that morning, Emily."

"What?" Emily said in disbelief.

"Lucas and I became friends when he offered to help me out with an apartment building I was maintaining. That day, two years ago on Christmas Eve, a water heater broke in that building. There were families with small children in need of heat and hot water."

Emily's legs felt weak over the shock of hearing Rick's confession. "Oh, Rick," was all she could say.

He moved closer, and she felt the heat of his body as he continued to wipe away her tears. "You see, Lucas would never let a bunch of kids down on Christmas, so he stopped at his garage that day to get a water heater he had in stock and—"

"And he helped you," Emily interrupted.

"Yes," Rick said as his own tears were forming. "Yes, he did."

Emily took her gloves off, offering the same gesture of wiping a single tear from Rick's cheek. "It's not your fault, Rick. I...I suppose we both had sad secrets we kept from each other. Maybe we both wanted to forget."

Rick pulled Emily close to himself. Their lips joined, and each tasted the other's tears. Those tears washed away the pain and sorrow of the past and sparked a passion that had eluded them for the past two and a half months. They held each other in a long, tight embrace; neither one wanting to let go.

"You know what Lucas told me before he left to go home that day?" Rick whispered warmly in her ear. He then looked into Emily's eyes that were beginning to fill up again. "He told me he needed to be home with his beautiful wife and didn't want to leave her alone, especially on Christmas Eve. He told me you'd be waiting for him at the door."

Emily collapsed against Rick's body. She felt weak remembering the hopelessness of that day. She did wait at the door for hours worrying. When the police showed up, she was shattered. But now, something was different; Emily felt safe in Rick's arms. She wasn't alone in her sorrows anymore. She looked up at Rick. "I love you Rick, so much," she said, sniffling.

Rick kissed her again and then held her face in his hand. "You have no idea how much I have wanted to hear you say that." He kissed her again. "I love you too, Emily."

They held each other for what seemed like an eternity when suddenly the snow stopped, and the air became strangely calm and warm. Emily and Rick looked overhead. It was still snowing above, but none of it was falling on them. A magical dome hovered overhead, protecting them from the elements. A distant haunting voice came from the direction of Magic River. "Emily? Emily?"

The two looked at each other. "Do you hear that?" she asked.

Yeah, I sure did," Rick answered.

The voice became stronger when an apparition of a dark-haired woman appeared. She was the same woman in the mist, the one with the mark of a brown heart on her wrist, and she spoke slowly, emphasizing each word.

"My name is Sandra Easton known as Orenda. My child born in the depths of despair in a dark prison was reunited with his Easton family. His life was spared, and he lived on to further a long line of Eastons. Now thou stands before the resting place of Lucas Easton, the last of his descendants," she said in a commanding, mystical voice.

"I don't understand," Emily said.

"Lucas Easton was married and loved by thee, a Stanford under my deadly curse. Therefore, his death had become an unintended consequence. Thou hast suffered from the curse cast upon thy families. The curse began to disintegrate by the love of God thou hast shared with thine ancestors through time."

Sandra was still young, Emily noticed. She looked to be the same age as when Emily last saw her. Now though, Sandra wore white, and her dark hair waved gently in a warm breeze. Her eyes were a penetrating blue-green, and she had a milky complexion. Emily thought she was stunningly beautiful and listened as Sandra continued to speak.

"Thy love shared between thy two families has broken my curse on thee forever, for no curse has any power over love. It is no longer upon thy death but by thy love within thee that has saved thee from such an egregious curse."

Sandra's voice grew fainter as she began to fade away. "After three hundred years, I can rest in peace from this costly mistake of casting such a destructive curse. Thou hast set thee free."

And just like that, Sandra "Orenda" Easton disappeared, leaving Emily and Rick stunned over her appearance and relieved that the curse she had cast upon their families over three centuries ago was now gone forever.

"Lucas is Sandra or Orenda's descendent?" Rick asked, shocked.

"It seems so," Emily said.

She turned to look at Lucas's grave and noticed something that wasn't there before. A dozen fresh-cut red roses stood in the flower holder attached to Lucas's stone. "Did you put those roses there?" Emily asked, pointing down towards the stone.

"No. Where did they come from?"

"Maybe the roses are Sandra's way of making amends," Emily offered.

"I guess that was her last magic trick," Rick said with a smile returning to his face.

As she kissed Rick on the cheek, Emily's puffy eyes lit up. "I've missed your humor."

The two hugged each other tightly just as the dome of warm, calm air faded soon after Sandra's departure. The wind and cold came blustering back, causing Emily to shiver. She grabbed Rick's arm. "Come on. Let's get out of here."

"No, wait. I have one more thing to do."

Rick stood at attention, staring down at Lucas's stone. "Well, buddy, I know how much you loved Emily and how you didn't want her to be alone. If it's all right with you, I wouldn't mind taking over for you."

Emily noticed Rick giving her a side glance. He looked back at the stone. "It would be my honor to care for and protect Emily always. And if you have no objections, it would be my greatest honor to take Emily as my wife."

Emily could hardly believe her ears. Rick turned towards her and pulled out the small gift tucked away in his coat. He flipped open the top and presented a sparkling diamond ring with tiny diamonds wrapped around the band. Emily was speechless.

"Will you marry me?" Rick asked.

Emily's mouth dropped open. All those sorrowful tears she had cried earlier turned into joyful ones now. "Yes, I will marry you," she said and watched as Rick placed the ring on her finger. Emily looked down at Lucas's grave and saw the most amazing thing happen right before her eyes. One of the red roses turned entirely white. She held onto Rick's arm, looking right into his eyes with more joy than she could imagine. "I think we have Lucas's blessing." she said, pointing at the single white rose among all the red ones. "Thank you, Lucas. Rick, I love you."

They kissed again long and hard with the same familiar desires they both shared for one another. They held each other, watching the mist disappear from the river. Finally, the Magic River turned to ice after three hundred years of being shrouded by the foggy mist called the curse.

Chapter 28

THE VOWS

THROUGH THE OLD TRINITY CHURCH, the voices of the choir echoed with songs of Christmas. Away in a manger, silent night/ holy night. The angelic voices carried heavenward and bounced off the cathedral ceiling. The organist mastered the keyboard, so the music played in harmony with the singers. Each year the church had an early children's mass. Emily enjoyed listening to the children whispering excitedly over Santa's sleigh filled with toys; she loved the sounds of giggles from babies throughout the church.

Emily and Rick sat in the last pew in the back of Trinity Church, after experiencing the mystical encounter with Sandra Easton. Emily tucked her hands under Rick's arm, soaking in the warmth of his body and her joyful feelings of hope and happiness. She felt him pull her hand to his lips, kissing it gently and holding her a little tighter, basking in the love that ran through them both. It took a little while, but they both warmed up from their time in the cemetery.

When they were in the cemetery earlier, Emily had heard the church bells ring as families gathered for the early mass. Rick had suggested they go to the church service and Emily agreed. She said she would be happy no matter where she was as long as it was with Rick. She also wanted to thank God for blessing her, Rick, and all the other people through time, grateful they had been saved by the love of God. Emily felt the need to pray for all those lost that couldn't be saved and hoped they went to heaven for all eternity.

When mass was over, people filed out the main entrance into the falling snow with holiday greetings on their lips. Someone rushed back into the church, saying that something strange had happened to the Magic River. "It's frozen over!" the person yelled and then quickly exited the church to spread the news. Emily and Rick exchanged knowing looks; only they knew the true secrets of the Magic River.

The church became quiet, and only Emily and Rick remained behind. Rick turned in the pew facing Emily. He stroked her hair gently and then his fingers traveled down her cheek. He lifted her chin and softly kissed her. He pulled back, and Emily saw a twinkle in his eyes. "Let's get married," he said.

Emily looked up at him, amused. "You know, Rick, I did already say yes."

He glanced down at Emily and lifted one eyebrow. "No, I mean right now."

"Now?" Emily said, caught off guard.

"Sure. Why not?" he asked.

Emily stared at Rick, waiting for the punch line, but none came. He was dead serious.

"Um, for one thing, we didn't get the marriage license and—"

"Doesn't matter, for now," Rick interrupted Emily's excuse. "Let it be just us for now, two people in love, committing to each other." Rick lifted his chin towards the altar. "And with God's blessing. After all, we're in a church, right? And there's the altar," Rick said, pointing to the front of the church.

Emily loved how Rick was so carefree. He was a man who wasted no time, and he wanted to be with her, not wanting to wait for a formal event that would take weeks, if not months, to organize. She kissed Rick, realizing she needed him just as much. Saying their vows to each other would be a beautiful expression of their love for each other with or without a priest. "Okay. Let's do it," she said.

They linked arms and walked to the front of the church. They stood face to face in front of the altar among dozens of poinsettias and the nativity scene where baby Jesus lay. The scent of incense lingered in the air among the soft light of several flickering candles, which cast a reverent glow to the holy place at which they stood.

"I, Richard Douglas Miller," Rick began.

"Are you kidding me? Douglas was Captain Miller's first name," she gasped.

"Nope, not kidding."

Emily knew there was much more to tell Rick about Captain Miller, but that would have to wait until later. She nodded and held Rick's hand and his prosthetic hook.

Rick cleared his throat. His thoughtful, loving eyes settled on hers. "I, Richard Douglas Miller, take my sweet Emily Stanford Easton to be my wife. I promise to always take care of you and love you no matter what comes our way. I will stand by you, defend, and protect you with my life. I will be there for you in sickness and in health, for richer—" Rick leaned in closer with a humorous grin. "Which will never be me—or poorer—which will likely be me. But most of all, till death do us part."

"Aww, so sweet," Emily said. She gazed at his lips in anticipation of kissing them again. She then cleared her throat. "I, Emily Stanford Easton, take my handsome hero, Richard Douglas Miller, to be my husband. I promise to care for and love you through times of trouble, sadness, and pain. I promise to never walk away in your time of need. I will take care of you for always whether it be in sickness or in health, for richer—" She pulled Rick slightly closer to her and smiled—"and, yes, for poorer, and I promise to be by your side till death do us part."

"You have a deal, sweetheart," Rick said, winking.

"You may kiss the bride." A voice abruptly came from the side of the church altar. There stood Father Joe, watching the proceedings.

"So, ah, Father, how long have you been eavesdropping?" Rick asked.

The priest came over and stood in front of Rick and Emily, and she saw the pleasant expression of approval on his face. "Long enough to know how devoted and in love the two of you are," he said.

Emily thought an introduction might be appropriate at that point. "I'm Emily Stanford, and this is my—"

"Husband?" the priest offered.

"Ah, yes, in our hearts, of course," Emily said, wanting to avoid trouble with the church. She offered her hand to the priest.

She noticed that Rick stuck his hand out with much more confidence. "I'm Rick Miller, Emily's husband."

The priest shook their hands. He was a short man in his fifties with thinning gray hair. "In God's eyes, he sees your love and the beautiful words spoken to each other. But for now..." The priest reached up and put one hand on Rick's head and the other on Emily's. "I, Father Joe, bless your commitment towards one another. I ask that God gives you great joy for the rest of your lives and that he keeps you safe and healthy to enjoy the fullness of the love you have for each other. I ask this in Jesus' name. Amen." Father Joe took two steps back, as if waiting for a response. Then he said: "Well, Mr. Miller, aren't you going to kiss your bride?"

Emily was surprised over Father Joe's beautiful gesture in blessing their makeshift informal wedding. Then Rick turned and kissed Emily. She sensed that it was not the kind of kiss he would have given if they were alone on the altar.

"Now, when you're both ready, get your marriage license and come back. We'll make it official. That is, in the eyes of the church," Father Joe wore a mischievous smile.

Later that night, the bed felt warm as their bodies mingled together. Rick kissed Emily softly on her nose, eyelids, and forehead, making his way to her lips where their lovemaking surged strongly, making them yearn again for more. They explored each other's bodies with each touch igniting uncontrollable passion. They achieved the ultimate closeness when their intimate parts joined together. She felt the intense heat of his body over hers. He moved swiftly inside her, a place where she never wanted it to end. Finally, one last thrust of his body released the feeling of ecstasy for both.

They fell asleep, awakened by the sound of the church bells that drifted from the town over the countryside through the bedroom of Emily's house. The same room in which they had last made love. She stretched her legs, bathing in the warmth of the sheets and the sweet aroma of sex. She felt Rick turn his body once again towards her as an invitation to repeat the lovemaking from the night before.

She couldn't resist him and wanted him to kiss her. His tongue dragged across her lower lip, passed her chin, and down her neck leading to her nipples. He kissed every curve of her body as he made his way lower to where the source of her desire erupted, causing a feverish passion for both. They had more of the same, more exploring in secret places as he entered her once again. Their bodies moved together, intensifying the need for that euphoric moment. They were both addicted to each other's touches. She could hear his moans of pleasure mingled with her own. Then came the final climax. They lay tangled together in each other's arms with a sense of satisfaction momentarily achieved.

Reluctantly, Emily pulled herself away. She stepped into a pair of slippers while wrapping a fluffy white robe around her naked body. "I'll go make some coffee," she said.

"Breakfast in bed then?" he asked in a sultry voice. He patted the empty space next to him.

She stood admiring his naked body still showing signs he was ready for more. It took all her will power to back away, as she wanted desperately to accommodate his obvious arousal for her. "I'll be right back," she said and gave him a seductive look.

On the way to the kitchen, Emily decided that coffee could wait a bit and detoured to the living room to retrieve the Miller wooden box. She returned to the bedroom and set the box on the bed.

"What's this all about?" Rick asked as he sat up in bed, leaning against the headboard.

Emily took out Captain Miller's three-page letter. "Here, I want you to read this. There's a little surprise in there for you and Merry Christmas," she leaned over to kiss Rick on his cheek. "Now I'll get the coffee."

Emily looked out the kitchen window over the sink as she poured water into the coffee pot for brewing. She liked the old-fashioned way of doing things, and brewed coffee was no exception. She noticed that the fresh snowfall covered the yard with a white blanket of glittering diamonds, caused by the reflection of sunbeams poking through the early morning clouds. "Christmas Day," she sighed happily.

The windowsill displayed Sam's "Lucky" bottle. She picked it up and sat down at the table, holding part of him in her hand. "Merry Christmas, Sam," she said, placing the bottle next to the roses that Rick had left for her. So much has happened in the past twenty-four hours, more good things than bad, she thought. Emily was splendidly happy for the first time since Lucas's death. Her grief had crippled her until Rick came along with his handsome face; sexy blue eyes; his strong, well-built body; and his irresistible charm. The thought of him stirred her passion within seconds.

When the coffee began to perk, she went over to turn the burner down and took two Christmas mugs from the cupboard. Each mug displayed a Christmas tree and the words "Maple Sugar Barn" that were written along the rim. Emily heard footsteps behind her and then felt those strong arms of Rick's, wrapping around her waist. He placed a gentle kiss on the back of her neck.

"You do need coffee now, right?" she asked and turned around.

"No, not exactly," Rick said. "I could go with more of something else, but I suppose coffee will do for now." He kissed the tip of her nose and took one of the mugs from her. They sat at the kitchen table.

Emily had questions for Rick, a few mysteries he would be able to solve. "So," she began, "how did you find the wooden box in the basement?"

"I pried it out of the hole in the wall with that," he said pointing to his prosthetic hook, which sat on the kitchen counter. "Then after finding the old article with you in it, I ran up two flights of stairs with the box and placed it on the desk in the office. I figured it was a safe place and out of sight from anyone else except for you. Also, you might not have found it in the basement."

"I see. And so, when you were in the basement, you also found my box of pictures. Is that when you found out about Lucas?"

"Yup, and I was pretty shocked," Rick narrowed his eyes at Emily. "Why didn't you tell me about Lucas?"

Emily started to reply, but Rick interrupted. "It's okay, sweetie, I get it. It must have been awful losing your husband that way." Rick held Emily's hand, and she saw the warmth reflected in his eyes. "I understand now," he continued, "and don't worry, I'll always be here for you from now on." He kissed Emily's hand. "Anyway, seeing you in that old newspaper clipping felt urgent. I needed to get to you before you were sucked back into 1918, or at least that's where I thought you had gone."

Emily nodded. She stood to attend to the freshly perked coffee. She poured it into their Christmas mugs and then placed the pot on a potholder. They each took much-needed sips. Emily gazed at the bottle containing Sam's tiny resting place.

"I did end up in 1918…where I saw Sam," she said. "He was a doctor, doing what he always wanted to do." Emily chuckled, reflecting on Sam and his special keepsake, which sat on the table. She picked up the bottle, holding it as if it gave her energy.

"Sam?" Rick pointed to the bottle that had "Lucky" written on it.

"What's left of him anyway," Emily said and sighed.

"Yeah, I was wondering what was in that bottle. I saw it in the box that day." He turned a serious face towards Emily. "You came back pretty beat up, your arms bruised," Rick touched Emily wrist. "What the hell happen to you there?"

Emily felt the place where the shackles had cut and bruised her wrists. "I left 1918 and ended up in Salem, all the way back to 1692. It's where I saw Sandra giving birth to her son on the dirt floor.

I couldn't help her. The guard came and took the baby and when I tried begging them to help Sandra, well, that's when the guard grabbed my arm." Emily stared down at her wrists. "The guard took my shackles off and told me get out, but I couldn't leave Sandra. That's when she told me about the curse on my family and yours."

"Why didn't you want to be with me when you came back?" Rick asked.

"Because Sandra looked directly at me and told me the curse would die upon the death of the Stanford bloodline and that my loved ones would suffer at the hands of the Magic River. She went on to tell me that I would be cursed until none is left." Emily shook her head just thinking about how awful that moment felt. "I knew it had to end with me, which meant the curse would end upon my death. I couldn't risk losing you, Rick. I wasn't going to let there be another victim of Sandra's curse, so I stayed away."

Rick kissed Emily's hand gently. "I'm so sorry, Emily. Even if that were true, I would have taken my chances with you a million times over."

"I know you would have. That's why I stayed away. I guess...I was afraid...that is, until I read Captain Miller's letter, which by the way, what did you think of Captain Miller's letter?"

Rick had that humorous look on his face that was so appealing to Emily. She suddenly felt the need for him again. A need that didn't take much for either one of them to want to satisfy. Her eyes focused on what little he was wearing. A pair of sweatpants and nothing else, making it hard to keep herself in control. Her desire needed to be suppressed, at least for now.

"First of all," Rick said in answer to her question. "It was very clear that the Captain was quite infatuated by your beauty and those penetrating green eyes." He leaned over and kissed Emily's eyelid. "And just for the record, I totally agree with his sentiments. The man had good taste, just like I do."

"Why thank you, sir," Emily said with a formal bow of her head. "But I don't think the Captain said anything about my green eyes."

"No, but if he's a Miller, believe me, those eyes and that sexy red hair didn't go unnoticed by the man. As for the part where I'm a half-breed Native American, can't say I'm disappointed. In fact, I kinda like it." Rick leaned forward again this time and patted Emily's arm. "Most of all, sweetie, I'm grateful to the Captain for his honesty and giving you that last bit of information about what his grandmother foresaw about us."

Emily appreciated the sincerity in Rick's voice. Although he sat there without a shirt on, which was pleasing to her eyes, her mood suddenly changed when she became distracted by the tattoo on his arm. She had first seen it the last time they were intimately together before she went back to 1918. It was an American flag with an eagle holding three dog tags, each with a name written on it. On a banner underneath the eagle was written: "All Gave Some, Some Gave All." Emily knew it had a special meaning but had never asked, thinking it too personal or even painful to mention. She saw that Rick noticed her studying the tattoo.

"The three guys who got killed," he said. "You know, the ones I told you about that day on your front porch through the opened window."

"Yes, I remember, and I heard every word," she said with a little grin.

"I wish I could have saved them," he sounded a little melancholy as he rubbed the spot where the tattoo displayed his loss. "I'll always remember their names. If nothing else, their families were able to bury their loved ones in one piece."

Emily touched each name that would be etched onto Rick's arm forever. She glanced up at the shadow of sadness on his face. He ran his fingers through his hair, looking down at the table as if he could see those men alive again.

Then Emily's touch went to where Rick's hand was missing. "You are so brave and strong. Those other soldiers you did save have lives because of you." She squeezed his one hand. "Look at me, Rick." He gazed up, and his features softened as he looked at Emily. "You are a hero; you're MY hero," she said.

"If I'm your hero…then you must be mine. If it wasn't for you, Emily, I might not have reunited with my son, and I'd still be alone, just existing."

"Well, Rick, I suppose as hard as it is, all you can do is try and put the past behind and forget the pain the war has caused you."

Rick held up Sam's bottle of ashes and looked into Emily's eyes. "And what about you, Emily? Are you ready to forget?"

She stared at the bottle. "Not yet. I suppose I'm not ready to say goodbye to Sam yet."

"I also noticed there was an unopened letter from Sam in the box," he said.

"If I read his letter, it would most likely be a farewell letter. I…I'm not ready for that," she shook her head letting out a long sigh. "Even in the cemetery, I stayed clear away from his sister Sarah's grave where he, too, is laid to rest or—" She took the bottle out of Rick's hand. "At least most of him is laid to rest. The connection I felt for Sam was so special, so unique. In the short period of time I knew him, he was like a son to me and I like a mother to him. Then…when we met again, it was only a few short months for me since I last saw him yet fifty-four years later for him. Poor Sam, you had to see the look on his face when he first saw me and noticed how I hadn't aged one bit." Emily rubbed her thumb over the word "Lucky." "Sam was my friend, a friend that I loved dearly, and I miss him."

Rick put his hand lovingly around Emily's hand as she held Sam's bottle. "Well, then, in that case, I guess Doctor Sam Stanford will be our guest for Christmas dinner." Rick took the bottle and put it once again in its place of honor at the center of the kitchen table.

Emily looked at the refrigerator, knowing she didn't have anything special to cook and wondered how she would pull off a Christmas dinner.

Rick smiled and tapped Emily's shoulder. "Check it out," he said lifting his chin towards the refrigerator.

She squinted her eyes giving him a suspicious glance and then got up and opened the refrigerator door. To her surprise and delight, she saw a large, ready-to-be-put-in-the-oven turkey—stuffing and all—sitting on one of the shelves. "How did this get in here?" she asked.

Rick walked over to Emily, hugging her from behind, kissing her once more on the back of her neck. "Santa is not the only one with little helpers."

She turned her head giving him a sly look. "Derek? Meghan?" she guessed.

"Hmm, hmm, and they will be here at 2 p.m."

She turned around, hugging him close, feeling the tremendous happiness flowing over her. Finally, Emily had a family of her very own.

Chapter 29

UNDER THE CHERRY BLOSSOMS

THE FOLLOWING SPRING WHEN the cherry blossoms were in full bloom, Emily stood in the warmth of the sun and gentle breezes. Sunbeams cast a bright shimmering light over the white wooden chairs, facing a beautiful gazebo built by Rick and his son, Derek. Rick had replaced the old rotted swing hanging from the big maple tree that her grandfather had planted long ago and replaced it with a new swing made for two. Meghan had decorated the love seat with white ribbon, wrapping it around the chains that held the swing. Both Derek and Meghan were a big part of the preparations for Emily and Rick's wedding.

Emily was impressed with how Meghan used her interior decorating skills to the fullest when accessorizing the gazebo with white lacy curtains that draped to the ground and were tied back with the white roses Emily had requested. Meghan had arranged the large tent so it was set up off to the side and closer to the house for the reception. The whole scene had a romantic, vintage charm making it perfect for a country wedding. All things were in place and ready to go.

The guest list was small, consisting of Rick's friends from the VA, the Maple Sugar Barn, and Meghan's family. Emily invited some co-workers from the nursing home and mutual acquaintances of both her and Rick's from the town office such as Mark Johnson, the editor-in-chief of the *Maple Ridge Gazette*. Emily had not returned to the paper and had told Mark the job wasn't for her. Although he understood, he had still left the door open in case she changed her mind. Might she change her mind in the future? She didn't know, but for Emily the reasons had more to do with another unforeseen trip back in time.

In Emily's eyes, she and Rick were already married. They had lived like a couple throughout the cold winter, where they kept warm by their love for each other. But now it was time to make it official, pledging their love for one another in front of family and friends.

At the appointed hour, Rick waited at the gazebo with Father Joe and Rick's best man, Derek. Rick stood at attention in his military dress, sporting a button-down blue coat, a white semi-formal dress shirt, and a black bow tie with several medals on the jacket, including the Purple Heart. Although he had been reluctant to draw attention to himself in this way, Emily had insisted. He had agreed and told her, "All I care about is making you happy no matter what." And that had settled his wedding day attire.

Emily heard the music of "At Last" beginning to play. Meghan had suggested the song. For Emily, the first two words summed up this official day. She also remembered the Etta James classic as the song that she and Rick had romantically danced to at Meghan and Derek's wedding.

Knowing that the song was her cue, Emily emerged from the farmhouse's back door with the sound and memory of those enchanting lyrics describing to a tee the love they had for each other. She could see Rick in the distance, and she held tight to her bouquet, a dozen ivory and pink roses, for support. Meghan walked two steps in front of her for guidance more than anything.

Emily wore a long, ivory gown with see-through eyelet-lace sleeves down to her wrist. The plunging neckline and form-fitting lace bodice accentuated her small-framed figure. The ivory color enhanced her flaming red hair accented by blonde highlights, which she had swept up and secured with combs decorated with pink and ivory flowers, matching the cherry blossoms. She felt as if she were floating through the air as she walked towards and finally reached Rick. She couldn't believe how handsome he looked in his military uniform. He had cut his hair shorter on the sides yet kept the top a little longer, showing off his thick, silver locks.

In front of Father Joe, they repeated the same promises to each other they had made in Trinity Church on a cold, wintry Christmas Eve. Emily and Rick were now officially husband and wife, fully bound by a love that would take them on a journey till the end of their days.

The morning soon blended into the afternoon. The big white tent enclosed several round tables, a dance floor, and a brunch buffet filled with all kinds of appetizers and all things breakfast and lunch. Soon, everyone was gliding their way towards the dance floor with jazz, blues, and some old-fashioned disco songs. Emily and Rick hardly left each other's sides, greeting guests and thanking them for coming. Finally, Emily sat down and removed a tight-fitting pair of shoes and immediately felt wonderfully relieved.

"Is it time to take this bow tie off?" Rick asked, running his finger behind his collar to loosen what looked like a stranglehold on his neck.

Emily grinned, answering his question by leaning over and taking his tie off and unbuttoning the two top buttons of his shirt for more comfort. "There. How's that, Mr. Miller?" she said playfully.

"A total relief, Mrs. Miller." He kissed his bride on the nose. "All we need now is for everybody to disappear," Rick said.

"No such luck." Emily saw that Mark Johnson was coming towards them.

Having worked at the paper with Mark Johnson, Emily knew he tended to speak to people loudly as he ordered them around with every chance he'd get. She figured that no formal occasion would prompt him to change his tone.

"So, Miller, you finally did it. I was wondering when you'd stop all that flirting and take the plunge. Emily, we need you back at the *Gazette* as soon as posable. It hasn't been the same without you"

"Really? I thought maybe you would have forgotten me by now," Emily said.

"Nope. Nobody writes articles like you. It's as if you actually experienced the stories yourself."

Emily and Rick exchanged side glances and grins. Mark leaned in, shaking Emily's hand. Rick stood to offer a handshake. "Congratulations, Miller!" Mark said.

"Thanks, Mark," Rick said.

Mark started to walk away when Rick spoke up.

"Hey, Mark, just so you know. Even though she's my wife now, I have no intention of stopping the flirting."

Mark gave a little chuckle and added. "Hey, Miller, when you get your ass back to work? You need to find an AC technician. Now the damn air conditioner conked out."

Rick sat back down, kissed Emily on her forehead, and chuckled himself.

"What?" Emily said, knowing Rick had some other kind of remark pertaining to Mark.

Rick lifted his chin in Mark's direction. "When is that guy ever gonna stop barking orders?"

They both laughed and waved goodbye to Mark as he left the reception.

"Want to share what has the two of you in a hearty laugh?" Derek asked as he and Meghan came over to sit down.

"Nah. Just an inside joke is all," Rick said.

Emily looked at her young friend with great appreciation. "Thank you for everything." Emily took Meghan's hand and looked around at the festive atmosphere surrounding them. "I couldn't have done this without you, Meghan."

"Aww, Emily, you're welcome. Actually, it was a lot of fun," Meghan said.

Emily noticed Meghan giving Derek a look, as if trying to get permission to say something that was clearly on her mind. Emily sensed that Rick seemed to notice something was up, too. "Everything okay?" Rick asked.

Derek ran his hand through his hair just like his father did when nervous or stressed and cleared his throat, obviously trying to get something off his chest. But Meghan took the reins instead and let out their news. "We're pregnant!"

Emily and Rick were stunned, which immediately turned into excitement. "WHAT!" Emily said happily.

Rick stood up in front of Derek. "Congratulations, son! That's incredible. Way-da-go," Rick said, patting Derek on the back and then shaking his hand.

Emily hugged Meghan. "I'm so happy for you! When are you due?" she asked.

"December and..." Meghan held out a small box wrapped in gold paper. "We'd like to give this to you as a wedding gift." She handed the box to Emily. "What is it?" she asked.

Rick put his arm around Emily's waist. "You'll never find out unless you open it, sweetie."

Emily removed the paper and opened the top. Inside was a tiny pair of pink ballet slippers with a card that read: "It's a girl!" Once again, Emily felt overwhelmed with such good news and hugged Meghan again and saw Rick hug his son.

With a serious look on her face, Meghan held Emily's hands. "Emily? I want you to be there when the baby comes. Besides, I hear tell you've helped deliver a couple of babies before and under conditions that were less than ideal."

Derek stood close to Emily, looking her in the eyes. He was as handsome as his father, Emily noticed, and he smiled with a look of appreciation on his face.

"Our baby will be so lucky to have a grandmother like you." He then put his hand on his father's shoulder. "And Dad, our little girl will have a hero to look up to, just like I do."

Rick embraced his son, and each patted the other hard on the back. "Thanks, Derek."

Emily took her turn hugging both Derek and Megan. "It will be my honor to be there for your baby's birth, and I'm bursting with joy to be her grandmother."

"Wow! A lot of hugging going on, I see," a woman said, standing by one of the primary poles that held up the tent. She was a striking woman with dark hair, penetrating eyes, and features matching her daughter, Meghan.

"Mom! Come here," Meghan said, waving for her mother. "Emily, Rick, this is my mom, Sylvia."

Rick reached out, shaking Sylvia's hand. "Nice to see you again."

Emily had met Sylvia once and briefly at Meghan's wedding. It mainly was a nod and a cordial "nice to meet you" greeting. Emily held out her hand to Sylvia, and at the moment they touched, a strange spark of energy shot up Emily's arm. The energy gave her the same unusual sensation she remembered just before going through the mist and finding herself back in time. Emily abruptly let go, praying it was only an anomaly. She thought for sure she would never have to feel that impending doom ever again. Emily saw Rick's reaction, and he immediately and instinctively put his arm around her. "Emily? What's wrong?" Rick asked, concerned.

Emily snapped out of the daze and tried her best to recover from her bad manners. "Oh, I'm sorry, I just…er, a little indigestion is all." Emily hoped the excuse was convincing, but she didn't fool Rick by the look on his face.

Sylvia's expression told Emily that she had the same experience, only she was much more successful in covering it up. Instead, Sylvia added another layer of mystery. She asked Emily if she liked her two-times great-grandmother's book, *Diary of the Witches' Testimonies*. "Just so you know, there's more to the story," Sylvia added.

Emily dismissed the additional comment and stuck to commenting on the book instead. "Yes, it was an interesting read and very helpful in, well, understanding witches, I guess."

Emily could see Meghan's awkward demeanor by the way she nervously shifted her weight from one foot to the other. Sylvia seemed to notice, too. "Now, Meghan, I'm sure Emily knows that you and I are, after all, Spencer witches," Sylvia said in a matter-of-fact way.

Meghan rolled her eyes. "Mom, we don't need to discuss this now." She glanced towards the newly married couple.

Sylvia smiled. "Yes, of course, darling. You're right." Sylvia reached out again to shake Emily's hand, but Emily hesitated. "It's okay, Emily. We're all connected," Sylvia offered.

Emily shook Sylvia's hand and, this time, felt the power of friendship instead. The experience was similar to her first meeting with Lily Spencer. Still, the strange encounter with Sylvia gave Emily an uncomfortable feeling, but she decided to not let it overshadow her perfect day.

Although Rick had asked her about it, Emily didn't want to talk. Emily had appreciated Rick's not pressing the subject either; after all, it was their special day. Besides, Emily had something else she needed to do before the day was over. Something she had put off for far too long.

Emily stared out the kitchen window. The day had been long, and all the guests were gone. She held a letter to her chest, feeling heartbreaking waves of sadness creep in through her bones. She felt a presence behind her but wanted to be alone where time stood still and remained that way forever.

Time to her was a funny thing, she thought, which time, in what place? Did she always belong in one place or another? Love came to her wherever she found herself; this moment, she was between a love for a man who swept her away towards a new beginning and a love that had filled her past and far beyond. Emily had said her goodbyes to Lucas, knew he loved her and approved of Rick. The white rose Lucas had sent was a symbol of his love and approval. That miraculous gesture had given Emily peace; now she had to face one last, painful goodbye.

"Are you okay, sweetie?" Rick asked, coming to stand beside her.

"I never knew what it felt like to have a child." Emily put her hand on her stomach as if reflecting on what it would have felt like. "At least three time periods I was in, I had helped someone else give birth. I saw the joy on their faces, even anguish when unable to touch their babies. I could almost feel what they were feeling." She looked up at Rick. "I also knew what it was like to love a child. A child that felt like my own. Then, came the time I had to say goodbye twice." She remembered Sam as a boy and as an old man.

"And now for the third time," Rick said as he touched her arm gently.

Emily took Sam's bottle from the windowsill and looked up at Rick, feeling tears starting to form.

"What can I do for you, sweetie? How can I make it better?" he asked.

She kissed his ear and then whispered. "It's time. Give me a few minutes and then come to me," she said.

The bottom of Emily's wedding dress moved gracefully over the freshly cut grass as she made her way towards a bench next to the old log alongside the Magic River. She sat letting her eyes take in the beauty of the river and held what was left of Sam. "Lucky," she sighed gazing at the bottle and then looking overhead at the cherry blossom tree. "Your favorite time of the year," she said to the breezes that blew softly through the trees. She could almost hear the echoes of Sam's little boy voice drifting in the air. It's my favorite place in the world, the voice said.

"I miss you, Sam," Emily whispered, responding to the echoes. She looked down at the letter in her lap and smiled at Sam's hand-writing on the envelope: "To my dearest friend, Miss Emily, from Sam." Cracking the seal, she read:

My dear Miss Emily,

As you know by now, I'm dying or by the time you read this, I'll be gone. I didn't want to leave you like this when we had just begun to know each other again. I want you to know above all else: I have always loved you. My heart broke when you left me at twelve years old and broke again when I knew I would soon die from this terrible virus and leave you forever. I remember telling Louis Miller once that I would see you again someday. I just never realized it would be at the end of my life. It saddens me deeply to have never spent a lifetime together with you. You are and always will be my dearest friend. Emily, go live, love your man who dances with love in his eyes for you. Enjoy the laughter, but most of all, let us both say goodbye for now—until we meet again in a place called heaven.

Your dearest friend forever,

Sam

Emily held the bottle with Sam's ashes and kissed it with tears streaming down her cheeks. She stood and opened the bottle, pouring out the ashes in Sam's favorite spot in the world. "Goodbye for now, Sam. I love you."

The ashes lay still as if reluctant to leave, and every heartbreaking emotion filled her body. She felt loving arms come from behind, wrapping around her heartache, and she leaned into the embrace of the man who would carry her through her pain and sadness. "Do you think he knows how much I love him?" she asked.

Suddenly a wind kicked up, swirling across the ground, picking up Sam's ashes, carrying them through the cherry trees and over the tops of Emily and Rick's heads. Moments later, the wind unleashed the white and pink petals that rained down like the snow squall Sam loved so much and covered Emily and Rick in a blanket of peace.

Rick kissed Emily gently on the side of her cheek. "Yes, Emily, I think Sam knows; and I think he just said: 'I love you, too.'."

If time stood still, she would choose this moment to last forever, as the pink and white petals brushed across her cheek in a kiss that said goodbye. Emily focused her gaze on the breezes above, which gently carried the cherry blossoms—and Sam—far away on an amazing journey through Magic River.

Acknowledgments

It was at midnight when one single light shined on my keyboard as I typed the last lines of *Journey Through Magic River.* I fell in love with these characters, especially the two main characters who carried me through this journey of loss, adventure, and love on an epic scale. Since that night, the world I have created remained in a work file on my computer. Work that was far from over. I have many people to thank as they helped me through the ups and downs of being a writer and the long process of editing this body of work to be as close to perfection as possible.

Once again, I found myself asking the same nagging questions. How in the world am I going to complete this project, and who will read it? There was one person by my side to remind me that I am both a writer and an author and that my story is worth telling. That person is my husband, Ned. Thank you for planting the idea in my head over thirty years ago to write a book, and now all these years later, I have written and published two of them so far.

I want to thank both my son and daughter for their words of encouragement.

Nathan: In the very beginning, I had asked you to read the first chapter before I even wrote the second. You told me that it sounded like a great story and to keep going, and that's just what I did. Thank You

Laura: You listened to me rambling on about my book and how I worried whether my book would be good enough. Thank you for being so patient and reminding me never to doubt myself.

I want to thank my son-in-law, for doing some quick editing at the end of this process. He encouraged me on this writing journey and occasionally provided unsolicited advice in the form of, "Take a minute and breathe." With those deep breaths, the few times away from my work, and help along the way, I was on my way to finishing up this project.

I could not have done any of this without my editor Pauline Bartel who has taught me so much about writing. Thank You

I want to thank my publisher, The Troy Book Makers, for their help with all the fine details of publishing my book. Thanks to Jessika, who once again created another fantastic book cover.

I want to thank those incredible unnamed individuals who have inspired me as I created the characters throughout this novel. Extraordinary people such as nurses, doctors, war heroes, wounded warriors, and all the veterans from past and present wars. As always, when writing my characters, I am inspired by their dedication to others and service to our great country. Thank You for being my inspiration.

Through it all, I want to thank GOD, an ever-present spirit in my life. I have God to thank for this wonderful gift of writing. His love has always been with me when I am creating a story. It is said in the Bible, 'God is love.' These words have inspired me to include his love throughout this amazing story.

ALSO BY ANN MARIE PICHE

Spiritual Journey of an Ordinary Girl

You can order this book at your favorite bookstore
or find it on amazon.com
Publisher; The Troy Book Makers: order copies at:
www.shoptbmbooks.com

Visit Ann Marie's website: **annmariepichewriter.com**
Check out her blog and sign up for the newsletter for a more
in-depth look at Ann Marie's author journey.

Find Ann Marie on:
Facebook: **Ann Marie Piche - Author**
Instagram: **annmarie_inspiredwriter**
Goodreads: **Ann Marie Piche - Author**

Please feel free to leave a review on
Amazon, shoptbmbooks.com and Goodreads.